Rock the Boat

Rock the Boat

Olivia Harvey

HOT KEY BOOKS

First published in the UK in 2025 by
HOT KEY BOOKS
an imprint of Bonnier Books UK
5th Floor, HYLO, 103–105 Bunhill Row, London EC1Y 8LZ
Owned by Bonnier Books, Sveavägen 56, Stockholm, Sweden

Copyright © Olivia Harvey, 2025

All rights reserved.
No part of this publication may be reproduced, stored or transmitted
in any form or by any means, electronic, mechanical, photocopying or
otherwise, without the prior written permission of the publisher.

The right of Olivia Harvey to be identified as author of this work
has been asserted by them in accordance with the
Copyright, Designs and Patents Act 1988.

This is a work of fiction. Names, places, events and incidents are either the
products of the author's imagination or used fictitiously. Any resemblance
to actual persons, living or dead, is purely coincidental.

A CIP catalogue record for this book is available from the British Library.

ISBN: 978-1-4714-1671-2
Also available as an ebook and in audio

1

This book is typeset using Atomik ePublisher
Printed and bound in Great Britain by Clays Ltd, Elcograf S.p.A.

MIX
Paper | Supporting
responsible forestry
FSC® C018072

bonnierbooks.co.uk/HotKeyBooks

For Joe. Same time next year?

1

'I don't think I can do this,' I tell Adam, stopping dead on the path, the Mallorcan sun beating down on the back of my neck, my hair ruffled by the breeze.

I press one hand against my stomach and try to breathe in for four, breathe out for four. It doesn't help.

'Of course you can.' Adam hitches his backpack higher onto his shoulders. 'It's just nerves. You'll be fine once we get there.'

There is a yacht somewhere in this long line of yachts that range in size from 'Harry Styles in Italy with his latest model girlfriend' to 'Jeff Bezos post-divorce' and stretch the length of the marina.

'Can you tell which one it is?' I ask Adam, squinting because the morning sun is too bright, even through the sunglasses I bought at the airport because I somehow forgot my own.

Adam shakes his head. 'Not yet.'

I start walking again. Probably best to just put one foot in front of the other and not overthink it. It's okay to be nervous. My wheelie case judders over the cobbles, my hand fizzing with the vibrations, my forearm aching.

I've read that nerves and excitement are basically the same emotion. I can choose to be excited instead of, well, terrified. Maybe

I should've brought a backpack too, but I haven't a clue how Adam fitted everything into his. Knowing him, he probably only packed underwear and a toothbrush.

'I didn't expect it to be this hot,' I say, even though everyone kept telling us it was going to be hot.

'I know. There's sweat running down my crack.'

'Do you ever think we've lost the magic?' I ask, deadpan.

Adam laughs, his hazel eyes crinkling at the corners in the way I've always loved. 'Never.'

He glances around to make sure no one's watching, then crowds me up against the trunk of a palm tree, his hands sliding down to my waist. 'In case we don't get a chance to do this for a while . . .'

His voice is low and makes my belly flutter, the same as it did when we first got together. I tip my face up as he dips his head down to kiss me and despite the heat and my nerves, I relax. Not completely – I'm still clinging to the handle of my case – but enough.

'It'll be sexy,' Adam says, pressing me against the tree. 'Sneaking around.'

We did a ten-day course to qualify for these jobs and one of the instructor's catchphrases was 'Don't screw the crew.' I'm pretty sure it's intended for new colleagues rather than actual couples who've been together since secondary school, but Adam insisted we shouldn't tell anyone we're together, that it would be better for us to pretend to be just friends. He doesn't want anything to jeopardise this job. And, of course, neither do I.

'I know,' I tell him. He smells like orange and herbs, the Old Spice deodorant he's used for as long as I've known him. 'I've been thinking about it.'

'Oh yeah? What have you been thinking?'

I slide my free hand around the back of his neck and brush my thumb over the stubble on his jaw. 'About crawling into your bunk . . .'

'Yeah?' He rests his forehead against mine. 'We'd have to be quiet.'

I smile. Oh, I've thought about that. It'd be like when we first started seeing each other; when we'd skip school and go back to his and get each other off in his bed with his 'All You Need Is Klopp' Liverpool posters staring down at us.

'You'll have to put your hand over my mouth . . .'

Adam groans and pulls back, his hands still either side of me, caging me against the tree. 'We need to stop or we'll be arrested before we even find the yacht.'

'Just wanted to give you something to think about.'

We eventually spot the yacht – *Serendipity* – at the far end of the marina. It looks the same as it did online: long and sleek and gleaming white with a wooden deck separating two rear staircases. On the very top the silver radar domes spin slowly. The sun bouncing off them is dazzling.

'Someone's beaten us here,' Adam says, pointing to a guy at the bottom of the stairs, crouching to pull off his shoes. Brown skin, a closely cropped beard, a short bleached afro. He reminds me of someone, but I can't think who.

'Barefoot on deck,' I say.

One of the first things we were told on the course is that you don't wear shoes on board, so you don't damage the teak floors.

'You know it,' Adam says. 'Welcome to our new life.'

My stomach lurches with excitement-is-the-same-as-nerves.

Our first proper professional jobs. In a whole different country. Together. Even if we have to pretend not to be. It'll be worth it.

I want to kiss Adam, but it's too late. I settle for a quick squeeze of his arm instead.

'Hey!' The guy on board waves, his biceps bulging against the short sleeves of his black T-shirt. 'Are you new?'

Between joining him on the yacht and climbing the stairs to the main deck, we learn that his name's Nico, he's the lead deckhand (and so Adam's immediate boss), he's from south London, he's been crewing for a couple of years now – mostly in the Caribbean – and he hasn't worked in the Med before.

'Did you two come together? No pun intended.'

I roll my eyes, grateful for my sunglasses.

'Yeah,' Adam tells him. 'Not like that though. Just friends.'

'We were at uni together,' I tell Nico. 'And secondary school before that.'

'And you're not banging? What's that about?' He laughs. 'I'm only messing. I'm capable of being friends with women. I'm a modern man. I sleep in the wet patch.'

While Adam and Nico do the standard introductory bro-chat bullshit, I wander around the deck, having a look at everything. There's a long table with six chairs on one side and, on the other, a padded bench built into the curve of the yacht. At the back of the deck, towards the double doors that I think probably lead into the main salon, there's a well-stocked bar with brightly coloured bottles of spirits – orange, blue, lilac – and silver cocktail shakers lined up alongside an ice bucket.

After a few minutes, one of the double doors slides open and a woman steps out to join us. She's short and slight, barefoot like the rest of us, but wearing fitted navy pants and a polo shirt with the ship's logo, her hair pulled back into a sleek ponytail, sunglasses hiding her eyes.

'Nico,' she says with no apparent enthusiasm.

'No. Way,' Nico deadpans. And then he laughs loud and long, skirting the dining table to approach the woman, stopping a metre or so away. 'Permission to hug?' He salutes.

I suspect she's also rolling her eyes behind her sunglasses, but she lets Nico hug her, saying, 'Knock it off!' as he picks her up off her feet.

'I don't believe it,' he says, setting her back down and rubbing a hand over the back of his neck.

'I know,' she says, sardonically. 'Of all the yacht crews in all the world.'

Nico cackles again, before turning back to me and Adam. 'This is Louise. She's the . . . What are you? Second stew?'

'Chief stew,' Louise says.

'Wow!' Nico throws his hands up. 'You've gone up in the world! Kudos!'

'Thanks.'

Moving past him, she makes her way over to Adam and me, holding out her hand for me to shake. It's cool and dry and I feel instantly self-conscious about my own hot clamminess.

'You're the two greenies on this crew,' Louise tells us. 'Everyone else has varying amounts of experience, not necessarily on this boat or in the Med. They'll point you in the right direction, but probably not more than once. Any problems – Hope, you see me. Adam, you'll be reporting to Nico here, or Ben, the bosun. You'll meet him later, along with the captain. I thought Adam could bunk with you, Nico.'

'Sure thing.' Nico picks up his bag and hooks it over his shoulder. 'Follow me.'

Adam throws me a quick smile before following Nico inside. Watching the door close behind him, leaving me alone on a strange boat in a strange place with a strange person, I think I might actually puke.

It must show on my face because Louise says, 'Don't worry. Once everyone arrives, you won't have time to be nervous.'

'When will everyone get here?' I ask.

'The rest of the crew, today,' she tells me. 'And we have our first guests on Friday.'

So we've got three days to learn, well, everything. This is fine.

We don't have to wait long before the next arrival – a tall, willowy girl with light brown hair in two braids wrapped around her head.

Louise introduces us and Kelsey hugs everyone, her face open, smile huge and blue eyes wide.

'You two are in together,' Louise tells Kelsey and me. 'Why don't you come and get settled?'

Kelsey and I follow Louise through the salon, which is all glossy wood-panelled walls, twinkling chandeliers and filled with expensive-looking furniture, and then down a curved set of stairs that's both steep and narrow. I have to hoist my case up into my arms and I wish again that I'd just brought a backpack.

I hadn't expected much from the cabins but once the two of us are inside, there's barely room to even turn round.

'Isn't it crazy?' Kelsey smiles. Her teeth are very straight and very white. 'At home my wardrobe's bigger than this. Top or bottom bunk?'

'Oh, I don't mind.' It doesn't actually feel real. This glorified cupboard is where I'm going to be living for the next few months. 'You choose.'

'Since it's your first time, you should probably take the bottom. Sometimes when it's windy, we can get thrown right out of these bunks.'

'Seriously? My mum was worried about that, but I said people can't be falling out of their beds all the time!'

She takes out a lip balm and applies it with her index finger. 'It doesn't happen often, but it does happen. I was on a boat once and the storm was so violent we all had to sleep in the guest rooms because it was too dangerous to sleep in the bunks.'

There's not enough space for me to do anything but stand back and watch as Kelsey makes quick work of unpacking her bag into the various drawers and cupboards half hidden around the cabin, and then she climbs up onto her bunk and lies down.

'I'm just gonna nap for, like, fifteen. Wake me if anything exciting happens, yeah?'

'Where's Kelsey?' Louise asks me when I get back up on deck.

Everyone is gathered around the table. Nico is sitting at what is effectively the head of the table, even though it's an oval, and there's a guy in a baseball cap at the opposite end and someone else with his back to me. Adam is on a bench seat, his arms spread out across the back. He beams at me and I almost head straight over to sit next to him, but I realise I shouldn't – as far as everyone else on board is concerned, we're not a couple, we're just friends – and wave instead, pulling my sunglasses back down from the top of my head.

'She said she was going to have a nap,' I tell Louise. And then immediately worry that maybe I shouldn't have told her that.

Louise rolls her eyes. 'Captain's coming down for a chat, so could you go and wake her?'

I nod, pushing my chair back and bumping the table with my hip as I get up. The boys cheer as the bottles and glasses rattle and I scarper down the stairs to our cabin.

Kelsey's not actually asleep. She's sitting up against a pile of pillows and scrolling on her phone.

'Can you come up?' I ask her. 'Captain's coming for a chat apparently.'

'Sure.' She pushes her duvet back and swings her long legs off the side of the bed. She's only wearing a tiny vest and knickers, and I'm reminded that I'm going to have to get used to the lack of privacy. I've always been the type to get changed under my clothes, but it seems Kelsey is much more relaxed.

She pulls on a pair of shorts, drops her phone into a pocket and says, 'Ready!'

Captain Liz has short dirty blond hair and if I had to guess, I would say she's in her fifties. She's wearing a red polo shirt with beige shorts and deck shoes. She's got a bunch of what look like friendship bracelets and festival wristbands up one arm and a tattoo of a seashell on her ankle.

'I won't do the icebreaker thing,' she tells us. 'You'll all get to know each other soon enough anyway. And probably better than you ever expected to. Some of you have experience; some of you are new. I expect you all to work together kindly and efficiently and help each other out without being asked. I know it's a cliché to say that we work hard and we play hard, but it's a cliché because it's true. You will work harder than you ever have in your life, guaranteed, but when we don't have guests, you get to enjoy this beautiful place.'

She gestures at the marina and I follow her gaze across the water to the palm trees and golden buildings beyond.

'And I recommend that you do enjoy it. But not too much.' Her eyes crinkle at the corners as she smiles. 'So! Enjoy the next couple of days because once the guests arrive it will be full on. If you have any questions or problems, Louise is your first port of call but I try to be approachable. As long as I've had coffee. I'll hand you over to Ben for the safety walk-through.'

The bosun in charge of the deck crew, Ben, is Scottish, and possibly the most handsome man I've ever seen. Like a younger, softer Henry Cavill. Timothée Chalamet if he looked less like a Victorian ghost. Thick, dark hair swept back off his forehead, perfectly shaped eyebrows, deep brown eyes, and just enough five o'clock shadow to make him unpretty.

The other deckhand is Liam, who is also hot, but just normal hot, not film-star hot like Ben. He's got a tattoo sleeve all down one arm and smaller tats dotted on the inside of his other arm. His hair is cropped and a small scar bisects one eyebrow. At least I hope it's a scar and he hasn't had that shaved in.

Ben shows us the life jackets and rafts, fire extinguishers, fire-safety doors and water-tight doors. We learned some of this on the course, but all yachts are different. It's a reminder that we're actually going to be out at sea, which obviously I knew but it still freaks me out a bit.

'Obviously there's no drinking when we're working,' Ben says, once we get back to the aft deck. 'There's plenty of opportunities for that when we're off duty.'

'Tonight doesn't count though, right?' Nico says. 'Tonight we can get shit-faced.'

'Absolutely not,' Ben says, but he's laughing, revealing – inevitably – perfectly straight, white teeth.

'The first night's always a big one,' Nico tells Adam and me. 'No matter what Ben says. You in?'

Adam is smiling behind his sunglasses and looking totally comfortable already. 'I'm in.'

'Hope?' Nico asks. 'You in?'

This whole thing is meant to be about new experiences, new adventures, new friends.

'I'm in,' I say.

2

I promised Mum I'd call her as soon as we arrived, so I leave the men, who are sounding increasingly raucous – no doubt checking each other out like chimps in a nature documentary, all thumping chests and crotch displays – and walk to the bow, the front of the boat, where it's much quieter. I stand for a little while, holding on to the railing and staring out over the water, watching the waves ripple away towards the horizon, and then I call Mum.

'So you made it then?' she says, her voice immediately pulling me home.

I can only just hear her over the sound of the TV and I can picture them all: Mae on the sofa with her blanket wrapped around her fist, thumb in her mouth – she sucks it so much and so enthusiastically that she's worn a permanent blister on her knuckle; Alfie's probably there too but stretched out on the floor, headphones on, playing *Pokémon* on his Switch. Riley is most likely in her room, learning TikTok dances or watching something inappropriate on Disney+.

'Yeah, it's great,' I say. 'How are you feeling?'

'Oh, you know. My back's killing. My feet are buggered. I thought my waters had broken this afternoon but turns out I'd just peed myself. All fun and games.'

'That's rough.'

'Eh, what are you gonna do? So what's it like? This yacht?'

'It's amazing. It's huge but my room is tiny and I'm sharing with a girl called Kelsey. From Cheshire.'

Mum snorts. 'Posh?'

'Not *not* posh.'

'Mind out for her. Posh girls are the worst.'

'She seems nice. Haven't seen much of her so far.'

'What does Adam think?'

'Of Kelsey?'

'I meant of the yacht. But, yeah, her too.'

'I don't think he's seen much of her yet, but he seems happy enough with the yacht. We're all going out tonight to get to know each other a bit better.'

'Don't be getting too drunk,' Mum says. I can tell that she's moved into the kitchen. The tap is running as she fills the kettle. As she gets a mug out of the cupboard, the door bangs against the wall like it always does, always has. There's a perfectly round dent in the wall now from the handle that no one's ever thought to remove.

'The kids are missing you,' Mum says.

She'll be unscrewing the jam jar we use for sugar and spooning too much into her tea.

'I miss them too.'

Mae always asking me to tickle her back to help her fall asleep. Alfie acting like he doesn't want anything to do with any of us, but then cuddling into my side whenever we put a film on, wrapping his hand in my hair like he did when he was a baby. Riley, seven going on seventeen, always messaging to ask me to bring her McDonald's or to show me a video of the raccoon she follows on Instagram.

'When's your next appointment?' I ask Mum.

She's not due for another five months, but the health visitor was a bit concerned the baby might be huge so they're monitoring her more closely than they usually would.

'Next week, I think. I'll have to check. Did I tell you they've got me on these iron tablets? They're huge. Like choking down a shoe.'

I laugh.

'I'd better go,' she says, and I can tell she's back in the living room with the kids. 'Have a good time tonight. Be careful.'

'I will.'

'Oh, hey, I know what I wanted to tell you. I saw Maddie at the hospital. The doctor was like, "I have a medical student with me today. Is it okay if they sit in on your examination?" and then it was Mads! She looked knackered. And then I had to get up on the thing with the stirrups for an examination and I thought she'd be on the other side of the curtain, but, no, there she was, looking right up my chuff.'

'Well that's great,' I say, sarcastically. 'I'll text her and ask what she thought.'

Mum laughs. 'Don't do that. I mean, text her. But maybe don't mention how she saw my vag.'

I close my eyes and sigh. 'I am definitely not going to mention that, but I imagine she will.'

'She can't, can she? Confidentiality and all that. Anyway, it was mortifying. Reminded me of when I had you and they asked if I minded students watching and when I looked up there was a whole line of them peering at me. Like they'd brought a coach tour in.'

I've heard this story many times.

'Right. Deffo gotta go now. Give Adam my love. Look after him. And tell him to look after you.'

'Don't worry,' I tell her. 'We'll look after each other.'

I glance around in case anyone's nearby, but I'm still alone.

'I know you will,' she says. 'You always do.'

'Give me a ring after your appointment,' I say. 'Or whenever. You can leave a message if I'm busy.'

'Yeah, I know how phones work, soft girl.'

I smile, shaking my head.

'Anyone want to talk to Hope?' Mum says and is greeted by a chorus of *no*s.

Charming.

'Tell them I love them anyway.'

'Will do. Love you.'

'Love you too.'

I feel a bit self-conscious about joining everyone back on deck – I can hear their laughter from here – so instead I head back to my cabin to unpack. Despite – or because – it's so small, the storage has been well designed. Between the bunks and the bathroom is a small, shared closet with drawers at the base. I hang up some clothes alongside the uniforms that are already hanging there, and tuck T-shirts, shorts and underwear away in the drawers. I take the photo album Mum made for me out of my case. It folds out into a triangular frame so I can choose different pictures to display.

I pick the one of all of us in Gran Canaria a couple of years ago. We're on the beach, the sun setting behind us, the pink and apricot sky reflected in the ocean. My stepdad, Mick, took it on timer and he's pretty much a blur as he tried to fling himself into frame in time. The little ones – pink-cheeked and sand-blasted – are laughing. Mum, holding toddler Mae, is grinning at Mick; Adam's smiling at me. I'm the only one looking at the camera. I love it so much.

I put it on the shelf that runs along the wall next to my bed, along with a Jellycat Snowball I caught Riley sneaking into my bag. At first she denied it and then said she doesn't like it and wanted to get rid of it, which made me laugh since I bought it for her last Christmas. I brought some battery fairy lights to string up in my bunk too, but I've no way to attach them right now, so I leave them in my case and slide it under my bed, alongside Kelsey's.

When I open the door to head back on deck, Adam's at the end of the corridor.

He grins at me. 'Fancy seeing you here.'

I'm ridiculously happy to see him and we haven't even been here for a day yet. He looks like he's already caught the sun – his cheekbones and browbone are pink.

I smile back at him. 'We have to stop meeting like this.'

'You okay? How's your cabin?'

I push the door open to show him. 'Titchy.'

He steps closer to look past me into the room. 'Right? I knew they were going to be small, but I didn't think they'd be this small.'

He's close enough that I can smell him. Beer. Deodorant. The heat of his skin.

'How's yours?' I ask, nodding towards his door.

'The same, pretty much.'

I close my door behind me and follow him up the corridor to his cabin. He pushes the door open and then reaches back to pull me inside with him.

'What if Nico comes down?'

He grins again. 'We're not doing anything. I'm just showing you my room. Totally innocent.'

'Right.'

He's already crowding up towards me, my back against the door, but I crane past him to look around the room.

'How is it this untidy already?'

It looks like the two of them upended their cases on their beds. There's trainers and flip-flops tangled together in a pile and the bathroom floor is carpeted with towels.

'Let's get you out of these wet things,' Adam says, tugging on the hem of my T-shirt.

'They're not wet,' I argue, but I'm already softening against the door, my hands on his hips to pull him closer.

He dips his head and licks the shoulder of my shirt and I honk out a laugh, which he stops with a kiss, leaning into me. He tastes of beer and crisps and I don't even care. It's Adam. I love him. And I'm so glad he's here. I'm so glad we're doing this together.

His hands are under my T-shirt, thumbs brushing over my nipples, and I arch against him, my head banging back against the door.

'Do you think we can –' I start to say, but then Adam drops his hands and straightens up, his eyes looking panicked.

'I can hear Nico.'

I shake my head. 'I didn't hear anything.'

But then I almost fall backwards as the door opens.

'Hello, hello. What's this then?' Nico says, stepping into the room with us, even though there's no space. 'Did you two sneak away for a bit of afternoon delight?'

'Nah, mate. Just showing Hope where the magic doesn't happen.'

16

'It's a pigsty,' I say.

Nico snorts with laughter and then snorts again like a pig. 'I know, right?'

He goes into the bathroom and starts peeing without closing the door.

I widen my eyes at Adam who pulls an apologetic face.

'We're going in about an hour,' Nico says. 'Bagsy first shower.'

Only then does he close the bathroom door.

Adam kisses me quickly, before opening the cabin door and ushering me back out into the corridor, leaving me high and dry.

Or low and wet. I head back to my room for a cold shower.

3

The restaurant we go to that evening is on a terrace in the harbour – we can literally still see the *Serendipity* from here. The sun is starting to set, the sky streaked with hot pink and peach.

Nico insists that we sit boy/girl/boy on the long table to get to know each other. I end up with Adam on my left and Nico at the head of the table to my right. Liam is at the other end, next to Kelsey. Liz, the captain, didn't join us – apparently she rarely goes out, preferring to stay in her cabin and watch Danish crime shows while FaceTiming her wife back in Canada. The chef, a cute Italian man named Carlo, arrived just before we left, but said he was too tired from the journey to come out.

Nico orders jugs of margaritas for the table and then there's a brief lull in the chatter and noise while we all study the menus.

'How are you finding it so far?' Nico asks me.

I'm trying to decide between a burger and salmon, but I glance up at him. He's still wearing his sunglasses, but he pushes them up onto his head to look at me. His eyes are deep brown and twinkly, like he's about to tell a joke. I realise who he looks like – the footballer Neymar Jr. Alfie's got a poster of him on his bedroom wall.

'It seems great. Everyone is nice so far.'

He nods. 'It's a good crew, I think.' He raises his voice. 'Apart from Louise!'

'No one cares what you think,' Louise calls back in a sing-song voice.

When I look down at her she's smiling at her menu. Nico is grinning. Interesting.

I decide on the salmon and fold my menu, reaching for one of the water bottles in the middle of the table.

Nico gently knocks my hand away and pours me a glass. Is he flirting? I can't tell if he's flirting.

'It's super busy on charter,' he tells me. 'And *knackering*. But it's fun.'

'How long have you been a yachtie?' I ask him.

The word *yachtie* sounds silly coming out of my mouth, like I'm using slang I haven't yet earned, but everyone else says it so I have to try it.

Nico screws up his face in thought. 'Four years, I think? Maybe five now. Had to take time out for Covid, so it's probably five actual years, four yachting years.'

'So what made you . . . ?' I start to ask, but the waiter arrives to take our order and once he's gone, Nico's turned to talk to Ben on the opposite side of the table. Adam is chatting to Louise and Liam has turned in his seat towards Kelsey, and he's smiling at something she's saying as she twirls one of her silver hoop earrings between her fingers.

The margaritas arrive and I grab the nearest jug before Nico can, and pour his, mine and Adam's.

Adam catches my eye and flicks one eyebrow up, which makes me smile. I can't believe he booted me out earlier after getting me all worked up (I sorted myself out in the shower), but it's sort of sexy too. No one here knows we're together. There's so many of us at home; I never get to have any secrets. I kind of like it.

'Do you know where we're going after this?' I ask Nico, as I slide his drink towards him.

'Not far,' he says, gesturing vaguely. 'Still in the marina.' He does one of those chin-ups that boys do. 'So what's your deal? Left some poor dude pining for you back in Liverpool?'

'No. Just many little siblings.'

'No boyfriend?'

I shake my head. 'No boyfriend back in Liverpool, no.'

Under the table, I feel Adam's hand on my thigh and I roll my shoulders back, straightening in my seat.

'How about you?' I ask Nico. 'No girlfriend?'

'Nah,' he says. 'I'm a free spirit, me. Can't be tamed.'

I hear a snort from further along the table and I look up and see Louise scoffing.

'It's terrible, you know,' Nico says pointedly in her direction. 'Being judged. All I want to do is work hard, save money and keep myself to myself.'

Pretty much everyone laughs at that and even Nico can't keep a straight face.

I gasp as Adam starts to bunch my dress in his hand, his fingers brushing up my inner thigh. I pick up my wine to hide my face and focus on Nico's story about his first job.

'We were in the tender – me, the chef, the bosun – going to this beach,' Nico's saying. 'The bosun was drinking, which I didn't think was the best idea, but, like, I was new, I wasn't going to argue.'

Adam is talking to Louise. I can't hear what he's saying, just the tone of his voice over the hubbub of the restaurant and other conversations. His fingers are sliding higher, but painfully slowly. Heat pools in my stomach and I want to reach down and hurry him up, but I make myself focus on Nico.

'We went to this beach. Beautiful. He kept drinking.'

I hold my breath as Adam's thumb hooks into my underwear.

'On the way back, I can see we're heading for this channel marker, right?' Nico says. He pauses to take a drink and I do the same. 'I thought he must've seen it – it was red and they're not small. By the time I realised he hadn't seen it, god knows how, I yelled out, but it was too late. We hit it. We all went flying.'

'Oh my god,' I say. Adam's fingers are brushing over me, curling and probing.

'Right?' Nico says. 'He's fuckin' laughing. I was . . . like, I was new, right? I didn't know if this was like an initiation type of thing, you know? So I didn't think I could throw my weight around or anything. And he's my boss, right?'

I nod. I can't speak. Adam's thumb is circling, the pressure perfect, his fingers curling exactly where I need them. I squeeze my thighs together and try to regulate my breathing. I can't believe he's just casually talking to Louise, not even looking, so he's not going to know when I'm almost there and there's no way I can do a *When Harry Met Sally* here in front of everyone, but I'm not going to stop him either.

'The chef lost his shit,' Nico says. 'Literally had me sitting on the bosun on the way back. He was almost passed out, so it wasn't that big of a deal, but, you know, I'm still the new guy, sitting on the boss.'

I widen my eyes, say 'No. Wow. That's a lot.'

I'm leaning forward, my thighs trembling, feeling the pressure build almost to the point of no return when the food arrives, the waiter leaning between Adam and me to put our plates down on the table. Adam pulls his hand away, pushes his chair back and says he's just going to the bathroom. I wonder if he wants me to follow, to finish what he started, but I don't think my legs would even hold me up.

The club is only a few minutes' from the restaurant, around the harbour. I walk with Louise and Nico. Adam is behind us with Kelsey and Liam. Ben's gone back to the boat to jeers from Nico that he accepts good-naturedly, warning everyone not to get too messy because we've got a big day ahead tomorrow.

'Surprised you didn't head back,' Nico says, dodging around a bollard to catch up with Louise.

'I'm not staying long,' Louise says. 'Too tired. But I can't let you lot out on your own with greenies.'

'Are we the greenies?' I ask, gesturing vaguely in Adam's direction. I can hear him laughing with Liam.

I feel a bit loose-limbed and spacey – I don't know if it's from the cocktails or the almost orgasm – but I know I need to move on to soft drinks in the club. We've got to be up early tomorrow and the last thing I want is a hangover. Plus I want to make a good first impression.

'You're the greenies,' Louise confirms with a small smile.

'So we're babysitting you,' Nico agrees.

I smile. 'Probably for the best.'

'Not our first rodeo,' Nico says. And then leapfrogs a bollard as Louise turns to me and rolls her eyes.

The club is far from busy since it's still relatively early, but it's buzzing even so, an LED wall flashing with light effects in time to thumping dance music.

I get a lime and soda and follow Louise and Nico to a circle of seating in a darker corner. Adam, Kelsey and Liam stay at the bar and I watch the coloured lights play over Adam's face as he throws his head back with laughter and leans in to shout into Liam's ear.

'Your boyfriend's having a good time,' Nico says, his mouth right up against my ear.

'Not my boyfriend,' I say. 'But yeah.'

'You're not jealous?'

'He's not my boyfriend, so no reason to be jealous,' I lie.

Kelsey's hand is on Adam's forearm and I wonder what happens if someone is interested in either of us. We probably should have discussed it and come up with a plan. But then Kelsey downs her drink, shouts something at the boys and moves down to the other end of the bar. I can just about see a barman with a huge beard and long hair leaning over the bar to kiss her on the mouth.

'She's got a bloke in every port that one,' Nico tells me.

When I look back at Adam, he's looking around the club, searching for, I hope, me. When he spots me, his face splits into a wide grin and the tension in my shoulders melts away. He and Liam cross the dance floor towards us and I can't take my eyes off Adam. He's changed so much over the last few years it's hard to believe. I look basically the same as I did when we met, when we were sixteen. I'm a little taller and curvier, my hair is better and I now only get spots once a month instead of all the time, but Adam . . .

He's tall – just over six foot – and broad. Strong from the gym.

He used to be cute with a cheeky smile, a unibrow and a buzzcut. And I'm not sure exactly when it happened, but now he's a man. With a strong jaw, hair that always looks perfectly dishevelled and neatly trimmed brows. He's hot. And he's mine. My secret boyfriend.

4

When my alarm goes off, I have no idea where I am. Dark. Enclosed. Like a cupboard. My breath catches in my chest with fear and then I remember. Mallorca. I'm a yachtie now. It's 7 a.m. and we didn't get back until, when? Two?

I stretch, feeling an ache in my calves from wearing heels last night, and swing my legs down and stand, careful not to bang my head on the top bunk. I turn on the bathroom light, blinking until my eyes adjust. Kelsey's bunk is empty, the bed still made, her washbag open with make-up spilling out, the way she left it when we went to dinner. Shit. We couldn't find her when we left and Louise said it was fine. She'd follow us back eventually; she was probably hooking up with the hot barman.

She's probably on her way back now, I tell myself as I stand under the steaming water of the shower. Doing the walk of no shame.

The boat is quiet when I leave the cabin. I make a coffee – there's something wrong with the machine, coffee splutters from the nozzle and milk pools in the tray, but coffee is coffee – and take it upstairs.

Through the windows, I can see the sun is rising, the sky a deep orange. Movement catches my eye and I turn, but it's a reflection of the water shimmering over the polished wooden wall. As soon as I see one, I see multiple others on the ceilings and surfaces. It feels magical. I wish Adam was up too and we could sit and watch the world wake up together, but I know he'll still be fast asleep. He is not an early-morning person.

Outside, I curl up on one of the daybeds on the aft deck. I warm my hands on the mug and look out over the water. I am here. This is now. I hold out my coffee and take a photo to post to Instagram and the family group chat.

'Morning.'

After a few minutes, Louise appears, also with a coffee, and sits down opposite me.

She's wearing shorts and a hoodie. Her feet, like mine, are bare, toenails painted dark red. She's not wearing make-up and she looks tired; the skin under her eyes is smudged lilac. 'Kelsey's back, yes?'

I shake my head. 'She's not in her bunk.'

'Shit,' Louise breathes, her eyebrows knitting together. 'I'll text her again. Not that she'll even be awake yet.'

While Louise is on her phone, I see that Mum is typing in our chat.

'Where is dishwasher salt???'

Bloody hell.

I tell her – under the sink – and she immediately asks how to refill it. While I'm googling for example photos I can screenshot and send, Louise says, 'She hasn't been on WhatsApp. The captain's going to lose it.'

'Is this not . . . ?' I start to ask, but then I'm not really sure what the question should be. Is it not okay to go out and not come back?

'You can stay out,' Louise says. 'But it should be pre-agreed.

Or she should have let someone know. You can't just disappear. Liam left with some woman, but he told Nico and he came back.'

I didn't even notice Liam had left.

Louise stands. 'We've got a full day today, so god knows what condition she'll be in when she does get back. Come and see me when you've finished your coffee, yeah? We need to get to work.'

The guests are arriving in two days – we have a meeting with the captain later to learn about them – so I spend the morning cleaning. I iron bedding and vacuum not just the carpets, but the furniture and walls, even the ceilings.

There's a list on the wall of everything that needs to be done before they arrive, from deep cleaning the seating, polishing cutlery, checking all the stock, and descaling the irons and coffee machines. It's a lot and I don't know how to do most of it, but there's pages of instructions in ring binders and if all else fails, there's the internet.

I google the coffee machine and after trying variations on 'nozzle leaking', 'pod bursting' and 'coffee machine messy', I find a YouTube tutorial on how to take the machine apart. The nozzle is completely jammed with impacted coffee powder and it takes me half an hour – along with much soaking, rinsing and jabbing with a wooden skewer – to get water running through it again. Once I've cleaned the rest of the machine and put it back together, I make a coffee to test it. It works perfectly and I actually feel really proud of myself. It's not time for my break yet, though, so I take the coffee through to the galley and offer it to Carlo the chef.

He looks appalled.

'From the machine? Thank you, no. Is not coffee.'

'Sorry, I didn't even think.'

'I only drink espresso.' He holds his hand up to mime a tiny cup.

I'm about to pour the latte away when Louise comes in, so I offer it to her. She almost snatches it off me, wrapping both hands around the cup.

'Thank you. I was just about to go and make one.'

'I cleaned the machine, so I just made it to test.'

She pulls a face. 'I should've told you not to bother. I think we need to buy a new one. That one leaks and sprays coffee everywhere.'

'That's why I cleaned it. The nozzle was blocked. I watched a YouTube video.'

Her eyes widen over the top of the mug. 'Seriously? Well done. This tastes so much better too. I think we were losing half the coffee and getting mostly hot milk.'

'Is not coffee!' Carlo says again, passionately.

By lunchtime, I'm aching, my fingertips sore from scrubbing the stairs down to the galley, along with 'detailing', which means I have to clear every crevice and crack with another wooden skewer, but it feels good to work hard, to feel a sense of accomplishment.

Louise and I stop for omelettes cooked by Carlo, who is smiley and friendly but busy sorting the provisions for the forthcoming charter. Adam joins us, sitting next to me and hooking his foot around my ankle under the table while Louise asks him about home, his family, how he's finding deck work so far.

After lunch, I polish mirrors and scrub sinks. I clean toilets, thinking about how Mum had said, 'It won't all be glamorous, you know.'

Louise keeps trying to get hold of Kelsey, but there's no reply and when the captain comes to find us, she's furious.

'How long before we call the police?' Louise asks.

Captain Liz shrugs. 'I honestly have no idea. What would they even do at this point? She's been missing for – what?' She looks at her watch. 'Less than twelve hours? I told her this mustn't happen! I can't believe she's done it again.'

I look at Louise whose lips are set in a straight line, her face wan.

My stomach churns at the thought that something might have happened to Kelsey. I wonder how well she knows the guy in the bar.

'Still nothing?' Nico calls, appearing from the salon. 'Want me to go and have a look around?'

'Where would you even look?' the captain says. 'She'll have gone home with someone and she'll turn up late and hungover, looking like shit, all embarrassed and apologetic . . .' She shakes her head. 'I'm not putting up with it. I told her.' She checks her phone. 'When she turns up,' she tells Louise, 'send her straight to me.'

'And if she doesn't?' Louise asks.

The captain sighs, rubbing a hand over her face. 'If she's not here by three, we call the police. In the meantime, can you get everyone together in the mess? I've got the preference sheets.'

'*Xander Barrett*,' Captain Liz reads, once we're all seated around the table in the crew mess. Adam sits opposite and we smile at each other.

'He developed an app for fine art auctions,' the captain continues, 'and he's bringing a couple of friends to celebrate his fortieth birthday.'

She slides information sheets across the table to each of us. Xander Barrett is American; white with cropped curly hair, a square jaw and a wide smile. In his photo he's wearing a blue polka-dot shirt, sleeves rolled up over muscled forearms.

'They mostly want to hang out and chill,' the captain says, 'but would like a special birthday dinner with a George Michael tribute act who's being flown in from London especially and he'll be staying in a hotel, not on board.'

'So maybe a beach picnic, jet skis . . .' Louise suggests.

'One pescatarian,' the captain tells Carlo. 'They would like kombucha in the morning, good coffee . . . The primary's requested ice-cream cake for his birthday . . . They like seafood, cocktails . . .'

Carlo's head snaps up from where he's been looking over the information sheets. He looks confused.

'Seafood cocktails? Cocktail di gamberetti?'

The captain laughs. 'No, no. Seafood. And cocktails.'

Carlo nods. '*Tutto bene.*'

'Although,' Captain Liz says, 'I once had a cocktail in Paris that was served in a shell. That might be nice.'

'I could do this,' Carlo says, making a note on his pad.

I turn to the second page where Xander Barrett's friends are listed. His former business partner, Jeff Hicks – who, in his photo, is wearing those gold-rimmed serial killer glasses and has a black and white beard like a badger – runs a company 'building omni-channel consumer products to launch or grow commerce verticals'. Whatever that means.

'Hipsters,' Nico says, tapping one of the other pages.

I flip through until I find the guy he's looking at – hair shaved at the sides with curls piled on top, wire-framed glasses and gold hoops curved along the edge of one ear.

'Aren't they too old to be hipsters?' Captain Liz asks. 'Or am I too old to know what a hipster is?'

'They probably call themselves mavericks or some bullshit,' Nico says, shrugging.

'I like that film,' Liam offers, still frowning down at the information sheet.

'What film?' Adam asks, as we all flick through the pages.

'*Top Gun 2*,' Liam says.

Everyone laughs and Liam asks, 'Is that not what you're talking about?'

'It's not, mate,' Nico says, kindly. 'Don't worry about it.'

'There's a boy called Maverick at my little sister's school,' I tell them.

'Yikes,' Louise says. And then, tapping the info sheet, adds, 'I bet at least one of these guys has a podcast.'

'I would not take that bet,' the captain says, smiling.

Kelsey arrives at two thirty, carrying her heels from last night and looking exhausted, hungover and basically a total mess, eye make-up caked under her eyes and hair a matted tangle.

Louise walks down the ramp to meet her and takes her directly to see the captain. Adam's polishing the chrome railing while I'm cleaning and refilling the bar fridge on the deck and he catches my eye, pulling a face.

I grimace back at him, but I don't think she's going to get fired. She'll probably just get a bollocking and a warning, surely.

But I'm wrong. The next time I see Kelsey, she's showered and changed, but also pulling her rolling suitcase.

She smiles wanly at me. 'I got fired.'

'I'm sorry.'

'It's fair enough really. Although I've never been fired this early in a job before.'

'Do you have somewhere to go?' I ask.

She nods. 'I met a guy last night who's heading to the Bahamas and said I can tag along, so I'll probably do that.' She takes her phone out of the pocket of her shorts, checks the screen briefly and puts it back.

'Wow! Okay. Is that, er, safe?'

'Oh yeah. I mean, probably. There's a full crew. It's not just me and him.'

'Right. That sounds . . . good then.'

She laughs, apparently entirely unconcerned. 'And if that doesn't work out, I can find someone else. Don't worry about me.'

I smile. 'Well, I'm sorry to see you go. We didn't even get to know each other.'

'Right?!'

She lets go of her case long enough to reach out and hug me.

'But you never know. We might still see each other again. Yachting's a smaller world than you'd think. Have a great time!'

And then she leaves. I can't believe we've lost a crew member and we haven't even left the port yet.

'So what happens now Kelsey's gone?' Adam asks me later that afternoon. We're both on break, flaked out side by side on one of the big sofas on deck.

Louise told us to make the most of any downtime because once the guests arrive it's going to be full on. I should probably be napping in my cabin, but I'm worried about oversleeping and also that once I relax my already overworked muscles will seize up and I won't be able to get up again.

'Louise said Captain Liz is calling around trying to find someone else.'

'I feel like she should have done that before firing Kelsey,' Adam says, dropping his voice and raising one eyebrow.

'I feel like you shouldn't be questioning the captain's decisions on our second day,' I tell him, smiling. 'Isn't that mutiny?'

'Yeah, okay.' He rolls his neck from side to side and I have to resist reaching over to press my thumbs into the muscles I can see straining there. 'I'm just thinking . . . what if they can't find anyone?'

'Louise doesn't seem to think that'll be a problem. I guess we just wait. We've still got a couple of days . . .'

Every time I think about guests arriving, my stomach cramps with nerves, so I'm trying not to think about it.

'You were pretty squiffy last night,' I say, sliding my foot across the cushions between us to gently kick the side of his leg. 'Did you feel rough this morning?'

'Not too bad.' He stretches again. 'Been worse.'

'Showing off in front of your new mates.'

He grins at me, squinting against the sun, then says 'lads, lads, lads' completely deadpan.

I've seen him drunk so many times over the years. From throwing up out of an upstairs window at a friend's house party to having to lurch away from the dining table at Sunday lunch at his gran's. And he never fails to remind me that an Uber driver once had to pull over just before heading into the Mersey tunnel because I'd mixed my drinks. And there was a Sunday when neither of us could get out of bed at all, until eventually we got a pizza delivery that Adam paid his younger brother, Ollie, a fiver to collect at the door and bring to us in the bedroom.

It's something I've always loved about us – we've seen each other at our best and also at our worst.

'I didn't mean to,' Adam says now, ducking his head and looking at me from under his fringe. 'I was nervous, I think.'

I nod. 'Me too.'

'It's a lot, right? And I don't know what I'm doing.'

If we were at home, in my bedroom or his, I'd roll over, shuffle up alongside him, put my head on his chest, hook one leg over his thigh, maybe even slide my hand under his T-shirt against the warm skin of his stomach. But I can't do any of that here. I can only say, 'I think we probably have to learn by doing. Pick it up as we go along.'

I hold up my little finger to show him. 'I've got my first yachting injury.'

He squints at the tiny purple bruise running along my fingernail. 'Shark attack?'

'Slow-closing drawer closed slowly on my finger.'

'Ouch.'

'Really bloody hurts actually.'

He purses his lips for a second as if he's going to kiss it better, which is what he'd do at home, but instead he stares at me for a few seconds before saying, 'You're getting freckles.'

I wrinkle my nose. 'Am I?'

'Nose and cheeks and your top lip.'

He looks at my mouth. The first time we kissed was at a house party where he told me I had something on my face.

'Just under your lip,' he'd said, pointing.

I told him it was a big freckle.

'No,' he argued. 'It's a bit of chocolate, I think. There.'

I wiped it with my thumb, even though I knew.

'You didn't get it,' he said.

'No, because it's a freckle.'

'It's not!' He was so insistent. 'It's just there.'

'I know where it is,' I'd told him, 'and it's a freckle.'

It was when he asked, 'Can I get it?' that I realised he'd been staring at my mouth the whole time.

'You can try,' I told him.

He held my jaw in his hand. Rubbed his thumb under my lip. Said, 'Bloody hell, it is a freckle!'

And then when I laughed, he kissed me. I almost lean in to kiss him now but catch myself just in time.

Secret. We have to be secret.

The sun is setting over the ocean as we all have 'family dinner' together on deck later – apart from the captain, who once again has plans to watch Nordic noir on FaceTime with her wife. I'm seated next to Ben. It's almost hard to talk to him because he's so handsome, but he's also friendly and warm and before long I can almost forget the ridiculousness of his face. He tells me he got into yachting after his husband left him.

'We had a business together and it was really successful,' he says. 'He told me he wanted to sell it and retire – he was much older than me. The plan was that we would sell it and then travel the world together. We sold the business. He met someone else and he's travelling the world with him.'

'Bloody hell,' I say. 'I'm so sorry.'

Ben smiles, sadly. 'It was pretty rough. And for a while there I had no idea what I was going to do. I'd always wanted to travel and I wasn't going to let him ruin that for me. But I also used to worry about bumping into him and his new man somewhere, you know? I know it's unlikely, but it made it hard for me to arrange anything. It was like a mental block.'

'I get that,' I tell him.

'And then a friend took me on a yacht to cheer me up.'

'Wow!'

'A rich friend.' He smiles. 'I loved the whole thing and I kept talking to the crew... At first it was just chatting, you know, asking questions. But by the end of the trip, I knew it was more than that. I was almost interviewing them. I'd started making notes, researching it all on my phone. That was ten years ago. And here we are.'

He smiles and once again I'm startled by his face. I wonder what it's like to wake up in the morning, look in the mirror and see that.

'And do you love it as much as you thought you would?'

He nods. 'I really do. It's hard work – I guess you know that already? But it's so rewarding. And I get to travel and make good money and meet great people –'

'And scrub floors and wash windows and polish steel,' Nico interrupts.

'Shut it, you,' Ben says. 'I was bigging up the glamour side.'

'One of my mates called me a glorified janitor,' Nico tells us. 'I know he's jealous, but also I was like, well, yeah, a lot of the stuff we do on board is, you know, scut work. But look at where we get to do it? And then on days off we can go snorkelling or whatever. And I'm seeing the world. On his days off, he's probably just, like, playing *FIFA* and wanking.'

'What did your friends think of you doing this?' Ben asks me.

'Well, it was Adam's idea,' I tell them, looking over at Adam, who seems to be deep in conversation with Liam. 'My friend Maddie was really supportive. I've talked to her a lot about not knowing what I wanted to do. She's training to be a doctor – she knew she wanted to do that from when we were little – but I just didn't have a clue really.'

'Did you go to uni?' Nico asks.

I nod. 'I did English though, so that didn't really help. Unless I wanted to go into teaching, which I didn't.'

'What do your parents think about it?' Ben asks.

'They think it's great,' I tell them. 'Mostly. My mum's pregnant – she had me really young – and she and my stepdad have got three other kids that I looked after a lot. So I think she was a bit worried about not having me around to help, you know.'

'She can't expect you to do that forever, though,' Nico said. 'You've got to have your own life.'

I nod. 'I know. And she knows that too. It's just a hard transition.'

'Talking of a hard transition,' Ben says, pushing his chair back. 'I'm off to bed.'

'Wow,' Nico says. 'Bit raunchy for you.'

Ben actually blushes, the tops of his cheekbones flushing pink. 'That's not what I meant.'

Nico and I laugh and Ben gives Nico the finger, before heading off to bed.

I look over at Adam and he's looking back at me. I hope he's thinking about finishing what he started in the restaurant the other night.

I'm showered and wearing one of Adam's old T-shirts over my knickers when I open my door to him and he wastes no time in crowding me back into the room and running his hands over my bare skin, dropping his head to kiss the side of my neck.

'Been wanting to do this all day.'

I turn my head to give him better access, as I press up against him, slipping my arms around his waist and pulling him closer. We kiss, his tongue sliding against mine – he tastes of wine and melon gelato – fingers tangling in my hair, and it feels so, so hot. It feels like when we first got together and we'd sneak into each other's houses after school, before our parents got home from work, curling up in bed and rubbing against each other, afraid to take any of our clothes off in case we suddenly had to jump up and pretend we'd been studying.

'You feel so good,' Adam murmurs against my mouth, moving one of his legs between mine so I'm straddling his thigh. I rub against him and let him manoeuvre me back into my bunk. I duck as I lie down on the mattress, but he bangs his head against the top bunk and blurts out a 'shit!'

I shush him, but I'm also giggling at the startled expression on his face.

'Oh, you're laughing?' He raises one eyebrow at me as he ducks all the way under and crawls into the bunk, on all fours above me.

'I'm not,' I whisper, even though I am.

He digs his fingers into my sides, tickling me, and I resist the urge to yelp.

'Oh yeah, have a good laugh,' he says, fingers moving up my ribs towards my pits. 'Get it all out of your system.'

I'm managing to laugh quietly, through my nose, but I can feel it wanting to burst out of me and I know once I start I won't be able to stop, so instead I grab his hands and pull them up over my head, pushing our clasped hands against the pillow.

He almost growls as he drops down on top of me, grinding his hips into mine, and suddenly I'm desperate, writhing underneath him, pulling my legs up to hook around his waist, kissing him fast and hard.

'God,' he whispers, letting go of my hands, so he can push his under my T-shirt to grab my breasts. 'This is the best idea we ever had.'

I tug at his T-shirt – I want him naked, on top of me, inside me, all around me.

'Agreed.'

'Oh, hey.' He lifts himself up for a second. 'How's your finger?'

I can't even think what he means.

'Shark attack,' he adds.

'Oh!' I pull my hand down and look at my finger, even though I can't see it in the darkness. 'Still sore.'

He dips his head and kisses my fingernail before sucking the tip of my finger into his mouth.

'Oh, absolutely not!' I say.

And then we're pulling each other's clothes off. Adam's arm gets caught in his sleeve and he bangs his elbow against the wall, knocking my photo frame down onto the bed. I pick it up and drop it to the floor, then pull my own T-shirt off and drop that too.

As soon as I lie back down, Adam's mouth is on my breast and my leg shoots out, kicking the wall at the foot of the bed.

He lifts his head long enough to shush me and I mime zipping my lips and throwing away the key. He grins at me and drops his head again, grazing my nipple with his teeth. I hook my legs around his waist and he moans softly.

'Quiet,' I whisper.

I push him back and roll him off me, wriggling out of my underwear.

He's just watching me with an almost stunned expression on his face, until I gesture at him and he pulls his underpants off too.

We both moan as I straddle him and I whisper, 'We're terrible at being quiet.'

'You could shut me up,' he murmurs.

His eyes widen as I put my hand over his mouth and then lower myself down onto him. I breathe in roughly through my nose. I don't know how I'm going to be able to stay quiet through this. He feels amazing. We feel amazing.

I take my hand away to kiss him and he wraps his big hands around the backs of my thighs, holding me firmly against him, as I move slowly, pushing him deeper inside me.

'Fuck,' he whispers against my lips. 'This is so hot.'

I drop my head to kiss his shoulder, the dip at the base of his throat, behind his ear where I know it drives him mad.

We stare at each other and he grips my hips as I ride him, holding myself up on my work-weakened arms for as long as I can before dropping down to lie fully on top of him. He bends his knees and starts moving into me too and it feels incredible. He slides a hand down between us and I squeak as he curls his fingers against me.

I press my face into the side of his neck as fireworks burst behind my eyes.

5

I wake up alone. The cabin is pitch black and I have no idea what time it is or what I did with my phone. I grope around the bed for a while, finding my abandoned T-shirt and the knickers Adam pulled off me, but no phone. I eventually find it on the floor just under the bunk. It's out of charge.

I yelp as someone knocks on the door and immediately pushes it open a few inches.

'You're not up?' Louise says, as I squint in her general direction, the light from the hallway hurting my eyes.

'What time is it?' I croak. 'Sorry, my phone . . .'

'It's eight fifteen,' Louise says. 'Captain's waiting on deck.'

'Shit.' I'm about to push the covers off but remember I'm naked. 'Sorry. I'll be five minutes.'

'No longer,' Louise says and closes the door.

When I get up on deck – I washed my face, cleaned my teeth, pulled my hair back into a ponytail and hoped for the best – everyone's waiting.

'I'm so sorry,' I tell Captain Liz. 'My phone didn't charge and –'

She holds a hand up to cut me off. 'It happens. But don't let it happen again.'

I glance at Adam, who gives me a sympathetic smile. And then I notice someone new: a short, curvy girl with light brown skin and deep red curly hair piled up on top of her head. She's wearing silver Birkenstocks, cut-off jeans and a T-shirt with an illustration of what looks like the cover of a children's book from the seventies of children sitting around a boy lying in the middle of a pentagram and the title 'Let's Summon Demons!'

'Now that Hope has joined us . . .' the captain says and I wince, 'I'm sure you'll be pleased to hear that I found a replacement for Kelsey. Berry's been working as a tour guide in Barcelona but kindly agreed to come and help us out in our staffing crisis. She comes highly recommended by Louise and Nico.'

'Not by me,' Nico jokes. 'I found her annoying.'

'I can't wait to get started,' Berry says, giving a little wave before twisting her hand to quickly give Nico the finger. 'But is there coffee? And can I get a shower?'

'Of course,' Captain Liz says. 'Hope, can you show her to your cabin?'

Berry smiles over at me and her face is so open that I instantly feel like we're going to get on.

'Follow me,' I tell her and turn towards the salon doors.

'This boat's awesome,' she says in the salon.

'It's amazing,' I agree. 'I saw it online before we came but it didn't do it justice.'

'So shiny!'

'I have done so much polishing. I think my fingerprints are starting to fade.'

Like Adam, Berry's brought a backpack and it bumps against the narrow walls of the stairs as she follows me down below deck.

'So you're new?' she asks me on the way.

'I am. Me and my friend Adam started a couple of days ago.'

'You came here together? That's cool. Enjoying it so far?'

I glance back at her over my shoulder. 'We did, yeah. And I am, thanks. There's a lot to learn though, so it's a bit intimidating. And we haven't even had guests yet.'

'Yeah,' she says. 'You need to jump in at the deep end really.'

'This is what everyone keeps telling me. Where are you from?'

'LA originally, but I've been working in Europe for a while.'

I show her into the cabin and she drops her backpack on the floor, pressing her hands into the small of her back and stretching.

'You're on the bottom bunk already?'

I nod. 'Kelsey had the top bunk.'

'Oh, sure. And is that okay? You want to stay there? I don't mind swapping if you do.'

'No, bottom bunk's fine with me.'

'Great.' She beams at me and then says, 'Sorry, I just need to get out of this.'

She pulls her top over her head, revealing a lacy black bra along with watercolour tattoos all over her shoulders and arms. 'It's hot as balls out there.'

As Berry rummages in her bag, I stare at her tattoos. There's a sprig of lavender that looks almost three-dimensional on the back of her neck. To the left of the lavender at the top of her shoulder there's a tiny shoal of fish, peach and pink and blue, and a cresting wave between her shoulder blades. They're so beautiful that my fingers are almost itching to touch them.

'Your tattoos are amazing.'

Berry glances back at her over her shoulder. 'Yeah? Thanks. I sometimes forget about them. You got any?'

'No. Not yet. I want one, though.'

'Do you know what you'd get?' She unzips her bag and pulls out a washbag. It's bright green and printed with the words *Pickle Slut*.

'No. Not really. I used to think I wanted a palm tree, but people keep telling me they're basic.'

Berry laughs, unzipping the bag and taking out a couple of bottles.

'You get what you want and don't worry about what's basic. Look.'

She pulls down the front of her shorts to reveal a tiny Dory from *Finding Nemo* just above the line of her knickers. 'Don't get much more basic than that. I love her though. Sorry, I'll get my shit off your bed and then I'm going to hop in the shower.'

'God, yes,' I say. 'Sorry. I'll make coffee. How do you have it?'

While Berry showers, I make lattes for us both. When she comes out to join me, she's wearing the crew uniform. Her feet are bare, her toenails are bright pink, her wine-red hair is wet and curling round her shoulders.

'This uniform clashes with my hair,' she says, taking her coffee from me. 'Thank you for this. I've been awake since four.'

I'm grateful for my coffee too, since I didn't get a chance to get one, thanks to oversleeping.

We take our coffees up on the deck and it's only then that I realise I have no idea what I'm meant to be doing.

'I made myself one automatically and I should be working,' I tell Berry, as she curls up on the sofa at the back of the boat.

'I think they can spare you for ten minutes to bring me up to speed,' she tells me.

'I guess so,' I say. 'So you were a tour guide in Barcelona?'

She nods. 'Wine and tapas tours. So everyone would get steadily more drunk and rowdy and by the end of each one I felt like a kindergarten teacher. Stone-cold sober, hungry and pissed as hell.' She grins at me. 'Sometimes it was fun. But, yeah, it got old fast. Lot of British stag parties.'

'Oh god,' I say. 'I'm so sorry.'

'Right? Your people can drink!'

'So had you already quit when Captain Liz called?'

She shakes her head, a curl bouncing against her cheekbone. 'I was thinking about it. But I wasn't sure what I wanted to do, whether I was going to go home or stay in Spain . . . My original plan was to save enough to go travelling round Europe, but it hasn't worked out that way so far. I had been wondering if anyone was hiring . . . someone I've worked with before and liked. I didn't want to just go on any programme, so it was perfect really.'

'You've worked with Captain Liz before?'

She nods and swallows some coffee before answering. 'Briefly. She's great. Kind. And fair. Which is not as common as you'd hope.'

'And with Louise and Nico?'

She nods. 'But not at the same time. Louise acts like she's got a stick up her butt, but it's more that she takes the job real seriously. She's pretty cool once you get to know her. And Nico, well . . .' She rolls her eyes. 'He's great. Most of the time. Your friend is Adam, right?'

I nod. 'We've been friends since school.'

'That's cool. It's good to have someone to talk to when you're new.'

'Yeah. He was the one who suggested doing this and I didn't know at first – I've got a big family and help out a lot at home – but I felt like it was time to get away for a while, so he wore me down.'

'But you like it so far, right?'

I smile at her. 'So far.'

Captain Liz appears and tells us, laughing, to stop chatting and get to work, so we do.

I spend the morning in the pantry cleaning all the shelves, cupboards and drawers. Huge bags of rice and pasta, sugar and salt need to be decanted into plastic tubs and I have to update the inventory of all the food, along with expiration dates. I also need to check the cupboard on the aft deck where all the bottled water is kept. It's a tiny cupboard, fitted into an awkward space, so I have to crawl inside, and haul the cases of bottles behind me to crawl inside further and reach the rest. I worry briefly that someone will casually close the door and trap me in here, so I work fast, scraping my arm on the door hinge as I drag myself out.

Because we don't have guests on board yet, we're all able to eat lunch together on deck. Carlo makes a tortellini and tomato salad with artichokes and olives with vanilla panna cotta for dessert, and everyone raves about every bit of it.

'Did you all know this is Carlo's first job on a yacht?' Captain Liz says.

'Where did you work before?' Nico asks him.

'I was the private chef for a very rich man in New York,' Carlo tells us. 'He live alone and I stay there and only see him when I cook. So it was lonely and I was very bored.'

'I can't even imagine that,' I tell him. 'Did he have friends round ever?'

Carlo shakes his head. 'I think he is a lonely man and I feel bad for him, but there is nothing in common. Sometimes we try to talk, but . . .' He shrugs. 'So I look for other job and think I need job with many people and not so quiet.'

'You've come to the right place,' Liam says. I notice that he's eaten his panna cotta but left the strawberries.

Carlo dips his head and lowers his voice. 'I worry this is too much the other way.'

Everyone laughs and Carlo grins.

'You definitely won't be lonely,' Louise tells him, smiling.

'No,' Carlo says, still beaming. 'I might die of tired, but I won't die of lonely.'

After lunch I'm on break – thank god, I'm exhausted – so once everything's cleared up, I go up to the sun deck and call Maddie.

'Oh my god,' she says. 'Show me everything. Is it amazing?'

'I can't show you everything because everyone else is working,' I tell her. 'But I'm on the sun deck and look.'

I turn my phone so she can see the bunny pad – the huge comfy seating area – the hot tub and the ocean beyond.

'I am so jealous,' she says. 'I'd show you my view but it's literally a grey wall with a hand sanitiser dispenser on it.'

'Mum says she saw you at the hospital.' I sit on the bunny pad, curling my legs up underneath me. 'The less said about that the better.'

'Oh my god, I was mortified. When we said we knew each other, I thought the doctor would say I had to step out, you know? But she asked your mum if it was okay and she said fine. Next thing the doctor's pointing stuff out to me . . .'

'Please don't tell me what stuff.'

'Everything's fine though. Your mum is incredible.'

'I know she is. I feel bad – that I'm not there.'

Maddie huffs. 'You've done plenty. It's your time now. Is it really exciting?'

'It's a lot of work and it's going to get worse when the guests arrive.'

'Do you know much about them? Are they super rich? Ooh, are they famous? If it's a Kardashian you have to tell me.'

'Obviously rich,' I tell her. 'But not famous. Not knowing what they're going to be like or what they want is pretty intimidating.'

'You can do it,' Maddie says. 'You've got a lot of common sense.'

I laugh. One of my teachers wrote that on my report in sixth form and it became our catchphrase for whenever one of us does something stupid.

I tell her about Kelsey and she tells me that our friend Molly's mum saw Molly's boyfriend on Tinder and Molly confronted him at his work in front of everyone and one of his mates said her mum had messaged him and it was a whole thing.

'How's Adam getting on?' Maddie asks once I'm up to date on the local gossip.

'He's okay,' I tell her. 'Same as me really. In at the deep end, trying to swim. You know.'

'That's good. And how's the sexy sneaking around?'

'Pretty good so far.'

'Ugh. Why don't I have your life?'

'Because you're training to be a doctor so you can actually save lives? Bit more important, Mads.'

She huffs. 'I'd much rather be on a superyacht right now, thanks very much.'

'If it helps,' I tell her, 'after my break I have to go and descale all the loos.'

'And I've got a colonoscopy to observe.'

'Okay,' I tell her. 'You win.'

6

'Want to join? You can have the mat,' Berry says, unfurling her yoga mat in the middle of the deck.

I'm curled up in the corner of one of the big sofas with my phone and a coffee and Nico is stretched out on the other sofa. We're picking the guests up in Palma, which is just over two hours away and since we got the prep done first thing, the captain said we can relax while we sail.

I shake my head. 'Thanks but no. I'm not that bendy.'

Berry raises her arms over her head and leans a little from side to side, before folding herself into downward dog.

'You don't have to be bendy. This is how you get to be bendy.'

'Stop saying "bendy",' Nico says without moving. 'You're getting me hot and bothered.'

'You haven't changed then,' Berry says, but she's smiling.

'It would take a stronger man than me to resist a sexy woman doing yoga in the sun.'

'Have you ever considered,' Berry says, moving up to kneeling, 'that not everything a woman does is directed at your dick?'

Nico pushes his sunglasses up onto his head and grins, squinting against the bright morning light. 'I have considered it, yeah. But I dismissed it as unrealistic.'

Berry shakes her head. She lowers to plank – triceps flexing – and then down onto her belly before pushing up to cobra.

'Keep away from this one, Hope,' she tells me. 'He thinks he's charming.'

'Don't worry, I plan to.'

'Actually, I know I'm charming,' Nico says. 'And I know you both know it too.' He lies back down, replacing his sunglasses.

'Keep telling yourself that,' Berry says, without any malice.

She arches her back, dropping her hands down behind her to hold on to her heels, her chest raised to the sky.

She looks so strong and powerful. She looks like a sculpture. I realise I'm staring, but I don't have muscles. I mean, obviously I have muscles – I'm not a jellyfish – but I don't have visible muscles. I think I'd like to.

When Berry's done with her yoga, she stretches out next to me for a while, texting, and then goes inside for a shower. Nico's asleep with his T-shirt over his face. I climb off the sofa and experiment with a quick stretch – arms overhead, bend side to side – before going for a wander around the boat.

I head for the bow and – along with blue sky, a few tiny, white clouds and glittering water – I find Adam. He's sitting on the edge of one of the big round daybeds, hand gripping the chrome railing.

'Hey,' I say, sitting down next to him. 'I thought you went back to bed.'

I glance around to make sure we're alone before reaching for his hand. It's cold and clammy, but I rub my thumb over his palm anyway.

'I did,' he says, his voice both rough and weak, like the morning after too much beer. 'I feel like shit and the cabin was making it worse.'

The colour's drained out of his face. He looks pale, almost green.

'Ad. Did you drink that much last night?'

'Not that,' he croaks. 'Seasick.'

'Oh shit. Did you bring anything?'

He shakes his head before curling over and dropping it into his hands, fingers pressing into the back of his neck.

'I can't believe this,' he says. 'Are you all right?'

'Yeah. I mean, it's a bit weird, especially below deck, but I don't feel sick, no. Want me to go and get something? They must have stuff on board for passengers.'

'Please.' He sits up, leaning back, turning his face up to the sky. He looks woeful. 'Thanks.'

Inside, I find Louise and she gives me wrist bands, along with a couple of tablets – she says it's too late for them to work, but they might just make him feel better psychologically – and she tells me to go and get some ginger from Carlo.

I go back to Adam first. He's moved closer to the railings, presumably so it'll be quicker and easier if he does need to puke, and he takes the tablets, washing them down with water. I leave the bands with him and go down to the galley to find Carlo.

The table that runs through the middle of the galley is covered with an array of fruits and vegetables – red and yellow peppers, a pile of greens, lemons, peaches, tomatoes, cherries. It looks so beautiful.

'Is this for us or the guests?' I ask him. I really want to steal a tiny perfect tomato, but Carlo has a big knife.

He stops singing tunelessly along to Ariana Grande and says, 'A bit for both. First the guests and then the crew. Is just a chopped salad. But good!'

He smiles at me, and I notice he's got a gap between his front teeth. It's funny, Carlo is almost as handsome as Ben, but he's cute rather than hot. I tell him about Adam's seasickness and he points to a gnarly-looking piece of ginger, already on the table.

'I put this for the dressing,' he says. 'Just in case.'

He picks it up and scrapes off some of the rough peel before cutting off a chunk.

'Tell him just hold in mouth for as long as he can, and then he can nibble it, but he might not like to,' he says.

When I take the ginger to Adam, he's lying flat on his back on the sunlounger, eyes closed and fingertips pressed to his eyelids.

'I've brought ginger.'

He groans as he pulls himself up to sitting, looking even worse than when I left him. I help him put the wrist bands on, rotating them so they're in the right position, pressing on the acupressure points that are meant to prevent nausea.

'Carlo said to just hold it in your mouth. You don't have to swallow if you don't want to.'

'I hate this,' he moans.

I know he must be feeling bad because he wouldn't usually miss a 'that's what she said' opportunity.

As soon as the ginger passes his lips, he lurches up and vomits over the side of the boat. I rub his back, as he clings to the railing, his knuckles white.

'I didn't even think of this,' he says, once he's stopped puking. 'How thick am I? I just thought, like, I'm fine on the ferry. It's not even rough!' He gestures at the gentle swell of the ocean. 'If I feel like this now, what about when there's a storm?'

'I think maybe it's something you get used to. Don't they say that? You get your sea legs?'

'Oh yeah.' He frowns and his eyes go wide. He covers his mouth, gags a little and then says, 'I'm okay. Isn't sea legs about keeping your balance, not puking?'

'I don't know. Maybe? But I guess if you can get used to one, you can get used to the other?'

'If I have to leave this job cos I can't stop vomming, I'm gonna feel like a right dick.'

'It'll be all right,' I tell him, still rubbing his back. I've got an excuse to touch him and I'm happy to take it.

'Thanks.' He bumps his knee against mine. 'You're always there when I need you. At least we're not working too hard today.'

'We will be once we pick the guests up.'

'Oh yeah. Shit.'

I lean into his side and relax against him. I'm so glad we're doing this together.

When we arrive in Palma, the Gothic cathedral glowing golden in the sun behind a row of palm trees, we change into our whites – the smart uniforms we have to wear to greet guests – and then line up on the marina and wait for Xander and his entourage to arrive.

I once again feel like I might throw up from nerves.

Berry gently squeezes my arm. 'They're just people,' she tells me, leaning sideways to speak directly into my ear; it makes the hairs on the back of my neck stand up. 'People with money, but just people.'

I nod. I know she's right. I just haven't been around people with money very much. Before Mum met Mick we didn't have much at all. And while they both earn good money now, they also have three children together. And me. I had part-time jobs all through university and of course I lived at home, but they still had to pay fees and expenses and I know it was a stretch. It's part of the reason I agreed to come and do this. It pays well and the tips are great and I can send some money back home. Mum will probably say she won't take it, but I can get around that.

When the guests appear, walking towards us along the jetty, they all have that sort of glossy sheen that comes from expensive clothes, skincare and haircuts. They walk down the line of the crew, greeting us all and shaking our hands, and they seem nice. Just people. Rich people. Rich people who want to have a good time to celebrate a birthday. It'll be fine.

While Louise takes them for a tour of the boat and shows them to their cabins, the rest of us form a human chain from the dock along the passerelle to bring all their luggage on board. I can't believe how much stuff they've brought for just three days of charter. We didn't take this much to Gran Canaria and that was seven of us for a week.

Berry and I set the table on deck, before heading down to the kitchen where Carlo is preparing the guests' lunch. Louise radios to say the guests are hungry and will be coming straight up so could we bring up some nibbles. Carlo has made fried courgette flowers with honey and I take them up to the deck, where Xander Barrett and his friends are already waiting and take their drinks orders.

They're all polite and friendly. They ask my name and where I'm from and Harry – the one with the curly hair who is, according to the information sheet, a 'TikTok tarot guru' – says he loves my accent, that he had a fling with a Scouser at college.

I wince before I can stop myself and, to my embarrassment, Jeff notices.

'Don't worry,' he tells me. 'He's not into women.'

'Oh god, no,' Harry says, before adding, 'No offence.'

I smile. 'None taken.'

'He's got a guy in every port,' Xander jokes.

'Talking of ports,' Louise says, appearing next to me. 'Captain Liz wanted me to tell you that we'll be setting sail in around thirty minutes and lunch will be served just after. And if it's all right with you gentlemen, I'm just going to steal Hope away for five minutes . . .'

I follow Louise down to the galley where we quickly put together a huge dispenser jug of iced water with lemon, lime, strawberry and cucumber.

'Can we get some tequila in there?' Jeff – beard like a badger – asks once we bring it up to the deck.

'Ignore him,' Xander tells us. 'But actually, maybe this evening we could get a punchbowl going?'

We set sail while I'm setting the table and after Berry's finished unpacking the guests' cases, she joins me on deck. Carlo radios to say that lunch is ready and we bring up platters of seafood, along with tempura vegetables and garlic ciabatta, and the guests praise everything.

'They're so nice!' I say, next time Berry and I are in the galley at the same time.

'They are,' she agrees. 'So far. Sometimes things are different once the alcohol starts flowing.'

'Right,' I say. 'Of course.'

'But you're doing okay?' she asks me, resting her fingers on the back of my hand. Her nails are short and painted Barbie pink, the same as her toes.

There's just so much to remember and not nearly enough time to think, but I nod. 'All good so far. Thank you.'

Carlo's made a strawberry and nectarine galette that looks and smells delicious, and my stomach growls as we take it up to the table. While the guests linger over coffee – teasing each other, laughing, talking about how fabulous everything is – I refill the water, clear away dishes and make sure to stay on top of as much as I can.

The guests spend the afternoon in the sea with the water toys – snorkles, jet skis and Seabobs, which are like underwater scooters – with the deck crew supervising.

Louise, Berry and I sit down with schedules for the week ahead. I'm on crew mess and the captain's cabin, which she likes to be cleaned every day, so I go and do that, making her bed, hoovering, polishing, cleaning the bathroom. I straighten the pile of books on her bedside – a couple of dark-looking thrillers and a novel about a woman's unlikely friendship with an octopus. I refill the water bottles in her fridge and then radio Louise to come and make sure I've done a good job.

'This looks great,' she says, hands on hips, big eyes scanning the room. 'Did you polish that mirror?'

'Oh! No, I didn't.'

Louise nods. 'Make sure you do all the mirrors. Also it looks like the tissues need topping up.'

There's a chrome tissue box on a small, recessed shelf under the mirror.

'Okay.'

'I'd say also give the TV and the monitor a wipe – there's screen wipes in the locker. Don't use normal wipes or sprays.'

'Okay,' I say again.

'Great.' She smiles at me. 'Good job. When you're done in here, go and see Carlo because we need to start setting up afternoon tea.'

Xander Barrett and his friends clamber out of the water and flop on the bunny pad and we bring up drinks and snacks: watermelon with halloumi, gazpacho shots, pinwheel sandwiches.

'The chef is incredible,' Xander Barrett says, picking up a cheese straw. 'Did he make these?'

'I think so,' I tell him. 'I can go and ask.'

He shakes his head. 'No, don't do that. It's too hot to move.'

He's right. It's so hot that the back of my polo shirt is soaking wet where it's tucked into my shorts. Every time I step out of the air-conditioned interior and onto the deck, my face prickles with perspiration. I can only hope my make-up's holding up in the heat because I haven't had time to stop and check it. I haven't even had time to pee.

Jeff is lying flat out on the bunny pad, a T-shirt over his face.

'He's the oldest,' Harry tells me and then fake whispers, 'He can't keep up.'

'I can hear you,' Jeff says, his voice muffled by the cotton. 'I just know how to pace myself. Unlike some.'

Harry rolls his eyes at me and then pats the cushion next to him, inviting me to sit down. I tell him thanks, but I can't – I don't know if I can, but I'm going to assume not unless someone tells me otherwise – and ask if they need anything else.

'We're all good,' Xander tells me. 'This is perfect.'

Dinner goes well – Berry and I set the table with bright striped round placemats topped with white dishes and a mini inflatable beach ball around a centrepiece of pink, orange and yellow flowers. The guests call for Carlo to come up and join them for a drink and he blushes while they praise him and Harry flirts outrageously. They take their drinks up to the sun deck and Berry and I clear the table. Again. It feels like clearing and then setting the table is a big part of the job.

Berry takes the dishes down to the dishwasher, and I wipe and polish the table and sweep the deck. I can hear the guests talking about cocktails – the first they ever had, the ones that gave them the worst hangovers.

'I remember exactly what I drank that night,' I hear Harry say. 'Wine. And then beer.'

'Makes you feel queer,' Adam says, making me jump.

I move towards him, before remembering I can't. I give him a weird little wave instead.

'How are you feeling?' I ask him.

'Been better, but I think these are working.' He holds his hands up to show me an anti-sickness band on each wrist. 'You?'

'Exhausted. But good.'

'We started with red and, when that ran out, I moved on to white,' Harry is saying. 'And then the beer after that.'

Adam takes the mop out of my hands and starts mopping under the table.

'And then I had a Black Russian,' Harry says. 'And then a White Russian.'

'Are we still talking about drinks?' Jeff asks, drily.

'On this particular night, yes,' Harry says. 'Then a tequila slammer. And then, to top it all off, a Brandy Alexander.'

'What the fuck is a Brandy Alexander?' one of the other two asks.

'I think the actual recipe is cognac and crème de cacao and cream,' Harry says. 'There's something else too . . . sherry?'

'Brandy?' someone suggests.

Harry snorts. 'Probably yes. But when I used to make it at home I just did it with brandy and chocolate milk. God, I miss chocolate milk! When did you last have chocolate milk?'

'When I was an actual child,' one of the other men – I think it's Jeff – says. 'Like most people.'

Harry groans. 'I miss it. I should never have stopped drinking it.'

When I take the mop down to the galley, I check the pantry and find a couple of bottles of Cocio chocolate milk.

'Can I take these?' I ask Carlo, who's cleaning the galley and looks exhausted.

He shrugs. 'I think they are for the children, but there are no children?'

I smile. 'One of the guests said he misses it, so I thought I'd put some in his room.'

Carlo stops scrubbing long enough to smile at me. 'Now I'm wondering if I should try some too.'

'You should!' I tell him. 'The guest puts brandy in it.'

'Ah,' Carlo smiles. 'Maybe for bed.'

I take the two bottles up to Harry's room. I knock on the door and when there's no reply, go inside. Berry did turn-down service earlier so everything is tidy, the bed is made and the lights are low. I put the chocolate milk in the fridge.

When I get back up on deck, the guests have come down from the sun deck and are talking to Adam and Liam. I skirt around them and go up to tidy the sun deck, taking their dishes and glasses down to the galley. On one of my trips back down, they call out that they're going to bed and I radio everyone to let them know.

I expect Berry to be asleep when I get back to our cabin, but she's not. She's propped up in bed, watching something on her phone.

'*Great British Baking Show*,' she tells me, pointing at the small screen. 'Helps me relax.'

'I get it,' I tell her. 'Have you watched the *Sewing Bee*? I love that too.'

'I haven't, but I will,' she tells me.

She pauses the show and rolls onto her side to look at me. 'How are you doing? Everything go okay out there?'

'I think so,' I tell her. 'I'm worried I missed something . . .'

'You probably did. It's your first day on charter, you can't be expected to remember everything, but from what I saw, you did a pretty great job.'

I must be exhausted because my eyes well with tears.

'Thank you for saying that.'

'No problem. Now get some sleep.'

7

'This is incredible,' Xander says, as he climbs out of the boat. Standing on the sand, he stretches his arms wide and looks back out over the water. 'It feels like a private island.'

'Is it private?' Harry asks, waggling his eyebrows.

'He wants to know if it's a nude beach,' Jeff clarifies, drily.

'Oh! I don't know. I could find out . . .'

'I mean, any beach is a nude beach if you take off your clothes,' Harry says.

He's currently wearing knee-length white shorts and a bright yellow shirt patterned with huge white flowers. It's unbuttoned halfway down his chest where a charm that looks like a green jellybean is hanging from a thin silver chain.

It's Xander's birthday, and we've brought a picnic lunch over to this little cove, along with a table, chairs, parasols, deckchairs and some inflatables. It's a bit nerve-wracking looking after guests alone for the first time, but it's also a relief to get some time off the boat.

'At least wait until the crew leaves,' Xander says. 'Hope doesn't need to see that.'

'Maybe not,' Harry says. 'Adam though . . .'

He looks off into the distance, where Adam and Nico are on the way back to the *Serendipity* in the tender.

I snort and then cover my mouth with my hand. 'Sorry. That was rude.'

'Oh, is there a story there?' Harry asks. 'Have you got your eye on Adam? Or another body part?'

'No, no,' I tell him. 'Adam and I are old friends. We came here together. But there's nothing going on between us. It's frowned upon for deck crew.'

It's Harry's turn to snort. 'It may be frowned upon, but I'm sure that doesn't stop it. What happens at sea . . .' He shrugs. And then shrugs off his shirt. 'Anyway! I am going for a swim.'

'Careful,' I tell him. 'It drops off sharply.'

He pats my arm. 'Good looking out! I appreciate you!'

Xander and Jeff sit in the deckchairs – heads back, eyes closed – while I unpack the contents of the cool boxes, pouring drinks and setting the starters out on the table underneath the parasol, its spokes threaded with pompom garlands.

I keep an eye on Harry, but there's really no need since he's constantly yelling back to the beach, launching himself out of the water, waving and generally seeming to have the time of his life.

Once Harry gets out of the water, shaking himself like a dog, the three of them sit at the table and I serve lunch – a melon and burrata salad, figs with prosciutto and honey and roasted tomato focaccia sandwiches.

'Have you eaten, Hope?' Xander asks. 'You're more than welcome to eat with us?'

'Thank you, but we're not allowed to eat with the guests.'

'We'll never tell,' he says, leaning in as if it's our secret.

I smile. 'That's okay. But I appreciate the offer.'

'Bet you're not allowed to drink on duty either,' Harry says, running his hands through his wet hair.

'Definitely not,' I tell them. 'Sackable offence.'

'Makes sense,' Harry says. 'But not fun. Tonight will be fun though!'

Xander grins. 'I can't wait.'

'Can you believe this man is forty?' Harry says, gesturing at Xander. 'He doesn't look a day over thirty-nine.'

Xander gives him the finger.

'And it only cost him around twenty grand in surgeries,' Jeff says.

The three of them laugh as they hold their glasses up and toast Xander's birthday.

'Come on, Hope,' Harry says. 'You can cheers too with your sad little Evian.'

Smiling, I touch my plastic bottle of water against their glasses. 'Happy birthday!'

I'm clearing the table and packing everything back into the bags, when Harry sits down at the table with a pack of tarot cards in his hand.

'Have you ever had a tarot reading?' he asks me.

I shake my head. 'I haven't actually.'

'I'd love to give you one, if you're interested. I'm going to do Xander's birthday reading later, but I thought I could do yours before you go back to the boat. What do you think? No pressure!'

'You can absolutely say no, Hope,' Jeff says from his deckchair.

'No hope,' Harry says. 'Isn't that just Jeff all over?'

It's Jeff's turn to give Harry the finger, which he does without even looking.

I look over at the boat. The boys are coming soon with the tender, but they're not here yet. Once I've packed everything, I'll just be waiting for them.

'Sure,' I say. 'Why not?'

'Perfect!' Harry says. 'Sit down then.'

Xander stands up, stretches and walks down to the edge of the sparkling water.

'Come on,' he tells Jeff. 'Birthday swim.'

Jeff gets up and joins him.

'That's them being discreet,' Harry tells me.

I smile. 'That's nice of them.'

'Don't be nervous.' He shuffles the cards. 'I'm not going to tell you anything bad. And some of the cards can look bad at first glance, but don't worry – their meanings aren't always immediately obvious. Think of a question you'd like the cards to answer. Doesn't have to be deep and meaningful; go with the first thing that comes to mind. And if nothing comes to mind, that's okay too. No stress.'

I think about my family. Mum, the baby, the little kids. But I don't want to ask about them. Instead I picture Adam. Will we be okay? Will coming out here, working together, doing this job work out? That's what I really want to know.

Harry turns over the first card. 'All right,' he says. 'So this one represents how things are right now. The Seven of Cups is about being rooted in reality. In our heads we can imagine anything we want – I don't know about you, but I'm a big rose-tinted glasses person. This card is about having the courage to get past the rosy reality and find out what's actually true.'

He turns another card. 'This card represents what action you need to take. The Ace of Pentacles. Right now, the world might be offering you something new, so keep your eyes open to what's around you.' He gestures at the beach, the ocean. 'Not difficult!'

I smile. 'Right. Everything feels new right now.'

'The final card is about the future.' He turns it and beams at me. 'The Sun. People are drawn to you because of the beautiful energy you bring into their lives. And you radiate love and affection towards those you care about the most. Practise joy. Embrace pleasure.'

My eyes have filled and my throat feels tight. I think about Mum and Mick and my siblings and how much I miss them. And about Adam and how we came here together to do this brave thing.

'Oh, hon,' Harry says, his head tipped to one side. 'All good cards!'

'I know,' I tell him. 'That was lovely. Thank you.'

'What?' Harry suddenly shouts, making me jump, and then I hear Xander shouting from the water. I turn around and see he's gesturing behind me.

'Is he saying "goats"?' Harry asks, his eyebrows appearing above his mirrored sunglasses.

Yes, he is saying 'goats'. There's a brown goat stepping gingerly down the cliff face behind the cove, and when I shade my eyes I can see a couple more.

'I've never had a reading interrupted by goats before,' Harry says.

I laugh. 'Does that mean something?'

'I think it means I'm the greatest of all time.'

8

Tonight is Xander's eighties-themed party with the George Michael tribute act.

I help Berry set up the dinner table with neon decorations, garlands and balloons, and then go down to the galley to find sparklers and paper umbrellas for the cocktails, which we're going to serve in triangular Martini glasses with bendy straws.

I walk through the boat, dimming the interior lights and checking everything is clean and tidy and in place. While the guests are getting ready in their cabins, we all take turns to change into our evening uniforms, but with the classic 'Choose Life' T-shirts Jeff brought on board and requested we all wear tonight.

'I had one of these the first-time round,' Captain Liz tells me, as I'm walking through the mess on the way to the galley. 'Begged my mom to buy me one but she wouldn't and then sneaked to New York one weekend with friends and bought a bootleg in Chinatown.'

'My mum's a huge George Michael fan,' I tell her, while thinking that sneaking away to New York with friends sounds so unbelievably cool. 'When he died, she and her best friend went to London to lay flowers outside his house.'

'I love that. You'll have to FaceTime her tonight to show her the guy. He's not here yet, right?'

I shake my head. 'I think Nico and Liam are going to get him now.'

She frowns. 'Has Adam talked to you at all? About the job?'

I shake my head. 'Not really. There hasn't been much time.'

'Ben said he's struggling a little bit. Which is normal! I just thought, since you're friends, you could maybe have a word. See if there's anything he needs and won't say. Sometimes the deck crew can be a bit, you know.' She waves her hand. 'Macho.'

I nod. 'Okay. Thank you for telling me. I'll talk to him.'

'I appreciate that. Everything else ready to go?' She shuffles along the seat and stands. 'I'm going to go check on Carlo, but the table's done?'

'It is. It looks great.'

'Good work.'

The tribute artist looks uncannily like 'Faith'-era George Michael. To the point where I wonder if he's had surgery to refine the look. He's got the hair and the stubble, a similar build. He's not wearing the jeans and leather jacket of the music video though; he's in a black suit over a black V-neck T-shirt.

When he starts to sing – opening with 'Fastlove' – I'm even more stunned. I've grown up with these songs – Mum's always played them in the car and in the kitchen while she cooks, she pulls them up on YouTube when her friends come round and they all drink too much wine and cry to 'Careless Whisper' – and to me he sounds exactly like him. It's spooky.

Adam is standing on the other side of the deck. He looks smart and hot in his blacks and I wish I could go over and properly share this with him, with his arms around me, but I stay where I am, singing along with everyone else while also keeping an eye out in case the guests need anything.

'Isn't he incredible?' Berry says, nudging me with her elbow.

I nod, but he's singing 'Father Figure' which makes me well up. My mum's got a tattoo of a line from this song, about loving someone until the end of time.

'Do you think it's okay if I call my mum?' I ask her.

'It's fine. Go for it.'

Once Mum answers, I hold the phone up for a minute so she can hear the singer, and then I go down to the galley so I can talk to her.

'He's brilliant,' she says. 'That's made me weepy.'

'Me too. I miss you! I can't talk now. I'm working. I just wanted you to hear him.'

'Oh, chicken. I miss you too.'

I hang up and cry a little while I empty the dishwasher. I love this job so far, but it's hard to be away from home.

'You okay?' Berry asks, coming down the stairs with some glasses and plates.

'Just a bit homesick.' My voice cracks and I shake my head. 'Sorry.'

'Don't apologise! The first one is the hardest and you're doing so well.'

Tears are properly falling now and I swipe at them with my fingers, apologising again.

She smiles at me. 'Stop apologising! Do you want a hug?'

I don't. Because it's likely to make me cry more. But also I really do. I manage a nod and she wraps her arms around me, hooking her chin over my shoulder.

'Breathe,' she tells me.

I suck in a ragged breath, my nose filling with the scent of her spicy cherry perfume, and as I breathe out again, I relax. A bit.

'There you go,' she says, rubbing my back. 'We've got, what? Less than fifteen hours left? And you'll be asleep for some of them. Not enough, but some. You can do it.'

I cling to her in a way I doubt I would if I wasn't so emotional, but she feels warm and strong and I miss my family and I miss being held by Adam, and I'm so, so out of my comfort zone.

'You good?' Berry says, untangling from me and setting me back upright.

I nod, but I still feel like if I speak, I'll cry.

She holds my face in her hands, brushing the tears off my cheeks with her thumbs. I feel about five years old.

'They're dancing up there now. Let's go join in.'

I laugh. 'Okay!'

'And earn a huge tip!'

I can definitely work with that.

9

'You've all been fantastic,' Xander tells us when we all line up on deck to say goodbye. 'I've had the best birthday.'

The three men hug all of us and seem to have individual thank yous for everyone.

After Harry hugs me, he presses the tarot pack into my hands. 'I feel strongly that this should be with you.'

'Oh no –' I start to say, but he squeezes my hands with both of his.

'Don't argue. And you don't have to use it if you're not comfy. But maybe turn a card every now and then and see what you think.'

I've teared up again and he laughs and hugs me again. And then they leave.

'Eighteen hundred euros each,' Captain Liz tells us in the salon once we've all changed out of our whites.

I look over at Adam who's already looking at me, his face split into a wide grin. Eighteen hundred euros is about £1,500, I think. Pretty much every job I had at uni paid minimum wage and I've never earned that much money in one go before. Nowhere near. And in only three days. It's unbelievable.

'You all did a great job,' the captain tells us. 'Obviously with it being the first charter, there were some hiccups but I'm confident we can get them ironed out and the next charter will be even better.' She stands. 'So! Enjoy yourselves. Enjoy the money. And don't spend it all at once!'

I'm sitting next to Berry who bumps me with her shoulder. 'See? I told you you could do it.'

I smile at her. 'You did.'

And I did do it. But the past three days have been the most exhausting of my life. Worse than when Alfie was a baby and barely slept and so none of us slept – I hallucinated rabbits hopping on my bed and tripped over what turned out to be my own shadow, hit my face on the door and gave myself a fat lip. Worse than the first couple of months at uni when we were out every night and sleeping on friends' floors in halls and I once fell asleep on the train and woke up in Chester with a chicken leg in my bra.

'Can I have a word?' Louise says, and my stomach lurches. Am I in trouble?

'Did you put chocolate milk in the fridge in Harry's cabin?' she asks me, which is not at all what I expected her to say.

'Oh! Yes. Sorry, was I not supposed to?'

She smiles. 'No, he was delighted. He said you must have overheard him? Well, he said maybe you're psychic, but that it's more likely that you overheard him.'

'I did,' I tell Louise now. 'They were talking about cocktails while I was clearing up after dinner service. He said he hadn't had chocolate milk for years and missed it, so I went down to the galley and found some. Carlo said it was okay for me to take . . . ?'

'That's absolutely fine. It's exactly that kind of small detail that makes a big difference for guests. And I love that you took that initiative.'

'Okay. Great. Thank you for telling me.'

'You're doing really well,' she says warmly.

I find Adam sitting up on the sun deck, looking down at his phone. I sit next to him and he puts his phone away.

'You okay?'

I nod. 'I can't believe the tip. Like, I knew it was going to be a lot, but . . .'

I'm sending £500 to Mum and putting the rest into savings, since we don't have to pay for anything here.

'I was hoping for a bit more,' he says. 'They were all so friendly and had a great time.'

I snort. 'I think fifteen hundred is plenty.'

He shrugs. 'I know. I'm just being greedy.'

'How's it going, Ad?' I ask him. 'Are you enjoying it?'

He slumps a little. 'I don't know. I keep fucking up. I got a bollocking from Ben about the radio cos I left it in my bunk. And then I keep keying the mic.'

If you press the microphone button on your radio, no one else can get through. Louise told us on the first day how important it is that the radios are always clear.

'Ben gave me this big dramatic spiel about how it could literally be life and death. Like, I get it. But I'm not doing it on purpose. I don't even know I'm doing it.'

'You'll get used to it,' I tell him.

'Sounds like you're doing great.' He nudges against me.

I smile. 'I'm enjoying it. I'm knackered though.'

He shakes his head. 'Never been so tired in my life.'

No one has the energy to go out that evening, so Carlo makes pizzas and we eat them with wine, all of us together on the deck as the sun goes down.

'So how was your first charter?' Liam asks me, as I cradle my wine and try to keep my eyes open.

'Exhausting.'

'Everyone did great,' Louise says from across the table. 'Like Captain Liz said, there's a few things we need to pick up on and talk about, but they can wait.'

'Oh, you don't want to do it now?' Nico says, teasing her. 'A Louise bollocking could really lift the mood.'

'Not a bollocking,' Louise says. 'Well, maybe for you.'

'Promises, promises,' Nico says.

Louise rolls her eyes, but the corners of her mouth are twitching.

'How's the seasickness?' Ben asks Adam. 'I notice you wolfed down that pizza.'

'I've never been so hungry in my life. But yeah. I dunno if it's the pills or these things . . .' Adam holds up his hands to show the seasickness bands. 'But something worked.'

'Not the ginger?' Carlo asks.

'I think I puked the ginger right up,' Adam tells him. 'Sorry about that.'

Carlo shakes his head, sadly. Presumably thinking about the waste of an ingredient.

'I was sick as a dog when I started,' Liam says. 'Thought I was gonna have to quit. And then one day it just stopped.' He shrugs. 'Now I feel a bit sick on land.'

'That's called Stockholm syndrome,' Nico tells him.

Everyone is sitting around happily talking, laughing, vaping, and it's lovely, but my eyes are closing. Even the short journey back to my cabin feels like too much effort. I consider sleeping on the sofa or even putting my head down on the table.

'Come on,' Berry says, standing and reaching for my arm. 'Let's go. You're falling asleep. Big day tomorrow!'

I notice Adam half get out of his seat, before dropping back down again.

'You okay?' he mouths at me and I nod.

I will be. I just need to sleep for twenty-four to forty-eight hours and I'll be fine. Although I can't, because tomorrow we're all going out for the day. Apparently between charters everyone wants to go out and do things, rather than just sleep. It makes sense, but also . . . ugh.

'We need to clean up,' I say and a couple of people boo me.

'Don't worry,' Louise says. 'We can do that.'

'Speak for yourself,' Nico says, but I know he's joking. 'Go on,' he adds to me. 'We'll sort it. You look absolutely done in.'

I feel guilty because I know that everyone worked hard and everyone's knackered, but I let Berry guide me through the salon. She lets go of me so we can both go downstairs and I stagger slightly – I didn't realise I'd been leaning on her so heavily.

'Thank you,' I tell her at the bottom of the stairs. 'Sorry I'm so pathetic.'

'You're not pathetic.' She smiles at me, her eyes bright. How are her eyes so bright? Mine feel like they're going to fall out of my head and roll across the floor like in a cartoon.

'You're just exhausted,' Berry says. 'Let's get you to bed.'

'This is better than staying in bed, right?' Berry asks me, the following morning.

I smile. 'It's incredible.'

We're at Formentor beach, where golden sand curves around deep turquoise water. Yachts bob in the distance. We're far from the only people here, but it's not at all busy. A few people are swimming and sunbathing, but it's quiet and tranquil.

We pay to rent sunbeds shaded by wide straw parasols and everyone immediately strips off, stashing their bags. I fasten the strap of my bag to the parasol, pull off my T-shirt dress and kick off my flip-flops, before following everyone into the water.

The sand is hot underfoot, the sea almost as warm as a bath.

Berry ducks right under, swimming even in the shallows and appearing a short distance away, laughing as she shakes the sea from her hair. She's wearing a red bikini, her hair held back with a red scarf.

Adam swims over to me, splashing like a golden retriever. 'How cool is this?'

'It's a lot warmer than the last time we were in the sea together.'

He fakes a shudder. 'Don't remind me.'

Last year, Adam's nan signed everyone up for the annual Boxing Day swim in the Irish Sea. We all shivered together on the beach and then plunged in, squealing and gasping, the temperature of the water taking our breath away. Some clambered out straight away – including Adam's nan, who'd only ever intended to splash and not swim, but Adam and I swam, considering it good practice for our future water-based career plans.

'It was fun,' I tell him now.

His hand glides up my side under the water and I remember how we showered together when we got back to his place, because everyone else went to get food. The hot water on our chilled skin. His mouth between my shoulder blades as he pressed me up against the tiles.

I want to step closer and push up against him now, lick the droplets of salt water running over his collarbones. His eyes are dark as he looks down at me, my mouth, lower. He hooks his fingers into the side of my bikini.

'Pretty sure you're not meant to do that,' Berry says, popping up alongside us.

'We weren't!' I say instantly, but then notice she's not even looking at Adam and me, but over towards a stone jetty.

I follow her eye-line and see Liam backflip off into the water, then hear Nico hooting as he follows suit. They swim the short distance to the steps, climb out and do it again.

'I'm just gonna . . .' Adam says, before splashing away to join them.

I roll my eyes.

'Idiots,' Berry says, without malice. 'How awesome is this?' She opens her arms wide, water dripping off her fingertips.

I duck down to my shoulders, shivering as the water runs over my hot skin, and slowly turn in a circle. The creamy yellow of the sand, the deep green of the trees behind the beach, the light brown of the mountains beyond, the blue and green glitter of the water, a small white sailing boat in the distance tethered to a bobbing bright red buoy.

'It's perfect,' I agree.

***

Berry and I swim out to the buoy together and hold on either side, squinting into the distance, trying to see the people on the yacht. A couple sits on the bow, their feet dangling, and there's music playing that I'm sure I know, but can't quite place.

'Is that Hall & Oates?' Berry says, tipping her head to one side and closing one eye. 'It is!' She grins at me. 'Talk about yacht rock.'

'What's that?' I ask, pushing myself away from the buoy and then pulling back in again.

'Yacht rock or Hall & Oates?'

'Both, I think?'

'I bet you'd know Hall & Oates if you heard some songs. "She's Gone"? "You Make My Dreams"? "Maneater"?'

'I think I know "Maneater"...'

'"Private Eyes"! You must know that one.'

She sings a bit – she's got a nice voice – and it sounds vaguely familiar.

'My dad's a big fan. All yacht rock actually. He's the whitest man alive.'

'So yacht rock is... rock you listen to on yachts?' I laugh because that is patently ridiculous.

Berry laughs too. 'I think so? Sort of. It's soft rock and I think maybe people used to listen to it on bay cruises in California? Or it just has that vibe? You know, the sun's going down, everyone's got a drink in their hand, probably some weed going on...' She closes her eyes, turns her face up to the sun. 'I think it's just... evocative. You know? R & B by and for white people.'

'Who else is yacht rock?' I push myself off the buoy and tread water.

'The Doobie Brothers.' She mimes smoking up. 'Kenny Loggins. My dad has seen him on tour so many times. Steely Dan, obviously.'

'Obviously,' I echo, even though I have no idea who Steely Dan is. Or are.

'Supertramp! You know Supertramp, right? They're British.'

I shake my head. 'Never heard of them.'

'Come on!' She starts singing another song, something about breakfast. I think it's vaguely familiar. Maybe. Or I just want her to think I know what she's talking about.

'I'll make you a playlist,' she tells me. She pushes herself back off the buoy, floating on her back, before flipping over and saying, 'Race you!'

She's a much faster swimmer than me. Strong like Adam, but she glides through the water rather than churning it up like he does. She doesn't beat me by too much though, and she high-fives me as I straighten up next to her, closer to the beach, my feet sinking into the sand.

'They're still at it, look.' She points at the jetty and we're just in time to see a small dinghy pull up and a couple of lifeguards talking to and gesturing at Adam, Nico and Liam.

'Uh-oh,' Berry says. 'They're in trouble. Pretty sure there's a sign saying no jumping.'

We watch, the warm water eddying around us, as the boys talk to the officials and then walk back down the jetty to the beach. Liam and Nico head over to the sunbeds, while Adam comes to join us in the water.

'Get told off?' I ask him.

'Threatened with a thousand-euro fine!' He's caught the sun.

His nose and forehead are bright pink. 'We're going to go and get some food. You want in?'

We sit outside the restaurant – up on a bluff overlooking the jetty the boys were jumping from – with ham and cheese baguettes, iced coffees and beers. Nico yanks open a bunch of different packets of crisps, shards flying everywhere, and tiny brown birds swoop over to collect them, getting braver and closer until they're perched on the edge of the table.

'The guy was telling me some Spanish dude broke his nose jumping off that,' Nico says, gesturing at the jetty. 'They were going to put railings up but they think people will just stand on the railings and make it even more dangerous.'

A couple walks over, stopping to stare out to sea, blocking our view. They look to be in their seventies. The woman is wearing a hot pink bikini and the man is in a yellow thong, his entire arse on show.

'I've never jumped in the water, ever,' I say, to distract us all from staring at the man's buttocks. 'I've always been too nervous.'

'Oh my god, you have to!' Berry says, reaching for a crisp. 'Not here, that's ridiculous.' She raises an eyebrow at the boys. 'But off the boat. It's so fun.'

'Maybe,' I tell her. 'But doesn't the water go all up your nose?'

'Not if you blow out as you hit the water. But you can just hold your nose. It's allowed.'

I eat my baguette and drink my coffee as Adam tells them about our Boxing Day swim and they ask questions about the Mersey and the Irish Sea and where one becomes the other.

I watch one of the birds approach an open packet of crisps, taking a few little steps before retreating, getting a tiny bit closer every time. I take my phone out to film and manage to catch the moment he plucks up the courage, grabs a whole crisp and flies away. The kids will love that.

'You okay there, birdwatcher?' Nico says.

'Just getting something to send to my brothers and sisters,' I tell him. And then spend the next few minutes telling everyone about my many siblings.

Nico has a sister he clearly adores but who is currently travelling around Australia. Berry's an only child and so is Liam. Adam has one older brother who lives in London and works for a music production company, and his younger brother, Ollie, who's still at home.

'That reminds me,' Berry says. 'Hope's never heard of yacht rock!'

'What's yacht rock?' Adam asks.

'Thank you!' I say.

'I think I've heard of it, but I dunno what it is,' Liam says.

Berry explains it to them and Nico says, 'Oh yeah . . .' He adopts a stoned-sounding American accent: 'The smooth sounds of Simon & Garfunkel . . .'

While Berry and Nico discuss whether or not Simon & Garfunkel are actually yacht rock, I send the video to Mum to show to the kids.

Mum texts back almost immediately. *Cute! Where are you now?*

I take a few photos – of the jetty, the beach, my coffee – and then the boys pose together, Berry throwing herself into the photo at the last second. The resulting picture is hilarious. Nico grinning widely from behind his sunglasses. Liam's face almost a blur because he turned to look at Berry. Adam laughing, mouth wide open. And Berry in focus but clearly in motion, laughing too.

I love it. Being here with Adam like this makes the secrecy, the work, the exhaustion worth it.

10

Later that afternoon, we get a taxi to Puerto Pollensa, ten minutes back along the coast road, and order paella and sangria at a beachside restaurant on the Pine Walk. Liam doesn't come with us, saying he's 'on a promise' with a woman he met on an earlier charter.

'That man is relentless,' Nico says, as we watch Liam walk away.

The warm air smells of pine needles and sun lotion, of seafood, garlic and jasmine. Berry's wearing a pink string dress over a white vest and boy shorts, her arms lined with bead bracelets. She's got her pink-tinted sunglasses pushed up into her hair, curled into spirals from the salt water. I didn't even think to bring a change of clothes for the evening, so I'm wearing the same sundress and flip-flops from this morning. The dress feels soft and greasy from the sunscreen.

'Look at us,' Nico says, gesturing at the four of us. 'Double date.'

'We're not . . .' I start to say, just as Adam says, 'Bagsy Berry.'

I gasp. 'You can't bagsy a person!'

Adam shrugs. 'Sorry, bagsy can't be argued with.'

'What's "bagsy"?' Berry says.

'Oh my god.' I shake my head. 'Like . . . he's claimed you.'

'Wow,' Berry says, slowly, her eyebrows shooting up. 'Feminism not reached Liverpool yet then?'

'Hey!' Adam says in pretend outrage. 'I once emailed Nintendo to say Princess Peach shouldn't be a prize in *Mario*.'

'Oh, Mario!' Nico mimics in a high-pitched voice, clutching his hands to his chest.

'Exactly,' Adam says. 'My mum was dead proud.'

'Typical male feminist,' Berry says lightly. 'Does the bare minimum and thinks he deserves a cookie.'

'Nah, I was only joking,' Adam says. 'Hope, tell her!'

I shake my head. 'You're on your own here. You and your bagsy.'

'I think you've done yourself out of both the girls there,' Nico says. 'We're all gonna have to go gay.'

'You do know I *am* gay, right?' Berry says, pouring more sangria for herself.

'I didn't!' Nico says. 'Fair play.'

I didn't know Berry was gay either.

'Thanks,' Berry says to Nico. 'Good to have your approval.'

'Oh, I definitely approve.' Nico waggles his eyebrows.

'Adam, you're in the clear,' Berry says. 'Nico has just out-grossed you.'

The waiter unfolds a small table next to us and then brings out an enormous pan piled high with paella. He dishes it out for each of us, finishing it with mussels and prawns in the shell. It's so good we have seconds, and Adam has thirds, the waiter scraping the last of the pan directly onto his plate. We get a second jug of sangria and the boys get increasingly raucous, while Berry and I people-watch and stare out at the moon reflected in the rippling water. I feel full and happy, sleepy from the sun and the sangria.

A shirtless man, barefoot in cut-offs and carrying a bag from the nearby Spar, passes us before hopping off the jetty into a small boat. We watch him repeatedly try and fail to start the boat.

'I should go and help,' Nico says, but he's leaning back in his seat, looking about sixty per cent asleep, and makes no move to get up.

'I'm not helping someone with a boat on my day off from a boat,' Adam says, leaning forward to pour himself more sangria.

The man clambers out of the boat, looks around for a bit and gets back in again, sitting down and taking out his phone.

'He's going to have to sleep there now,' I say. 'I wonder where he lives.'

'He's probably just going out to one of the moored ones,' Berry says, waving towards the dozens of small yachts anchored out in the bay.

'Maybe he lives over there.' I gesture at the hills on the other side of the bay. A road snakes down towards the water, bright headlights tumbling like marbles. 'Be quicker by boat.'

A man and a woman approach – he's balding in Bermuda shorts and a Hawaiian shirt and she looks cool and somehow Swedish in a flowing white shirt dress and rope sandals, blonde hair tied in a low ponytail. They stop and talk to the man in the boat, who looks up at them, smiling brightly.

'They're asking him directions,' I say.

'And he's telling them he can take them there if they can get his boat started,' Berry adds.

'She's probably got a little boat back home,' I say. 'She summers on one of those tiny Swedish islands and has to sail everywhere.'

'How do you know she's Swedish?' Nico asks, tipping his head back to blow a cloud of Coke-scented vape in the air.

'She looks Swedish,' I tell him. 'Blonde and . . . serene.'

'Ooh!' Berry leans forward in her seat. 'He's getting out!'

The Hawaiian shirt guy reaches a hand out to help him and, once he's back up on the jetty, the three of them stand for a minute, talking and laughing.

'They're going to a party,' I say. 'They asked him to take them, but he can't, so now they've invited him along.'

'Or now they're skipping the party,' Berry says. 'And they've invited him back to their villa.'

We all watch as the three of them head off together.

'He's left his Spar bag!' I realise.

'Doesn't need it now,' Berry says. 'It was provisions for a lonely night and a sad wank, but now it's all oysters, champagne and a threesome.'

'I might go and grab the bag,' Nico says. 'Microwave burger, bottle of Yazoo and a box of tissues? Can't go wrong.'

'Are you two writing a novel together or what?' Adam asks me and Berry.

'It's just more interesting to make up a story.'

'Don't you ever do it?' Berry asks Adam. 'What about that guy?' She gestures vaguely at a middle-aged man in yellow shorts and a white shirt, sitting on a bench and looking distracted.

'He's waiting for his wife?' Adam says.

'She's late because . . . ?' I prompt.

'She . . . er . . . I dunno. She couldn't find her bag.' He downs his drink.

'He came here once as a young man,' Berry says. 'And met a woman. They had a holiday fling and agreed never to meet again. They both married other people, but then –'

'She found him on Facebook,' I say. 'After her husband died. His wife had died too. So they agreed to meet here.'

'Bloody hell,' Nico says. 'You've got me wanting to stay to see if she turns up.'

We all laugh as a waiter comes over to see if we want more drinks.

'So who wants to play a game?' Nico asks, once we've all got a round of beers. 'First time, last time, strangest place?'

I glance at Adam before I can stop myself and widen my eyes at him. I wasn't his first, but what will he say about the last time?

He looks directly back, a smile tugging at the corner of his mouth.

'I'll go first,' Adam says. 'First time was when I was sixteen. On holiday with my family at this caravan park we always went to. Loads of people had caravans there and went back every holidays, so a bunch of us had been hanging around together for years. This girl, Grace, I'm pretty sure she'd decided in advance that she was just going to find someone to do it with and she found me.' He shrugs.

'Was it just that once?' Nico asks.

'Couple more times,' Adam says, which is news to me. 'But only that year. Her family sold the caravan after that.'

'Not surprised, mate,' Nico says.

'What about you then?' Adam asks him.

Nico says he was sixteen too and it was with one of his sister's friends, who made him promise never to tell his sister.

'Made me feel great, that,' he says now.

'Did you tell her?' I ask.

'Never did. I keep my promises.'

'That would be more admirable if you hadn't banged your sister's best friend,' Berry says, smiling.

'So, what's your story?' Nico asks Berry.

'It was actually with my best friend,' Berry says. 'Well, she was my best friend then. She's not now.'

I pick up my drink and twist the neck of the bottle between my fingers.

'We used to sleep over at each other's places all the time,' Berry says. 'And this time we bought beer. And got a bit of a buzz. Watched a film. Started kissing and, you know . . .'

'Bish, bash, bosh,' Nico says.

'Yeah, it's not really like that with girls,' Berry says, smiling. 'Neither of us knew what we were doing, but it was nice. Bit awkward the following morning though.'

'Hope!' Nico says. 'What about you?'

I shake my head. 'Nothing too exciting. He was my first boyfriend. Went back to his place after school. No one was home, so . . .' I shrug.

'Did you do it in his childhood bed?' Nico asks.

I have to try really hard not to look at Adam.

'We did. Everton wallpaper and all.'

I do look at Adam then and catch the look of Liverpool fan outrage on his face.

'That is cold,' Nico says, gesturing at Adam with his beer. 'I can't believe she disrespected you like that.'

Adam smiles. 'We're just friends.'

'Keep telling yourself that, mate,' Nico says. 'Last time?'

'A girl I was seeing back home,' Adam says and I wonder what story he's going to tell. 'Nothing serious. Went back to her place after a night out and . . .' He holds his hands out. 'You know.'

'What?' Nico says.

'We had sex,' Adam enunciates and everyone laughs.

'Cool story, bro.' Nico rolls his eyes. 'Berry, I know you can do better than that.'

Berry takes a long pull of her beer and then says, 'You know I was a tour guide in Barcelona? Often it would be stag or hen parties.' She says both in an English accent. 'But this one was a writing group. Four women on a sort of creative inspiration tour of Barcelona. There was this one woman who I was pretty sure was flirting with me right from the start. She asked me a lot of questions, hung back to walk with me, touched my arm when we were talking.' She reaches out and brushes her finger over my wrist and goosebumps thrill up my forearm. 'You know,' she says. 'Classic stuff.'

I nod. I do know.

'The tour usually ended in this tapas bar but the women wanted to go dancing, so I took them to this place I love in the Gothic Quarter – tiny, dark, jazz and cocktails.'

She pauses to drink some of her beer and we're all just staring at her.

'We danced together – the other women were there and dancing too, but me and this woman were dancing together. It was hot and sweaty and busy, so we were dancing pretty close. We had our cocktails, out on the dance floor – everyone did. Some of mine splashed out over my hand and she reached over, took my hand and licked it.'

'Fuck off,' Nico says.

Berry laughs. 'I know.'

'That? Is a baller move.'

'Right?' Berry drinks some more of her beer. 'And it totally worked. We left the other women there and went straight back to my place.'

Ignoring the fluttering in my chest, I drink the last of my beer.

***

In the car back to the marina, Nico's in the front, chatting to the driver and Adam falls asleep, his head bumping gently against the window. Between me and Adam, Berry is looking down at her phone, texting. I stare out through the glass, over the water, and all I can think about is the story Berry told.

The woman licking her hand. Berry sliding her fingers between the woman's and leading her out of the club and back to her place. Maybe they stopped to kiss in doorways on the way or maybe they were in too much of a hurry and didn't kiss until the door of Berry's apartment had closed behind them, by then so desperate that they didn't even take the time to get undressed, instead just pulling clothes out of the way –

'You okay?' Berry asks me. 'Did you have a good night?'

'I did,' I tell her. 'It was great. I'm just tired.'

'Work hard, play hard,' she says, smiling.

Then she goes back to looking at her phone and I go back to thinking about her, even as I try to stop myself.

11

I'm lying face-down on a sunlounger, a soft, warm hand is smoothing cool lotion over my shoulders, down my back, skimming my hips, before gliding along the backs of my thighs. The sun is too bright for me to see and I tilt my pelvis to get some friction against the canvas cushion, my breath coming fast and shallow. Fingertips trail up my inner thighs and I let out a moan that wakes me up.

It takes me a second to get my bearings. Am I at home? Adam's bedroom? And then I realise. I'm in the cabin I share with Berry. She's asleep directly above me and I'm pretty sure I just had a sex dream about her. I really hope I didn't moan out loud.

I put my hands up to my hot cheeks. When I thought about having to share a room with someone, this wasn't something I'd even thought to worry about. But then I didn't expect to hear a super-hot story about a woman licking her hand in a club either. I lie very still for a while and stare up at the underside of Berry's bunk. When I'm fairly sure she really is still asleep – if not, she's an excellent faker – I climb carefully out of bed and close the door gently behind me.

Adam is sitting at the table in the crew room, his head resting on his folded arms, a coffee steaming just in front of him.

'Morning,' I say as I get myself a coffee. My voice comes out rough and husky.

He lifts his head and smiles, his eyes crinkling at the corners. I push the dream out of my mind and sit next to him on the bench seating. He shuffles along until my thigh is pressed against his thigh.

'You okay?' he asks me.

I nod. If anyone came in, they'd probably wonder why the two of us are only using about twenty per cent of the seating, but I don't even care. It feels so good to be close to him. To smell his familiar Adam scent, to see the ends of his hair still damp from the shower.

Under the table, he rests his hand on my thigh and I shudder. This is what I wanted. This is what we talked about. Sexy sneaking around. We haven't done enough of it lately. There hasn't been time. He squeezes my thigh, his thumb brushing over my skin.

'Are you sleeping okay?' he asks me.

'Not bad.' I wash away the memory of the dream with coffee. 'Are you not?'

'Not really.'

He's never been a great sleeper. He can get to sleep just fine, but if he wakes up, he struggles to fall back to sleep again. Whenever I stayed over, I told him to wake me rather than just lie there. We could talk or kiss or have sex, something to help him relax enough to get a couple more hours. But he hardly ever did. He'd go on his phone instead and that never helped.

'I miss you when I wake up,' he says, his voice low, his hand moving higher up my leg. I want to catch it between my thighs and rub against it, finally get the friction I was trying for in my dream, but one of the cabin doors opens and then Nico staggers in, hair sticking up in clumps, eyes still half closed.

'Morning, lovebirds.' He heads straight for the coffee machine.

Adam slides along the seat away from me. My thigh feels cold when he takes his hand away. I glance at him and he shakes his head almost imperceptibly.

Louise comes through and opens the fridge, taking out a bottle of juice before sitting down opposite Adam and me.

'Hope, I'd like you to come with me to get some provisions after breakfast, okay?'

I nod. 'Sounds good.'

'We're cleaning the anchor locker,' Nico tells Adam. 'What a joy to be alive.'

He yawns loudly, stretching his arms over his head. His joggers sit low on his hips, his T-shirt riding up to show smooth, light brown skin. I notice Louise noticing, her cheeks flushing, her lips parting. It makes me wonder if Nico's comments about me and Adam are actually him projecting. Not that I can see him and Louise together. She's so serious and conscientious and he's . . . not.

Over the next few minutes, the others appear. Berry in the shorts and vest she sleeps in, but with a baggy black cardigan over the top, the edges of the sleeves unravelling around holes she's pushed her thumbs through. My cheeks heat at the sight of her and I pretend to be fascinated by my coffee.

Liam comes down the stairs in shorts and a vest too, his hair wet with sweat even though it's still early. He likes to go for a run first thing. And then he bypasses breakfast in favour of a shower.

As we all get breakfast and slowly wake up, Louise runs through our jobs for the morning – which include pouring water down all the drains in the boat, cleaning the vacuum filters and washing the doormats.

The next charter guests arrive in two days. I feel more prepared than the last time, but still barely prepared at all.

'How are you finding it so far?' Louise asks me as we walk around the huge store, Louise with the list, me pushing the trolley. 'You're doing a great job, especially for a greenie.'

I smile. 'Thank you.'

'What's your plan? Do you see yourself staying in yachting?'

'I don't know actually. Originally, we said we'd give it a year? But that already doesn't feel like long enough to me.'

'You and Adam said a year?'

I nod.

'You know you don't have to stay on the same programme as Adam, right?'

She reaches for a carton of coconut water and lowers it into the trolley.

'No, I know. It's just this whole thing was his idea, and I went along with it.'

I realise belatedly that this is probably not the right thing to tell my boss.

'Which is not to say I didn't want to do it! Just that the impetus came from him.'

She nods. 'Don't worry, I get it. I just want you to know that even if ultimately Adam decides one year is enough, you can make a different choice.'

'No, I do know that. Thank you.'

I can't really imagine doing it without Adam, but it's good to know she appreciates me.

She gives one of her tiny, fast smiles, as if she doesn't want to be caught being anything less than serious, and we keep shopping.

'How did you get started in yachting?' I ask her as we wander the wide aisles.

'After uni,' she tells me. 'I went to Australia with my sister and we had the best time. It was meant to be sort of like a last hurrah before getting a proper job – my dad works in finance and I did a business degree and the plan was always to get an entry-level job, climb the ladder, etc.'

She drops a huge sack of teabags into the trolley, which is well on the way to being full.

'Got back from Australia. My sister got a job in marketing. I applied for jobs, had a few interviews, but really just felt miserable about the whole thing. I kept making fantasy travel plans, you know? How much would I need to spend a year travelling around America? What if I did the whole South East Asia backpacking thing?'

We turn into the cleaning aisle and Louise looks at her list.

'Anyway, long story short. I got offered a job. A good one. But then I couldn't sleep. Felt sick all the time. Came out in a rash. So I turned it down. My dad was furious. In the meantime, I'd been doing all this googling about work and travel and I'd found yachting. So I applied to do a course and my certifications and then I got a job.'

She puts almost an entire shelf of cleaning products into the trolley.

'That first job was a nightmare. But I knew I was on to something, so I applied for another programme and that one turned out to be great. That's where I first worked with Nico actually.'

For a second, she looks almost soft and then she says, 'He was even more of a dickhead then than he is now.'

I laugh. 'I like him.'

'Everyone does,' she says.

* * *

When we get back to the *Serendipity*, Nico is on his way out for a run, so once I've helped Louise unpack and restock everything, I head to Nico and Adam's cabin. I'm hoping Adam might want to finish what we almost started this morning.

I knock on the door lightly in case he's sleeping and hear a grunt in response. When I push open the door, he's lying in his bunk – like me, he has the bottom one – looking at his phone.

'You okay?' I whisper, closing the door gently behind me.

'Knackered.' He drops his phone on the bed next to him and rubs his face with both hands.

I crouch down next to him, curling my fingers around his wrist.

'Nico's gone for a run . . .'

He yawns. 'Yeah, he asked me if I wanted to go but I thought it might actually kill me.'

'Are you aching?'

I ache constantly and his job is so much more physical than mine.

'Always.' He stretches, groaning.

'Want a massage?' I ask, flicking an eyebrow up.

He smiles, tiredly. 'I would love that. But I think I just need to sleep.'

'Okay.'

I lean in to kiss him, half expecting him to change his mind and pull me into the bunk with him, but he doesn't. He kisses me quickly, before saying, 'Sorry. I really am shagged.'

'Chance'd be a fine thing,' I say, bumping his shoulder with my head.

He gives me a weak smile. 'Sorry. M'just not up for it right now.'

'That's okay.' I drop a kiss onto his arm through his shirt. 'I just thought since you were alone . . .'

'I know, yeah. But I really just need to sleep. You prob should too.'

'Nah. I'm gonna get a coffee and call Maddie. She's not working today.'

'Maddie?'

'Yeah.' My legs are hurting from crouching, so I stand up and stretch. 'Did I tell you she was there for one of my mum's check-ups? She's seen things no one should see.'

He snorts. 'You didn't, no. So you've talked to her already?'

'Maddie? Yeah. I'll tell her you said hello.'

I lean down and kiss him quickly. 'Get some sleep.'

I turn the light out as I leave.

'Do I need to dress up?' I ask.

'Nah. Unless you want to.'

Berry has convinced me to go to dinner with her at a hotel owned by a friend of hers – despite his claims of tiredness earlier, Adam has gone out in Palma with Nico and Liam. Berry's wearing cut-off jeans with a ruched black off-the-shoulder top, her hair an explosion of curls. I put on loose white trousers and a dark pink vest and clip my hair up.

'Cute!' Berry says. 'I like your hair like that. You're just missing something . . .'

She takes a step back, as far as she can in this tiny room, and studies me until I can feel my cheeks heating up.

'Do you have any hoop earrings?'

I do. I find them and, once I've put them on, she declares us good to go.

***

The hotel is tall and narrow, a tower of balconies and glass, set slightly back from a busy street not far from the marina. I follow Berry past the terrace restaurant and pool and into the quiet and cool foyer.

She asks the smiling blonde woman on reception if Rubén is in, but before the woman can even answer, a man – short and stocky with cropped dark hair, a neat gingery beard and deep dimples – rushes over and envelops Berry in a hug.

'This is Rubén!' she tells me. 'This is his hotel!'

He doesn't look old enough to have a hotel and after haltingly apologising to me that his English isn't great, he and Berry chat for a couple of minutes in Spanish.

'He said to order whatever we want,' Berry tells me, as we head back out to the terrace. 'On him.'

'How do you know him?'

'He was a charter guest a couple of years ago,' Berry tells me, sliding a bowl of olives across the table to me. 'Try these – they're so good. And then I came to stay here for a couple of nights when I was between yachts. I didn't know it was his place, but he remembered me. And we became friends. He's great. I dated his sister for a little while; not so great.'

I pop an olive in my mouth and bite down. It's the best olive I've ever tasted.

Berry tells me about some of her previous yachting jobs as I drink my wine and eat too many olives. There's a band setting up in the corner of the terrace – just two men with acoustic guitars – and once they start to play, people get up to dance.

We order more drinks and a charcuterie and cheese board and I tell Berry about my siblings, about Mum and Mick, and Maddie. She asks about Liverpool, about uni, about the small crescent scar on my arm that I wish I could say was from something exciting, but I actually got taking a tray of chicken nuggets out of the oven.

When we've finished our food, we order more drinks and Berry says she wants to show me something. I follow her through reception and into a tiny lift with a wobbly door.

'Is that a mosquito?' she says, flinching.

'I can't see one.'

'It is! Hold this.'

She hands me her wine and flaps at the air, trying to kill it.

'Don't,' I tell her. 'You don't know where it's going.'

'Straight to hell if I have anything to do with it.'

She claps her hands over her head and groans in frustration when she misses it again.

'We're in a hotel,' I tell her, holding the glasses close to me so she doesn't inadvertently clap them out of my hands. 'Maybe he's a guest. Maybe he's got a date. There's a lady mosquito waiting for him right now. In a negligee. All perfumed.'

Berry snorts. 'Well, she's shit out of luck.' She claps again. 'She'll have to find herself a nice firefly or something.' She groans in frustration as the lift stops and the doors open.

'Have a nice evening, sir,' I tell the empty lift as we step out.

Berry takes her wine back from me, shaking her head. 'You're unbelievable.'

She peers into the glass for a second before huffing out a breath. 'I was hoping he'd drowned.'

'Heartless.'

We've arrived at a small, dark landing.

'Where are we?' I ask her.

She smiles. 'Follow me.'

I do. Along a corridor and through a dark spa room with a massage table and shelves piled high with folded towels. Berry opens a door, says, 'Mind the step' and I follow her out to a small terrace, where sunloungers point towards the glass balustrades.

'Don't look yet,' Berry says. 'Little bit further.'

I follow her up a short set of stairs to another terrace. This one also has sunloungers directed towards the glass, but they're arranged either side of a bright blue plunge pool.

'Rubén told me there'd be no one up here,' she tells me. 'It's one of my favourite places. Look.'

She walks around the pool and over to the glass, pointing out towards the marina.

'Can you see the *Serendipity*?'

I can see yachts, but I wouldn't be able to pick ours out. Mostly I can see the enormous cruise ships, lit up in red and white, steam drifting from the funnels like abandoned cigarettes.

Berry points to the left. 'There's the jetty. So it should be . . .' She wafts her hand. 'Somewhere along there.'

I laugh. 'Oh yeah, I can see it now.'

A dimple curves in her cheek as she smiles at me. 'So I thought I'd be able to pick it out and I overestimated myself. Still cool, though, right?'

'Very cool.'

We lean against the balustrade and drink our wine, looking out over the buildings to the water beyond. I turn and look at the castle, high on the hills behind us, lit up and glowing golden against the navy-blue sky.

'Thanks for bringing me here,' I tell her. 'It's great.'

'And the drinks are free!'

She puts her wine down on a small table and unbuttons her shorts, letting them fall to the floor around her feet.

I glance around to make sure no one's joined us without me noticing. Or maybe there's cameras. Berry pulls her top over her head. She's not wearing a bra and I whip my head around to look out over the water again.

'You not coming in?'

I shake my head. 'No, no. I'm good.'

Even at this time of night it's still humid and I would love to get in the pool, but I'm not taking off my clothes and I'm not getting into a tiny pool with an almost naked Berry. I can still feel her hands on my thighs in my dream. How wet I was when I woke up.

The water splashes as she lowers herself in. 'Pass me my wine?'

I do. And then I toe off my flip-flops and lower myself to the ground next to the pool, dangling my feet in the water.

'I knew you couldn't resist,' Berry grins up at me.

The water is cool but not cold and my swinging feet send ripples across the surface. Berry lowers her head back, her eyes closed, legs stretched out, breasts just under the surface of the water.

'We should probably be getting back soon,' I tell her.

She groans and arches her back. 'Don't say that. I could stay here forever.'

'You'd prune,' I tell her.

'And the mosquitoes would eat me alive. Okay, lemme just . . .'

She leans forward and glides the length of the pool, before flipping over onto her back again. I finish my wine. Berry rolls over and glides back again, then lifts herself out at the other end of the pool, grabbing a towel from one of the sunloungers.

I swing my legs out of the water, patting them dry before stepping back into my sandals and collecting both our glasses, purposely not looking at Berry. When I look up, I catch Berry looking at my legs where my damp dress has got stuck high on my thighs. I don't pull it back down.

The cab drops us off at the end of the long jetty and we've walking towards the boat when someone shouts my name. I turn to see Adam and Liam getting out of another cab just behind ours.

'Hey! Where've you two been?'

As they walk towards us, I see Adam stagger, holding his hands out in front as if he's trying to recapture his balance.

'Casino,' Liam says.

Adam sings, the '*no, no, no*' from Amy Winehouse's 'Rehab' and says, 'To the bar. Great bar.'

'Apparently!' I laugh. 'Did you spend your entire tip?'

He shakes his head slowly, loosely. 'I did not.' And then he taps his temple with his finger.

'Yeah. You're smart.' I smile. 'Smart and shit-faced.'

The four of us walk along the jetty, Adam occasionally losing his balance and, at one point, reaching for me and saying, 'Are you happy, Hopey?'

I widen my eyes at him in warning, but it's probably pointless when he's this drunk. We're lucky he's not trying to give me a piggyback or asking me for a snog.

'I'm very happy. Thank you for asking. Are you?'

'I am sound as a pound.' He laughs. 'Loads of pounds.'

When we get onto the boat, we have to shush Adam who is now attempting to sing 'Valerie' and can't balance well enough to take his shoes off. In the mess I get him a glass of water and then Liam helps him up the corridor to his room.

'They had fun,' Berry says, smiling, once we're in our cabin.

'I did too. Thanks for taking me.'

'Thanks for coming.'

We smile at each other and I don't know if it's the wine or because the cabin is so small or because I can't stop thinking about her body under the water, but for a second I can't quite catch my breath.

Berry blinks at me and then says, 'I'd better shower.'

I nod. She closes the bathroom door behind her and I pull off my shorts and bra and get into bed in my vest.

I roll onto my side. Squeeze my eyes shut. Pull my legs up towards my chest.

I've got a crush on Berry.

Shit.

12

'Looking gorgeous, ladies,' Nico says, as Berry and I join him and Adam on deck the following evening.

I'm exhausted and it took a while for Berry to convince me to go out again tonight, insisting I wear one of her dresses. It's very short. My legs are tanned from being in the sun, and I was surprised by how happy I felt when I looked in the mirror on the back of our closet door.

Adam looks good too in a black polo shirt that shows off his tan, jeans and trainers without socks. Maybe at the club there'll be a chance for us to sneak away together. I'd like to slide my hands up under that shirt.

I spent most of the day cleaning out a cupboard literally called the doghouse, and I had plenty of time to think. There's nothing wrong with a crush. It's normal. Healthy even. Doesn't mean I'm going to do anything about it. I have a boyfriend. He's hot. It's fine.

Berry's wearing what is effectively a mesh dress and sandals tied up her calves.

It's fine. I'm fine.

A few minutes later, Liam joins us and finally Louise, in a little black dress and thigh-high boots, her hair loose around her shoulders.

Her eye make-up makes her already huge eyes look like Disney eyes. She looks about ten years younger.

'Is this everyone?' she asks.

'Ben and Carlo said they might join later,' Nico tells her. 'The cab's already waiting.'

We follow Nico through the marina to the cab. The sun has set but the air is still warm, the sky a deep purple-blue, like a bruise.

Berry is on my left, singing along to SZA's 'Kill Bill' on the radio. Her thigh is warm against mine; I shift in my seat to put a bit of space between us. Nico and Liam are up front, talking to the driver about football, I think. I glance over at Louise. She's looking out of the window, her leg bouncing with excitement or nerves or just anticipation. I don't know which.

I relax against Adam, my body softening, my weight against his side. And I feel him tense. He leans forward so suddenly that I almost tip over into the space behind him.

'Did Yamal play?' he asks the other guys, the driver.

The rejection stings, even though I know we're in a car full of colleagues and he doesn't want to get caught. But no one's interested. And it's not like I was planning to climb into his lap and ride him all the way to town; I just wanted a bit of physical contact. I don't think that's too much to ask.

The club is dark and loud and absolutely heaving. As we push our way through the crowd, Berry turns back to shout something at me, her eyes shining as the lights – blue, red, pink – strobe across her face.

'What?' I yell and it makes me laugh.

She shakes her head, laughing too, and makes a 'drink?' gesture with her hand.

Shrugging, I try to convey that I'll come with her to the bar. Nico and Louise have already disappeared and Adam and Liam are heading to the bar too, so we follow them and join the crush of bodies waiting to be served.

Berry passes me a bottle of San Miguel, cold and wet with condensation. I press it to my neck, just under my jaw – it's really hot in here; a trickle of sweat is already making its way down my back and we've only just arrived.

Beer in one hand, Berry grabs my wrist with the other and pulls me out onto the dance floor. She twirls, throwing her head back, her raspberry hair swinging and then I'm dancing too, laughing as a young Spanish guy struts between us and slides his arms around another guy in a gold crop top and booty shorts.

At the opening notes of 'Padam Padam', everyone cheers and Berry throws her arms up over her head, some of her beer overflowing and running down her hand. She licks it off, her tongue slipping between her fingers.

I think of her again with the woman in Barcelona. The woman's mouth on Berry's hand. Berry's mouth –

'I love this song!' she shouts, bringing me back to the present.

'Me too!' I gulp my beer.

Berry moves up close to me and we dance together, rolling our hips, our shoulders, grinning at each other as we mouth the words. The beat moves through my body and everything else – work, my borked neck, Adam, the fact that we have to be up again in about seven hours – just goes away.

We dance as Kylie transitions into 'Rush' by Troye Sivan, through the Adam Lambert cover of 'You Make Me Feel (Mighty Real)', the Scissor Sisters' 'Filthy/Gorgeous'. I've finished my beer, my hair is stuck to the back of my neck and my face is burning. I press my bottle to my cheek, but it's not even cold any more.

Berry raises an eyebrow and mouths, 'You good?'

I press my lips up to her ear. 'Too hot!'

She nods and slides her hand into mine, guiding me off the dance floor.

'I want to keep dancing!' I shout, but she takes no notice, leading me through the crowd.

I let myself be led. And then we're outside on a terrace dotted with palm trees in planters with fairy lights threaded through the branches. It's busy with people smoking and vaping and just standing around, presumably getting some air too. I follow Berry to the far corner where the view stretches over tile rooftops all the way to the ocean and we sit on a bench.

'Next time we come out, do not let me wear heels,' I tell her, clenching and stretching my toes in my ankle boots.

'Noted. Are you okay? Just too hot? How's your neck?'

I roll my head, tentatively. I tried to use the almost-constant stiffness in my neck – caused, I think, by the daily hoovering – as a reason not to come tonight, but Berry was unmoved.

'Turn a bit,' Berry says. 'Let me see what I can do.'

I shift my body away from her slightly and then her hand is on the side of my neck, her fingers pressing gently, thumb pushing more deeply into the tight muscle of my shoulder. I know I should stop her, but it feels so good.

'Often when your neck is stiff, it's not actually your neck that's the problem,' she says, her voice just behind my ear. 'It could be your shoulder, your back, even your hips. It's all connected.'

Her fingers move up behind my ear as her thumb presses a line down the side of my neck. I automatically drop my head to the left and I feel Berry's breath on my skin.

'Feels good, yeah?'

I can't even answer her. Because it feels amazing. My mind is a jumble of the woman in Barcelona, the dream I had the other night, Berry lying back in the pool, water rippling over her bare skin.

I imagine her kissing me where her fingers are currently pressing. Of her hands moving over my shoulders, down to my breasts. Of her thumb press, press, pressing up my inner thigh.

I lean forward, roll my shoulders back, shake her hands off me.

I glance back but don't meet her eyes. 'That's much better. Thank you.'

'No problem.' She stretches. 'It's so cool out here.'

I can't help looking then, as she tips her head back, closing her eyes, long eyelashes feathered over her cheeks, the moonlight highlighting her cheekbones. We're sitting close enough that I can smell the beer on her breath, her salty sweat mixed with the cherry perfume she always wears.

She opens her eyes, catches me staring and smiles, her tongue between her teeth.

She glances down at my mouth and I feel something like a sigh rumble through my chest. I can't move. But even if I could, I don't think I would. I want to know what she's going to do. Her gaze flicks up to my eyes and then back down to my mouth and then she's leaning forward and touching her lips to mine.

Just that slight brush, that gentle sensation, floods through my entire body, like the first sip of beer on a hot day. Or stepping into a hot shower on a cold day. Like she's flipped my entire body chemistry. She leans in a little more, pressing a little more firmly, her lips sliding as she turns her head and that's when I wake up to what's happening and pull back.

'I'm sorry, I can't,' I say, before my brain has entirely come back online.

'No?'

I shake my head.

'It's okay,' she says, smiling. 'You know, "Don't screw the crew" is more of a guideline than a rule.'

I try to smile in response, but my mouth feels wobbly. I want to touch my lips, check if I can still feel her kiss.

'It's not that,' I say instead. 'I'm not . . . I don't . . .'

Her eyes widen slightly. 'Not into girls?'

I shake my head again.

'Oh shit. Sorry. I just thought . . .' She shakes her head. 'I thought I was getting flirty vibes. That's totally on me. I misunderstood.'

'No, it's probably me. I'm really sorry. I –'

'Honestly, don't even worry about it. We can just pretend this never happened, yeah?'

She stands up, ready to head back inside the club.

'Okay,' I lie.

13

When my alarm goes off I have a second to focus on the pain in my head before I remember what happened last night. Or rather, just a few hours ago.

Berry kissed me.

And, right now, she's asleep two feet away from me. I roll out of my bunk and practically crawl out of the cabin, grabbing a hoodie off the floor. I pull it on as I wait for a coffee and only then do I realise the hoodie I've picked up isn't mine; it's Berry's. It smells of her cherry perfume. I should take it off, but I don't. I don't want to.

Berry kissed me and I liked it.

What am I supposed to do about that?

My phone buzzes with a WhatsApp message from Maddie and I message back to ask her if she's free for me to call. I need to talk to someone. She says yes, so I head up on to the deck. It's not yet light; the sky's a deep royal blue with the egg-yolk orange sun a semi-circle on the horizon.

'What's up?' Maddie says when she answers.

'Are you sure you're okay to talk? Where are you?'

'It's fine. I'm driving. You're on speaker.'

I pull my feet up under me on the seat. 'You're on your own?'

'I am. That sounds ominous. Has something happened?'

I blow out a breath and stare at the line of gold starting to appear on the water as the sun climbs higher.

'We all went to a club last night after the charter ended.'

'Right . . .'

'And we'd been dancing – me and Berry. We share a cabin. We were dancing and then we went outside because it was too hot and crowded and I was a bit drunk and –'

I think about her hands on my shoulders. And what went through my head.

'She kissed me.'

'Oh shit,' Maddie says.

'Yeah.' I rest my head on the back of the seat and look up at the lightening sky.

'Where was Adam?'

'He was there too. In the club. Not outside with us.'

'And what did you do? Did you kiss her back?'

'No. I stopped her.'

'Okay. Well . . . that's good, right? Was she okay about it?'

'Yeah, she was. Of course. She's great.'

'But . . .'

'I don't know.' I stand up and cross to the railing. 'Things are a bit weird with Adam. He's not doing that well at the job – the captain asked me to have a word with him and I did, but . . . I don't know. He's been really drunk a couple of times, and he seems quite stressed.'

'Is everything okay at home, do you know?' she asks.

'I haven't heard anything. But I haven't really talked to him much. It's so full on; we don't get to spend much time alone.'

'No sexy sneaking around?'

'Nope. We're so busy all the time and so knackered and he's determined that no one knows about us, even though I really don't think anyone would care. Even Berry said last night that "Don't screw the crew" is more of a guideline.'

'When did she say that? When she was trying to get into your pants?'

I laugh, but at the same time a pulse flickers between my legs. 'She wasn't trying to get into my pants!'

'Says you. Sounds like you're a bit sexually frustrated and missing Adam and overreacting to a flirty kiss. God, I just thought – you're sharing a cabin; you can't even wank!'

I snort. 'I really hope you're still in the car.'

'Nope. Walking into the building now. The security guard's never gonna look at me the same again.'

'Jesus. But no. Exactly that. There's the shower, but not for long.'

'Also, it's nice to have someone be into you,' Maddie says. 'You and Adam have been together so long. I don't think a bit of a crush or a bit of flirting's going to kill anyone.'

'Right.' I nod. 'You're right.'

'I, for example, have the raging horn for the guy who runs the barber shop that's just opened underneath our flat. He barely speaks English. When I go in or out, he smiles and says "Okay?" and I say "Okay?" like we're in a John Green novel and then I think about riding him in one of his barber's chairs.'

'I can't decide if I'm sorry or happy I called you,' I tell her.

'Always happy! But I'm at work now so it's misery time. Get back to your glamorous superyacht and think of me draining bunions or whatever horrible shit I have to do today.'

'I'm definitely not going to think about that,' I tell her. 'But thank you.'

'You're welcome. And stop worrying so much.'

'I think I just swallowed a mosquito,' Berry says in our cabin after we've worked all day and had dinner with everyone in the mess. 'Bastards better not start biting me inside.'

I snort. 'Yeah, I don't think that's a thing.'

'You don't know what they're capable of! They will kill us all!'

She twists her torso, trying to scratch the middle of her back.

'Don't scratch!' I tell her. 'You'll only make it worse.'

'Well, I know that. But it feels so good.'

I shake my head. 'Put some ice on it.'

She wriggles, rubbing herself against the cupboard door like Baloo in *The Jungle Book* scratching himself on a tree trunk.

I try not to look at how her hips are rolling, the way her eyes are scrunched shut and her mouth open at the illicit satisfaction of scratching.

'I'm going to shower,' she says. 'Then I can scratch legally.'

'Again,' I say, 'I don't think it works like that.'

She stops scratching and looks almost nervous for a second.

'I made you a playlist,' she says. 'I've sent you the link on WhatsApp. It'd be so much better on an actual cassette, but I guess those days are gone.'

'Wow.' I blink. 'Thank you.'

'I was doing it anyway, but could it maybe also be an apology for last night?'

She leans back against the door again and smiles at me, her nose wrinkling.

'Oh god,' I say. 'You don't need to apologise. It was just –'

She shakes her head. 'I do. It was stupid. We share a cabin and I made it way awkward.'

'You didn't.' I smile. 'This is a bit awkward now though.'

She laughs. 'Oh god. I keep levelling up. Right. I'm going to shower. Let's never speak of this again, okay?'

'Okay.'

She closes the bathroom door behind her and I hit play on the playlist on my phone. It opens with a song by Kenny Loggins called 'This Is It.'

The bathroom door opens and Berry leans out. 'You can't listen to it now!'

'Why not?'

'The vibes aren't right.'

'We are literally on a yacht.'

'But we need to be in the sun with a cocktail. The vibe's the whole thing. That's what makes it yacht rock!'

'Fine! God.'

I pause the track and Berry closes the bathroom door again. I hear the water start as I scroll through the rest of the playlist. 'What a Fool Believes' by the Doobie Brothers, 'Rosanna' by Toto, the Hall & Oates songs she already told me about.

She's in the shower. Just the other side of the wall. Naked.

I scroll a bit more.

'There's literally a song called "Sailing" on here,' I call out. 'Bit on the nose.'

'Or is it a yacht rock classic?' she calls back.

I carry on scrolling and trying not to picture Berry in the shower because we are room-mates and I have a boyfriend. Her head tipped back as the water streams over her throat. Her hands – slick with shower gel – sliding down her body.

'Ride Like the Wind' by Christopher Cross. Chris Cross? Really? 'Lovely Day' by Bill Withers. 'So Into You' by something called Atlanta Rhythm Section.

The door opens and Berry comes out wrapped in a towel, like she's done numerous times before. I stare at my phone until my eyes get hot.

'I put Bobby Caldwell on there,' she says, a disembodied voice coming from somewhere in this seven-metre-square cabin. 'I'm not actually sure it counts as yacht rock, but it's perfect, so who cares.'

'Which one's that?' I ask, scrolling aggressively.

'It's called "What You Won't Do for Love". I asked my dad for suggestions too. He added the Eagles and "Right Down the Line" by Gerry Rafferty. He plays that one at home all the time.'

'Nice. Thank you!'

'Slow Hand' by the Pointer Sisters. 'Guilty' by Barbra Streisand and Barry Gibb.

'My mom walked down the aisle to it,' she tells me, heading back into the bathroom. 'I still sometimes catch them dancing to it in the kitchen.'

'That's lovely,' I say, relaxing a little. 'It must be nice to know you come from so much love.'

'Yeah. But it's a bit . . . I don't know . . .'

She's back again, this time in her underwear and the vest top she sleeps in.

I stare at my phone again. 'Killing Me Softly With His Song' by Roberta Flack.

It's not like Berry's ever been shy – she stripped off in front of me literally minutes after arriving – but I've never been so aware of it before. Her body. In this tiny room. I could literally reach out and touch her.

'Like, how often does that happen, you know?' she says, and it takes me a second to remember what we were talking about. Her parents. Still in love. 'It's given me really high standards for relationships. Sometimes, I think, too high.'

'I kind of got both sides,' I say, looking up from my phone but determinedly not at Berry who is rubbing moisturiser into her legs. 'Like, my dad left my mum before I was even born. But then she found Mick and they're really happy. They make each other laugh all the time. That's what I always wanted really. That's why I –'

I almost say 'that's why I liked Adam' but catch myself. I promised Adam I wouldn't tell anyone and I have to keep that promise.

'That's why I liked the guy I used to date. He was funny. And kind.'

'Kind is important.' She's done with her legs and is now smoothing the cream over her arms, its honey and almond scent filling the cabin. 'I dated a few hot but mean girls back in California and it's not worth it. I mean, maybe it is for, like, a week. But after that, no. My parents fight all the time,' she says. 'About everything. It's sort of their hobby. My mom once told me that fighting with my dad is sexier than sex with other men. Total TMI, but also kind of nice?' She shakes her head. 'Anyway. I haven't found it yet.'

She climbs up to her bunk and I listen to the mattress creak as she settles herself into her bed.

'Have you had many?' I ask. 'Relationships?'

I hear her blow out a breath. 'Not serious relationships, no. Two? Or, I guess, three. You?'

'Just one.'

I want to tell her that it's Adam. It feels like a huge thing to keep from her and at least then she'd understand why I didn't kiss her back. But I can't.

'Just one?' Berry says. 'For real?'

I smile. 'Yeah. We got together pretty young.'

'I bet. You must've had some flings, though, right?'

'Just one really.'

I didn't know I was going to say that until the words are out of my mouth. But if I can't tell her about Adam, at least I can tell her this. Although I still hesitate; I've hardly told anyone. 'Charlie,' I say, eventually. 'At uni.'

'Yeah?'

'It wasn't even a fling really.' I picture Charlie sitting across from me in the coffee shop we always went to between lectures. 'It was more of a crush.'

'Oh, crushes are the best,' Berry says. 'When you can't stop thinking about them and you're always hoping to run into them?'

She clicks off her lamp so the cabin's only lit by my fairy lights.

'The excitement and the nerves,' Berry says. 'Fantasising about all the cool shit you'll do together if you ever tell them – or if they work it out themselves.' She sighs. 'Makes life worth living.' The mattress shifts as she gets comfortable.

I reach out and turn off my lights too.

'Did you ever tell him?' she asks, her voice soft in the darkness.

'No,' I lie.

Berry falls asleep fast – I can tell by the change in her breathing, but I lie awake for a while. Thinking about Charlie.

We were in the same lectures and seminars and often just seemed to be in the Students' Union at the same time. Before long we were walking back to town together and meeting up at weekends. I knew she was gay; she'd told me early on. She had a casual thing going with another girl and of course I was with Adam.

But then I started to notice that I was thinking about her more and more. Making up little scenarios to help me fall asleep. Charlie waiting for me after a lecture and saying she couldn't stop thinking about me. The two of us alone late in the library, her hand brushing mine as she reached past me for a book, turning to find her standing so close that I hardly had to move at all before I was kissing her.

I mentioned it to Adam, sort of half joking, partly because I always told him everything and partly because I knew it would turn him on. And it did. But thinking about being with Charlie, telling Adam what I wanted to do with Charlie, turned me on much more than I'd imagined. And it scared me.

And then, at Christmas, everyone from our course went out in town. First to dinner and then to a club. I danced with Charlie and all I could think about was touching her, kissing her. One strap of the top she was wearing kept falling down and I wanted to put my mouth on the curve of her shoulder, run my tongue up the side of her neck.

I left early. Adam was at home waiting for me, but this time I didn't tell him anything.

Back at uni, after Christmas, Charlie and I met for coffee like we always did and she asked if I had feelings for her. Just straight out asked me. Her boldness was one of the things I liked about her, but it scared the shit out of me. I told her yes, maybe, I had been having some feelings. But I didn't think I was gay. I didn't know. I worried that maybe I was bored, making it up. Maybe Charlie would kiss me and I would realise I was wrong, that I wasn't actually into her at all.

Charlie told me she was into me too, had been for a while, but she wasn't interested in anything as long as I was still with Adam. And I wasn't going to end things with Adam. I wasn't going to cheat on him either. And then I did. Or at least, I tried to.

The next time we went out as a group, I got absolutely shit-faced and, at the end of the night, in the street, the two of us waiting for Ubers, I tried to kiss her. And she pushed me away.

The next morning, I woke up with a raging headache, a rolling stomach, and a text from Charlie that said, *I'm not here for you to experiment with.*

We still saw each other at uni, of course, but we didn't sit together in the canteen any more. We didn't walk home together. We didn't meet for coffee. I missed her. And I felt horrible. I'd ruined our friendship. And I'd been a dick to both Charlie and Adam. I wasn't going to risk doing anything like that ever again.

14

When I wake up I'm not thinking about Charlie or Berry, I'm thinking about Adam.

I miss him. I love him. I've loved him for so long. What Berry said about how it feels to have a crush? That's how it's always felt with Adam. If we could just spend more time together here, alone, I know I wouldn't be thinking about Berry so much.

We're docking at Port d'Andratx to collect the new charter guests, so everyone's busy and I take advantage of their distraction to sneak out to deck to find him.

He's washing the side of the ship – leaning over the railing with a hose. I dig my fingers into his waist as if I'm going to tip him over and say, 'Tell your mother I saved your life!'

'My mother would tell you to chuck me over,' he says, turning around, his face already split into a wide smile that makes my stomach flutter.

'Hey,' I say.

I make a show of looking up and down the deck before leaning against him, my hips against his hips.

'Hope,' he says, his voice a warning.

'I know. But no one's around. I miss you.'

I go up on tiptoes, leaning into him more, drifting my lips under his jaw, which I know he can't resist.

He looks towards the bow before ducking his head to kiss me quickly, his mouth somehow soft and firm at the same time.

His radio crackles – 'Adam, Adam, Ben.' – and he pushes me away from him so fast I almost lose my balance.

Ben tells him to come and throw the lines for docking and Adam squeezes my hand quickly and goes. I'm suddenly curious about what it's like for them up on deck – and how Adam is actually getting on – so I follow him over to watch the docking procedure.

Ben tells Adam to throw the stern line to the linesman on the dock. He throws it, but it falls short and splashes into the water.

'Go again!' Ben shouts.

Adam hauls the rope out of the water, loops it, throws again and misses again. God, did I distract him? Maybe it's harder to throw a line with the erection I felt brewing when I leaned into him.

The linesman on the dock gestures at Adam and I hear Ben groan in frustration. Adam tries a third time, and it spools into the water again.

'This is so fucking simple!' Ben shouts, his anger making his accent thicker. He takes the rope from Adam and throws it himself. The linesman catches it first time and starts tying up, winding the rope in a figure of eight around the bollard on the dock.

'I could've got it!' Adam says and I can hear the frustration in his voice.

'Didn't look like it,' Ben says. 'And we don't have time for you to practise basic skills.'

'When exactly am I meant to practise them then?' Adam almost shouts. 'There's no time to do anything. How am I meant to learn it?'

'Everyone else has managed,' Ben says, throwing up his hands in frustration. 'And you literally could've caused us to crash, so sorry if I don't have time to baby you.'

'Oh yeah, great,' Adam says, his voice cracking. 'Everyone else can do it. I'm the only useless fucker. Thanks.'

He storms around the side of the boat and out of my sight.

'Hope,' Ben calls, 'can you come down here and give me a hand?'

Ben shows me how to set the fenders and tie up the lines on the deck.

'I shouldn't have spoken to him like that,' Ben says while we work.

'You were frustrated.'

He blows out a breath. 'That's no excuse. It's literally my job to . . .' He shakes his head. 'He's right, there isn't time to handhold, but he should have it by now.'

'He's hard on himself,' I tell Ben. 'When he dropped it the first time and knew everyone was watching, waiting for him to get it right . . .'

Ben nods. 'I get that. I do. I'll have a word later. If you see him, can you ask him to come and find me?'

Once we've docked, I leave Ben on the deck and find Adam in his cabin, lying on the bed.

'Hey.' I crouch down next to him. 'You okay?'

He shakes his head. 'I'm pissed off. You didn't need to come and find me.'

'Ben wants to talk to you,' I tell him.

He huffs in disgust. 'Oh no, am I in trouble?'

'Adam.'

I know this mood. It's why I wanted to talk to him before Ben did. When Adam is embarrassed, he responds with passive aggression.

'Sorry.' He blows out a breath. 'I'm just so tired. And I could've made that throw if they'd just left me to it. I can't do shit when everyone's yelling at me.'

'I know,' I tell him. 'It's rough when everyone's watching. It's not a great way to learn.'

'I just . . .' He swings his legs off the bed, perching on the edge. I drop down to sit on the floor, legs stretched out in front of me. 'I don't feel like we get any time to learn anything, you know?' he says, rubbing a hand over his face. 'It's like we're just meant to turn up here, never done any of this before, and just do it. No one's got time to even really show you.'

'I know,' I agree. He's right. It's hard. You just have to figure it out yourself.

'I thought I'd be better at it,' he admits. 'I mean, I expected to be good at it. I thought it would be easier than it is. I keep . . . I'm doing everything wrong.' He shakes his head. 'I'm sure they think I'm shit.'

'Who?'

'The captain. Ben. I heard Nico talking to Ben about how they gave me some leeway at first but I should be better by now. How they have to show me everything over and over. And they're not even wrong. I just don't get any of it.'

'You felt like that when you started uni, though,' I say. 'Remember?'

For most of the first year and some of the second, I would do my own work and then help Adam with his.

He nods. 'Yeah. I keep telling myself that. But that felt different. Like . . . it was hard and I did struggle, but I could sort of feel it.

It's hard to explain. It's like I could see what I needed to do. I couldn't do it yet, but I could sort of see the path to getting there? And it was further than I wanted it to be, but I could still see it. This.' He shakes his head again, his face screwed up in frustration. 'This I can't even see. Even when they're explaining stuff to me, my head's just a blank.'

'You'll get there,' I tell him. He did at uni. I know he can now.

'Is Ben pissed off?' he asks.

'No. He's more unhappy with how he spoke to you. He's a good guy.'

Adam nods. 'I shouldn't have lost my temper.'

I smile. 'No.'

'I should go and apologise.'

'Yep.'

He smiles then. 'You're better at this than I am. You're in your element. You look so strong and happy.'

'I feel it,' I tell him. 'It feels right to me. I mean, it's exhausting. I've never been so tired in my life, not even with the babies waking me up all the time. But I love it and I'm good at it and I'm glad I came.'

He nods. 'I can see that. I thought I would feel that too, but I just don't.'

His face crumples and I shift up onto my knees and wrap my arms around him, but he pulls away.

'Don't.'

I sit back on my heels. He's hunched over, elbows on his knees, head hanging down.

'I need to tell you something.' He doesn't look at me. 'I did something shit.'

I lower myself back to the floor and lean against the bed next to his legs.

My heart is already racing in anticipation of whatever it is he has to tell me.

His jaw is clenched, a muscle twitching near his ear. He's still not looking at me.

'I kissed someone,' he says.

For a second everything tilts. I actually reach out and grab the edge of the bed.

'That night,' he says. 'At the club.'

The night Berry kissed me. My breath is caught behind my breastbone.

'I was drunk,' Adam says, finally looking up at me. I can't imagine the expression he finds on my face.

'That's not an excuse, I know,' he says. 'It happened really fast. We were just talking – she came over to us, I didn't approach her. We were by the pool, you know?'

I nod. A lot of the time Berry and I were dancing, Adam and Liam stayed over in the seating area next to the pool. It was busy, the seats all full, people standing around and weaving through to get to other parts of the bar.

'She came over, sat next to me. I knew she was flirting.' He shakes his head. 'Liam was talking to her friend and he was talking about us going back with them, to their hotel.'

Bloody Liam.

'I didn't know what to say. Like, there was no good reason for me not to, you know? I couldn't say I've got a girlfriend in front of Liam. So I got up and went to the bathroom. And when I came out, she was waiting for me.'

'And Liam wasn't there so you could have told her you have a girlfriend.'

'Yeah.' He dips his head. Grips the back of his neck. 'Except I didn't.'

I nod. 'Right. So what did you do?'

'She kissed me.'

The thought of Adam kissing someone else makes me feel like there's a hand inside my chest squeezing my heart. But Berry kissed me. And I liked it. And I've thought about it so much since. And I didn't even consider telling Adam.

'She touched me a bit.' He rubs the back of his neck. 'You know.'

'She touched you where?' I don't feel like I'm taking this in properly. Like it's a dream and I'm going to wake up relieved this didn't really happen.

'Come on, Hope.' He nods towards his crotch.

'She touched your dick?'

'Yeah.' He rolls his shoulders back. 'I'm sorry. I didn't . . . Like, that was it. We went back into the club and then you and Berry were there and we left.'

I swing my legs around so I can lean back against the bed.

'I . . .' he says, his voice behind me, 'I didn't think about how hard it would be here without being able to . . . you know. Touch you. Be with you. You know?'

My stomach is churning like we've hit a swell and my brain is swirling too; so many thoughts are trying to force their way out of my mouth.

'I can't believe you kissed someone,' I say.

My eyes are burning, but I'm not crying. Not yet.

'I know. I fucked up.'

This is wrong. All of it. Adam kissing someone. Berry kissing me. Even the fact that we have to pretend not to be together. It's all such a mess.

'Maybe we should take a break,' he says.

'And go home? How would that work? We can't just leave.'

'Not from the job.' When I turn to look at him, I see his eyes are shining with tears. 'From us.'

I shake my head. 'I don't want that. It was just a kiss. I –'

'I can't do it, Hope. I feel like I'm going mad. There's too much –' He shakes his head.

'Is there something going on at home?' I can't believe he's saying this. 'I don't understand.'

He pushes himself off the edge of the bed and sits on the floor opposite me, dropping his head into his hands. 'I can't lose this job. I can't. And I'm fucking it up. I need to focus.'

'Yeah. I get that. But –'

He shakes his head again. 'I can't do this. I'm sorry.'

'You're actually breaking up with me?'

It doesn't feel real. I want to pinch myself and for this to be a bad dream.

'I have to, Hope,' Adam says and he's openly crying now. 'I'm so sorry.'

15

It turns out that work doesn't stop just because your boyfriend dumps you.

You have to carry on doing the job he convinced you to take. The job he sold to you on the idea that you would get to do it together. And now you're here together but apparently also apart.

It doesn't stop, even when that unbelievably now ex-boyfriend is sitting opposite you at a crew briefing an hour or so after telling you he kissed someone else and is deliberately not meeting your eyes.

'Paul Jennings is a film director,' the captain tells us. 'This is an anniversary trip – he and his wife have been married for ten years. His wife Marni is an artist. They have four children.'

'With them?' Louise asks, her voice high-pitched, her big eyes widening.

''Fraid so,' Captain Liz says. 'They really want to just chill out with nice wine, some entertainment for the kids, maybe a beach picnic. They'd like to go to Port de Sóller. And obviously an anniversary meal. Paul has requested a recreation of their first date as a surprise for Marni. It was an Italian restaurant!'

Carlo sits up straighter, looking delighted.

'They had rigatoni alla vodka, roasted aubergines, and beef carpaccio.'

'I can't believe he remembers what they ate,' Louise says.

I remember what I ate on my first date with Adam. We went to Nando's. He teased me for getting my wings with lemon and herb while he went for hot and tried to style it out as sweat pearled on his forehead and his eyes brimmed with tears.

'Wait till you hear this next part,' the captain continues. 'He says that on the dessert menu was something called Italian wedding cake. He wanted to order it that night – he already knew he wanted to marry her, but he didn't want to scare her off.'

'I love this man!' Carlo says, craning over the table to look at the information sheet.

'So, he'd like Italian wedding cake for their anniversary dinner,' the captain finishes. 'Do you know it, Carlo?'

Carlo nods enthusiastically. 'It is a, a *millefoglie* . . .' He waves his hands and frowns. 'In English . . . many-layer cake. Pastry and cream and fruit. It is for hope for the future.'

I am so not in the mood to think about hope. Even if it does come with pastry and cream.

All the preparation we have to do for a new charter at least works as a distraction from thinking about Adam. He's never far from my mind while I clean, tidy, make the beds and ensure everywhere is fully provisioned, but I can't let myself think about him too much or I'll lose it completely.

When the guests arrive, they're friendly and warm and very excited to be on board. The kids are shy, wide-eyed, quiet, but as Louise shows them all round, I can hear them all exclaiming

129

over everything from the shine on the mirrors to the colour of the carpets.

I set the table with bright rainbow bunches of dried wildflowers – bunny tails, pampas grass, gypsophila – and equally brightly coloured glassware, and it looks like a fiesta. It's the opposite to how I feel, but I'm pleased with it and so is Louise.

'This is fabulous.' She takes a photo on her phone for the file. 'Well done! The guests are just getting settled and then they'll be through. Can you go and tell Carlo ten minutes?'

After lunch, we sail to Port de Sóller, where we're going to anchor overnight. The guests have requested the water toys for later today, so Adam, Nico and Liam are getting them ready while Berry and I prepare an on-deck picnic area with bright, oversized floor cushions, an adorable wooden picnic basket play kit, a teepee tent and a giant snakes and ladders set.

I'm relieved that I don't have to work directly with Adam, but it's distracting knowing he's around. I could see him at any time.

The children do turn out to be adorable and it's lovely to be around little kids again. Mostly. At one point the oldest gets annoyed when the youngest can't play the game properly but wins anyway, and when he shoves him, the youngest rolls around on deck, wailing.

'I'm so sorry,' Marni, the mum, tells us. 'He's overtired.'

'I get it,' I tell her. 'I've got three little siblings.'

She seems hugely relieved. 'I think people think that's just an excuse for bad behaviour, but it's a real thing!'

'It definitely is. So is hangry.'

'Oh god, for me too, never mind the children.'

'Have you had enough to eat?' I ask her.

Carlo made the most amazing spread. Tiny sandwiches, mini quiches, pizza rolls, little pots of pasta and salads. Even adorable little cucumber boats with cheese-slice sails.

'Oh gosh, yes,' Marni says. 'It was all amazing. Please tell the chef. I'm going to go and put this one down for a nap.'

The youngest, Noah, is clinging to his mum's leg, thumb in his mouth and his eyes almost closed.

'Teddy, do you want to nap?' she calls over to the second youngest. He shakes his head, frowning, as if offended by the very suggestion.

'You should,' she says in a sing-song voice. 'If you don't want to be a nightmare later . . .'

He ignores her and, after rolling her eyes and smiling at me, she takes Noah through to the guest rooms.

The dad, Paul, lies on the bunny pad with the other boys, chatting and laughing. We bring drinks for him and ice lollies for the kids and tidy away some of the more perishable food.

When Marni comes back out, she crawls into the tent with Teddy, lying down next to him, talking quietly and stroking his face, and soon he's napping too.

'Could I please get a French 75?' she asks me, emerging from the tent and blinking into the sun. 'I have been dreaming about this trip for so long and all I kept thinking was a French 75 in the sun. With no kids on me.'

By the time the two youngest are awake and Marni has had her French 75, the floaties and slide have been set up and Paul is quick to head down the slide with Scout and Arlo, the older two. Noah doesn't want to go on the slide, so I hop into a dinghy with him, Marni and Teddy and we paddle around to the bottom of the slide to watch the bigger boys having fun.

'Is it scary?' Teddy asks me, eyes wide, looking up at the slide.

'I don't think so,' I tell him. 'Not too scary. Doesn't it look like fun?'

'I don't like the splash in a-water,' Noah says. 'At a-bottom.'

'I don't like going under the water,' Teddy tells me, his little face serious. 'When we go to swimming, she –'

'Amy,' Marni corrects, gently.

'Amy,' Teddy repeats, 'Amy is the swimming lady. She maked us go under water and Noah cried and cried.'

'I don't yike it,' Noah tells me.

Marni smiles at them both. 'But it's important to learn to swim so you can stay safe, right?'

'And!' Noah says, apparently remembering some more indignities of swimming lessons. 'We hafta wear a hat and it hurted my ears.'

'My little sister has long hair,' I tell them. 'Down to her bottom. And when she had swimming lessons, we had to pile her hair up on top of her head to fit in the hat and when we pulled it on . . . POP! It jumped right off!'

They both dissolve into giggles.

'So she didn't couldn't do it?' Teddy asks.

'Well, they taught us a trick,' I tell him. 'You fill the swimming hat with water and flip it over onto your head and then it doesn't pop off.'

'But the water goes on you?' Teddy asks.

I nod. 'It does.'

'All down-a face?' Noah asks, looking appalled, and sounding like a tiny Super Mario.

I nod again.

'Did she cry?' Teddy asks.

'She did a bit.' She did a lot. 'But then she tried again and she got used to it and then she loved it. One time we went and she didn't want to take the hat off! She wanted to wear it home.'

The boys both laugh again.

'I'm gonna wear it to school!' Teddy almost shouts.

Noah's laughing so hard he keels over sideways into the bottom of the dinghy.

'So are you two going to get in the water?' I ask them. They're both wearing life jackets and there are floaties and pool noodles all around us.

'Can I go on the slide with you, Mummy?' Teddy asks.

'I don't think so,' Marni tells him. 'Because what about Noah?'

'I stay with . . .' He stares up at me, his forehead scrunched. 'I forgot-a name.'

'Hope,' I tell him.

'I stay here with 'ope. And not get wet!'

Marni and Teddy clamber back on board and I wait with Noah in the dinghy. I can tell that as soon as his mum's out of sight, he starts to fret a little, so I suggest a game I've played with my little siblings – trying to think of rhyming words.

'Boat,' I say first.

He shakes his head, eyes big.

'Goat!' I throw in a 'maa' for good measure and the corners of his mouth twitch in an almost smile.

'Can you think of anything that rhymes with "boat" or "goat"?'

He shakes his head.

'No?' I joke. 'That doesn't rhyme with "boat" or "goat". How about "coat"!'

He nods.

'And – ooh! Float!' I point to one of the unicorn floats tied to the back of the dinghy.

I mentally run through the alphabet. 'Moat. Do you know what a moat is?'

He shakes his head.

'It's water around a castle. To protect it, if anyone wanted to attack it. How about . . . vote?'

He shakes his head again but he's smiling now.

'I vote that when we see Mummy and Teddy we give them big waves. What do you think?'

He nods and, just in time, his mum and brother appear at the top of the slide. Noah and I wave and they wave back, Teddy jumping up and down before apparently deciding the slide is too big to tackle and disappearing behind his mum's legs.

Noah and I watch as Marni crouches down and chats to him and then sits at the top of the slide, Teddy in her lap.

'He frikened,' Noah says in a small voice.

'I think he is,' I agree. 'But I think he's going to be brave.'

Marni and Teddy push off and Noah screeches with laughter as they zoom down the slide and splash into the water. Teddy bobs to the surface, hair all over his face, but he's laughing.

'You brave, Teddy!' Noah shouts and even from here I can see Teddy's eyes light up.

In contrast, mine fill with tears. What am I even doing? I'm just meant to carry on working alongside Adam as if none of this has happened. No one knew we were together so no one will even know we've broken up.

And now I'm playing with someone else's kids while my siblings are at home without me. What if Mum has the baby early and I'm not there? What if she needs me?

I need her.

I wish I could just go home.

16

'Oh!' Marni says through tears. 'This is all so beautiful!'

The table is covered with a red-and-white-checked tablecloth. A central row of candles in old wine bottles is surrounded by cut lemons and bunches of fragrant basil, rosemary and thyme.

Jack Savoretti's half-Italian version of 'You Don't Have to Say You Love Me' – requested by Paul – is playing and the deck is lit with fairy lights.

'I just heard the song!'

Marni turns to Paul, who slides his hand down her arm to take her hand and twirl her. She wraps her arms around his neck and they start to dance, really just swaying in place.

It feels like we shouldn't be here. I feel like I'm intruding. But at the same time it's all so beautiful and romantic and my heart is cracking. I don't understand how everything could have gone so wrong with Adam so quickly. How can he not want to be with me any more, after just one kiss? I feel like there must be something I'm missing. My Adam, the Adam I've loved for so long, would never do this.

But he did.

The song ends and I watch Paul and Marni whisper to each other, giggling, their eyes sparkling, and I want to run back to my cabin and cry. But I can't, because I have to bring up the meal and serve the guests and pour the wine and pretend not only that everything is fine but also that I'm so happy and thrilled at how in love the two of them are.

The Italian wedding cake is a massive success. Marni and Paul both cry and then, once they've eaten, they get up from the table and dance. We try to stay as much out of the way as possible, just keeping an eye out in case they need anything.

When one of the big cruise ships in port sets off fireworks and they go up to the sun deck to watch, I take the dishes down the stairs to the galley. Adam is in the corridor. He's staring down at his phone and his face looks so stricken that my first thought is that someone's died.

'What's happened?'

He startles and shoves his phone in his pocket before turning to me, shaking his head. 'Nothing. It's fine.'

'Adam.'

I know him. I've known him. I know he's not fine.

'Leave it, Hope.'

He starts to walk away and I grab his arm. He shrugs me off, but when he turns to look at me, his expression is soft and tears immediately spring to my eyes.

'It's nothing,' he says. 'I promise. Don't worry.'

I know he's lying, but I don't know how to make him tell me the truth.

'I was planning to start the *Sewing Bee* tonight,' Berry tells me, after everything's cleared away and we're back in our cabin. 'Do you want to watch?' She gestures at the small TV on the wall at the foot of her bed.

I was thinking more about crying myself to sleep or obsessively searching Adam's Instagram for some sort of clue as to what's going on with him, but I can't do any of that with Berry here. And I'm not even sure I'll be able to sleep.

'I can cast it from my phone,' she says. 'I think . . .'

'To both TVs?' I ask her. Maybe *Sewing Bee* with Berry will relax me enough to get some sleep.

'I don't think I can do that.' She frowns. 'But I could squeeze into your bunk.'

My brain goes white. It's a terrible idea. But if it helps me stop thinking about Adam, I don't even care.

'We don't have to . . .' Berry says.

'No. We totally can,' I agree. 'That's a good idea.'

'It'll be cosy.'

I pile our pillows and cushions behind us and Berry manages to get the show to play on the TV, although the sound is very slightly out of sync.

We're pretty much pressed together all down one side – my right side against Berry's left. It's definitely cosy.

'Oh my god,' Berry says, shifting on the bed so her knee brushes against mine, sending a buzz of electricity up my leg. 'It's Claudia Winkleman!'

I laugh. 'How do you know Claudia Winkleman?'

'*The Traitors*. A British tour guest told me about it and I was obsessed! I watched the whole thing one weekend when I was horrifically hungover. I love her!'

'She's the best,' I agree.

It takes a while before I can relax completely with Berry so close, but I'm so tired that by the high-street challenge I feel almost boneless. I'm starting to drift off when my phone buzzes with a message from Mum that just says, *Bed rest, ffs*.

I push myself up against the pillows. 'Oh no,' I tell Berry. 'My mum's got to go on bed rest.'

Another message comes through before I can reply.

I'm fine. Don't worry. They're being extra cautious because I'm geriatric. Cheers for that. She's added the gran, the knife and the skull emojis.

I show Berry and she laughs.

'God, she's going to be a nightmare,' I say, but my eyes are pricking with tears. 'I wish there was something I could do.'

Maybe I should go home. I shouldn't be so far away when Mum is struggling. How is she going to look after the kids when she's on bed rest? I type a message to Mick.

Don't worry, Mick replies. *Everything's under control.*

I shake my head at my phone. I don't see how it can be.

'Could you send her, like, meal kits?' Berry suggests, pausing the *Sewing Bee*. 'Do you have Blue Apron in the UK?'

'We don't,' I tell her, 'but we have loads like it and that is a brilliant idea. Thank you.'

While the *Sewing Bee* contestants work on their made-to-measures, I pick and schedule meal kits to be delivered over the next few weeks, along with a box of doughnuts to arrive tomorrow, and, despite still being worried – of course I'm still going to be worried – I feel better.

'You doing okay?' Berry asks, once the show's finished and the TV's off, but she's still in my bed. 'Must be hard to be away from them.'

Tears well again and I see her face go soft.

'Sorry,' I say, wiping under my eyes. 'I'm fine. I just miss them.'

She smiles. 'Of course you do. I bet they miss you too.'

I laugh. 'None of the kids will even speak to me. Riley's even stopped sending me TikToks.'

'It sounds like you're really close to them.'

I nod, swallowing down the lump in my throat. 'Yeah. Mum works, so I looked after them a lot.'

'While you were at college?'

'Yeah. I know. It sounds like a lot, but I did English so I didn't actually have to be there that much; it was mostly reading.'

'But could you do all the reading when you were looking after the kids?'

'Sometimes. It was fine, though. I wanted to help. I mean, there wasn't really any other option.'

'They're not your kids, though,' Berry says, gently. 'Wasn't it up to your mum to sort?'

'I like helping,' I say, shrugging.

'I've noticed,' Berry says, smiling.

'And, honestly, I'm making it sound like more than it was.'

'I bet you were called "most conscientious" at school.'

'I was! And I was happy about it too.'

'Typical oldest child.'

'Are you a typical only child?'

'I think so? Probably. Hyper independent. I don't like to share. Had imaginary friends for much longer than I should have done.'

'Yeah? Are they here with us now?'

Berry snorts. 'No, but I could seriously conjure them up. I sometimes think, like, I wonder what Beeper's doing now . . . And then remember.

Nothing. Because it was literally a beeper I found in the trash.'

'Your best friend was a trash beeper?' I say. 'This is the saddest thing I've ever heard. How did it even start? Like . . . you found a beeper and . . .'

'I found the beeper. I thought it was like an adult Tamagotchi and I was so pleased with myself. Like, "Aha! I knew you guys did this too!" It didn't work, but I just pretended it did. Like I imagined a little face on the screen.' She closes her eyes. 'I can see it now. Blinking eyes. A shy smile.'

'This is the most adorable thing I've ever heard. I hope you know that.'

She gives me a look. 'Then there was a hurricane. I woke up in the night and the power was out and the rain was hammering. I can remember this clap of thunder that I seriously thought had hit the house it was so loud. Like, it was right outside my window. I ran to my parents' room. My mom still talks about it sometimes. She said the thunder woke her up and as she was coming to get me, I was running down the hall in my PJs, going, "No, no, no, no, no, no," with the beeper in my hand. I remember being in their bed, in the middle, between them. They never let me do that. I was sort of sitting up because I didn't think I'd be able to sleep. I remember seeing fork lightning through their window, even though the curtains were closed. I saw this jagged . . .' She draws it in the air with her hand. 'I thought the sky was splitting open.'

'That sounds so scary.'

She nods. 'I'm still afraid of storms. Which . . . is not great in this job. I thought it would be like aversion therapy, you know? Like, if I can stand a storm on a yacht, I can cope with a storm anywhere. Hasn't worked out like that. I still freak out.'

'And no beeper.'

She shakes her head sadly. 'No beeper. My mom was amazing, though,' Berry says. 'Because before the storm, there'd been a drought. There's almost always a drought in California, you know? But there'd been a drought and then this terrifying storm that caused floods and landslides and power outages and traumatised little me. But then she took me to see the superbloom. Do you know what that is?'

'I think I've seen it?' I tell her.

'Probably on Instagram. It's a whole thing now. There was one a few years ago and, like, hundreds of thousands of people turned up and there was gridlock and people trampled the flowers or pulled them up . . . It was awful. But this was before all that. It wasn't even called a "superbloom", I don't think. My mom just drove us there one day and it was just all these flowers, all different colours, as far as you could see. I remember that when we got out of the car I thought it was painted. Like someone had painted the grass purple and yellow and orange. I remember being confused but thinking it was pretty cool, you know? And then we walked through it, along this path. It was like *The Wizard of Oz*.'

'It sounds so beautiful.'

She nods. 'It really was. And then Mom told me that it was caused by the storm. That if we hadn't had the storm, we wouldn't have the flowers. And that sometimes bad things, scary things, can turn into something more beautiful than you could imagine.'

'Wow. She sounds incredible.'

Berry smiles. 'She is. And it really works for me as a metaphor, you know? And some of the seeds that caused it had been dormant for years and years just waiting for the rains to bring them alive. She said they were like the stars, you know? The past made visible.'

'That's amazing.'

She nods. 'One day I'd like a whole tattoo sleeve of flowers. It doesn't help me when there's a storm though. I'm still terrified.'

'Well, I'm here now,' I tell her, nudging her with my shoulder. 'I can be your beeper.'

She smiles. 'You can be my beeper.'

17

Having four small children on board is exhausting. We're obviously all on high safety alert all the time, plus they need to be constantly entertained. Every bit of me is aching. One upside is that they all, including Paul and Marni, go to bed early.

I've barely seen Adam. He's avoiding me. And I'm avoiding him right back. I cry quietly in the shower each morning and then make myself get on with the day. It's the only way I can deal with it.

'My lower back is killing me,' I groan that night, trying to get comfortable in bed.

Berry sings it back to me to the tune of '. . . Baby One More Time'.

'It's not funny!' I say, but I'm laughing. 'Teddy had me pretending to be a horse for hours.'

'You're right,' Berry says, deadpan. 'That's very serious.' She grins, her tongue between her teeth. 'You know what you need? Yoga and then a hot shower.'

'I think I'm just going to sleep.' I've put a pillow between my knees and that seems to be helping a little.

'No, don't – you'll seize up. Come on.'

She reaches out and, when I take her hand, hauls me out of my bunk. The two of us head up to the sun deck where it's quiet and

Berry puts down a yoga mat for me, saying she can manage fine without.

She leads me through some poses – triangle, forward bends, extended child's pose, which makes my hips and shoulders complain and then almost relax. We do cat-cows and pigeon, downward dog and sphinx, and end by lying on our backs looking up at the darkening sky.

'Corpse pose,' Berry says.

'Wait, really?'

'Yep. Savasana. It's really good for you. Relaxes every muscle. The first time I did it in a class, I fell asleep.'

I snort. 'Did they just leave you there or . . . ?'

She laughs and out of the corner of my eye, I see her turn her head to look at me. When I turn mine to look back, my neck pops audibly.

She lifts one leg and then the other, pointing and flexing her toes. I do the same. She crosses her right ankle over her left knee and then pulls her legs in towards her chest. I copy her again and actually moan at the relief of the stretch.

'Yeah,' she says. 'This is a good one.'

'Thank you for making me do this,' I tell her, as we change legs. 'I don't think I can get up, but I'll just sleep here. Throw a waterproof over me.'

'We don't need to get up yet,' she says, pointing up at the sky. 'Look. Orion's Belt.'

I squint. 'Is it?'

'No idea. Could be.'

I smile. 'We should have an app or something.'

'Nah. We don't need one. See that row of stars and then there's two underneath? That's a cock and balls.'

I snort. 'Ah yes. I've heard of that one. Cass—'

I start laughing at my own joke and the more I try to say 'Cassiopenis', the more I laugh. Berry laughs too and I don't know if she knows what I was about to say or if she's just laughing at me laughing, but soon tears are streaming down both our faces and I can't catch my breath.

'Oh god, stop,' she hoots. 'My ribs are hurting.'

She sits up, reaching a hand out for me again.

I let her pull me up, still giggling. It feels really good. It feels like a release.

'What were you gonna say?' She's grinning at me, her eyes bright.

I manage 'Cassiop—' this time before I'm laughing again.

'Oh god,' she says. 'I know it now.'

It takes another couple of minutes for us to get ourselves together before Berry squeaks out, 'Cassiopeen—'

'Don't,' I gasp, trying to catch my breath.

'Gives new meaning to the Plough,' Berry says and then we're both cry-laughing again.

'God,' I say, lying back down on the mat. 'I'm surprised no one's come up to check on us. We must sound deranged.'

Berry lies down too and I turn to look at her. I think about rolling onto my side to face her. What would it be like to lie like this in a bed? To know I could touch her? Reach out and pull her over to me. I wonder what she'd do if I did that now. My stomach lurches at the thought of it. She's staring back at me, eyes wide in the dark, and I wonder if she's thinking about it too. She could do it. She could reach for me and pull me in. I'd go so easily.

***

I'm back in bed and texting my mum when Berry comes in with a cup of sleepy tea she's made herself.

'I feel like Elvis,' she says, as she climbs up onto her bed. 'Sleepy tea to get me off at night and coffee to get me going in the morning.'

'Just don't eat squirrel burgers on the loo and you'll be fine,' I tell her.

She laughs, then says, 'Oh shit!' as hot liquid sloshes onto my bed.

'I knocked my tea over.' She jumps down. 'Did it burn you?'

'No, don't worry.' I clamber out of my bed, wadding up my blanket to catch the still-dripping tea before piling it onto Berry's bed to soak up the rest.

'Wow,' Berry says. 'That was quick thinking.'

'Three little siblings,' I tell her. 'I have dealt with so many pee accidents.'

'Ugh, I'm so sorry,' she says, moving next to me to reach up to her bed. 'I'd only had one tiny sip to see if it was one of the disgusting ones. I dropped the full cup!'

'It might not have gone through,' I say, hopefully.

We pull the bedding off her bed and ball it up, ready to take down to the laundry, but her mattress is soaked.

'Damn.' She pulls it towards her. 'Are there spares downstairs, do you think?'

I shake my head. I just did inventory a couple of days ago. 'They're on the list of things we need.'

We have guests on board so there's no way she can sleep in any of those cabins.

'Nico's bunk's free, right?' She pulls a face.

That would mean sharing with Adam. And as much as I want to find out what's going on with him, there's no way in hell I'm willing to spend any more time with him than I absolutely have to.

'You could just bunk in with me for the night,' I suggest to Berry, my belly fluttering with nerves.

'Yeah?'

I don't look at her. 'Yeah. I know it'll be a bit of a tight squeeze.'

'It's not too bad,' she says. 'Your bed's bigger than mine.'

I nod. It is. A bit.

'And it's just for one night,' she adds.

'It'll be fine,' I agree.

While Berry drags her bedding and mattress down to the laundry, I grab another blanket from the cupboard, pee again and climb back into my bed. The bed that I'm going to be sharing with Berry. Another terrible idea.

The lights are off, the room lit by the fairy lights along my shelf. I hear Berry come back into the cabin, and I shuffle over in my bunk until I can't go any further. I'm pressed against the wall.

The mattress sinks as she slides in next to me. I can feel the warmth of her body, smell her cherry scent and the almond oil she uses on her hair.

'I was thinking,' I tell her. 'Did you ever see the gardening *Bake Off*?'

'Gardening *Bake Off*?' She pulls the covers up over us both.

'Yeah. It's not called that, but it's another of those shows. Like *Sewing Bee*. But for flowers. These huge, amazing arrangements.'

'Sounds good. You wanna watch one now? What's it on?'

We bring it up on the TV at the foot of the bed and watch until both of us are drifting off to sleep.

I wake up to darkness and my body wrapped around Berry's. My leg thrown over her thigh, arm wrapped around her midriff, face pressed into the side of her neck. She's breathing slowly and deeply, still asleep, thank fuck.

I jerk myself away so fast that I hit the back of my head on the wall. I think the sound it makes will wake her, but it doesn't seem to. I lie on my back for a while, staring blindly up at the underside of the top bunk. I knew this was a terrible idea.

I check the time on my phone, shielding the screen so the brightness doesn't wake her. Only 2.30, so I can't get up. But how would I get up anyway? I'd have to climb over her and that's not happening. I roll onto my side with my back to her and try to will myself back to sleep – relaxing all my body parts one by one, counting backwards from a hundred while breathing slowly – but it doesn't work. All I can think about is Berry in my bed and how it felt to be pressed up against her, curled around her, the bare skin of her belly under my hand, my lips grazing her neck.

I must drift off eventually, because I'm woken again by Berry pressing up behind me. Her boobs against my back, arm thrown over my waist. I hold my breath and wait for her to speak, but I think she's still asleep, her body soft and relaxed where I'm now stiff and frozen.

What if she really is awake and waiting for me to respond? I whisper her name and she huffs out a sound, shifts on the mattress, the hand draped over me curling and releasing, but then nothing more. She's asleep.

Heat pools in my belly as I make myself relax. There's a throbbing between my legs and there's no way I'm going to be able to fall back to sleep.

I don't know how long it takes, but eventually I feel Berry start to wake up. Her breathing changes and one of her knees brushes the back of my thigh as she stretches her legs, chest brushing over my back. And then, like me, she must realise what she's doing and, unlike me, rolls away smoothly.

I keep my eyes squeezed shut. Force myself to keep my breathing slow and steady, hopefully fooling her that I'm still asleep and haven't been lying here for hours thinking about all the things I'd like her to do to me.

The mattress dips as she slips out of bed, and I hear the click of the bathroom door and then the shower running. There's no way I want to still be here when she comes out. I shuffle across the mattress, letting myself pause for just a second in the warmth her body left behind, and then I pull on my leggings and a hoodie and leave.

I climb up to the sun deck – the lightening sky is frilled with orange clouds, the water gleaming almost gold – and Adam is sitting by the railing, staring out to sea.

I sit next to him and he turns to look at me. He looks exhausted, dark smudges under his eyes, his skin pale and pillow-creased.

'I'm sorry,' he says.

My heart lurches. If nerves and excitement are the same emotion, I think the same must be true of falling in and out of love. I'm still aware of him all the time. I get butterflies when I catch a glimpse of him. But now none of it feels good.

18

The forecast is hot and clear with a cool breeze and the guests decide not to do anything but swim and get the water toys out again.

While Ben and Liam set up the inflatable slide from the middle deck, I hang out with the boys as they bounce on the floating platform, splashing each other and shrieking.

They've all grown in confidence so quickly – it's lovely. And it makes me miss my siblings. Mum told me that Riley's going on her first residential this weekend, which she feels much too young for, even if it is only overnight. And Alfie fell off the bed and screamed so much they thought he'd broken something but he was fine.

I wonder what it would be like to bring them on a trip like this. We could never afford it, but I know they'd all love it.

Marni joins us on the platform and tells me that Noah would like me to take him on the slide.

I beam at him. 'Really?'

He nods, shyly.

'Really really?'

His eyes are wide, but he nods again.

'This is going to be fun!' I tell him.

He clings to me – his hot little arms around my neck as we climb up the slide and the other boys wave at us from the platform. Marni shields her eyes with one hand and waves with the other.

'My mama,' Noah says in a tiny voice.

'We'll slide down,' I tell him, 'and then swim over to see Mama, okay?'

He nods and I hold him tightly as we tumble down, splashing into the ocean. He's giggling as I lift him onto the platform and the boys all cheer.

Teddy wants a turn next. And then Arlo and Scout, even though they could totally do it on their own.

I'm treading water, waiting for Noah to decide if he wants another turn or if he's been brave enough for one day when I feel a sharp pain in my leg. I've only got enough time to register it when pain radiates all the way up my side and then I go under.

I'm swallowing water and can't catch my breath. I can see the sun sparkling through from above and I try to turn, to pull myself back up to the surface, but I only manage to break through for a second before a wave hits me like a slap and my ears are ringing.

My throat, the back of my nose, the roof of my mouth are stinging. My leg feels like it's on fire and I try to look down to see what's wrong, to kick it out so I can see, but I can't make any of it work. There's a roaring in my ears and I know I should stay calm, I want to stay calm, but I know I need to get to the surface and I can't make it happen, I can't make my body do what I need it to do.

My ribs ache and I can hear shouting on the surface – echoing as if it's coming from very far away – and then hands are grabbing me and pulling me up. There's an arm across my chest and I know someone's got hold of me, but then we go under again. I try to remember my training, to stay calm, to relax, but pulling someone else down with me has scared me even more than going under myself. I kick my legs, feel my lungs burning as I run out of air.

The next time we surface, I hear Adam's voice saying, 'Hope. Relax. Can you breathe?'

I try, but the sun is bright and I can hear children crying and shouting coming from somewhere else, everything burns and I'm scared.

'Hopey,' Adam says, still calm, 'I've got you. It's okay. Relax.'

The next thing I know is I'm being pulled up onto the deck and rolled onto my side. I cough and spit, trying to wipe my face where salty strings of saliva stick to my chin and cheek.

'You're okay,' Adam says and I can hear in his voice that he's scared too. 'It's okay.'

I try to speak but my throat is tight and sore. When I try to open my eyes, they sting from the salt water, but when I close them, my head throbs. Everything hurts.

'I know,' Adam says. 'I know.'

I didn't realise I'd spoken aloud.

'We're getting some painkillers,' another voice says. 'I'm just going to pour some water over your leg now.'

Adam's holding my hand, squeezing my fingers. Water runs over my leg, cold and then warm and for a second I'm worried I've peed myself. Someone holds a bottle of water to my lips and I swallow two painkillers, choking a little. The other voice – Scottish, Ben – tells me he's going to wrap my leg with a hot towel.

'It'll feel too hot to begin with,' he tells me. 'Let me know if you genuinely can't bear it, but it's the best thing and it'll cool down fast.'

The pain from the heat is a good distraction from the pain of the sting. I realise that's what must have happened: I was stung by a jellyfish.

'Yep,' Ben says.

Again, I didn't know I'd spoken aloud.

'There's a bunch of them. Not dangerous. Just painful for a couple of hours.'

'Are the kids okay?' I ask, my voice croaky.

I hear someone make a sound like a whimper and I blink open my eyes just for a second.

Berry. Berry is there and I'm so happy to see her.

'I'm happy to see you too,' Berry says, her voice wavering. 'They're fine. The kids are fine.'

My eyes are closed again. The light through my eyelids is orange. It's nice. I really want to go to sleep.

'We're going to lift you now, okay?' Ben says.

Hands grip the back of my thighs, arms wrap around my back and then I'm being carried.

'I can walk,' I croak.

'Give over,' Adam says.

I think I'm laughing, but I sob instead.

I wake up in my bunk. My head is still banging, but nothing like earlier. I'm aware of my leg – it feels scratchy, almost like it's vibrating – but the intense pain is gone.

I got stung by a jellyfish.

And rescued by Adam?

And carried back to my cabin by Adam and Ben. And Berry was there. I can see her looking down at me, the blue sky behind her. Her eyes wide with fear.

I lurch over the side of the bunk and throw up salt water onto the floor.

The door opens and Berry comes in.

'Careful!' I croak. 'I've just puked, sorry.'

'Okay, don't move.'

The door closes again and then Berry's back. She cleans up, disappears again, and returns with a glass of water.

'How are you feeling?'

'Kind of like I got run over by a truck,' I tell her.

She crouches down next to my bed and reaches over, resting her cool hand on my forehead. It feels really nice.

'You scared the absolute shit out of me,' she says. 'Out of everyone.'

I blink my eyes open again. 'I'm sorry.'

'God, no, don't apologise! Are you okay? For real?'

'I'm fine, I think,' I tell her.

She reaches for my hand, gently squeezes my fingers.

'Captain Liz says take as long as you need. Oh, and I've got some more painkillers.'

She takes a bottle out of her pocket and shakes two into my hand. I prop myself up on my elbow and take them with the water and then lie back down.

'I'll come and check on you later,' she tells me.

The next time I wake up, it's the following morning and I feel fine. Well, my leg feels fine; my head feels like it's stuffed with cotton wool and my mouth feels worse. I need coffee.

I swing my legs out of bed and Berry says, 'Hope?'

'Sorry.' My voice is both rough and feeble. 'Did I wake you?'

'No, I've been awake. I was worrying about you.'

I stand up and lean against her bunk. 'I'm okay,' I tell her. 'I just need a coffee. And a shower.'

'Call if you need me,' she says, as I step through into the bathroom.

While the shower warms up, I check my leg. There's a red weal down my thigh and behind my knee and it feels tender when I touch it, but apart from that it seems okay.

'I made you a coffee,' Berry says when I come out. She's sitting on the floor, legs outstretched.

'Angel.' I take the coffee, blow it and as soon as I take a sip, I realise I'm incredibly thirsty.

'I'm going to get some water,' I tell her. 'Want to come and watch the sunrise with me?'

From the sun deck, the sky is swirled with pink and blue.

'Were you scared?' she asks me.

I run my fingertip over the raised red mark on my leg. It makes me shiver.

I nod. 'Not the sting so much as the . . .'

'Almost drowning?'

I huff out a laugh. 'Yeah. That wasn't fun. Imagine if no one noticed. Like the guests and the kids were all having fun with me just quietly drowning a couple of metres away.'

Berry leans against me. 'God, don't say that. Fuck.'

'Would've ruined their holiday. One star on Tripadvisor.'

She snorts and then says, 'Stop it. Tell me properly.'

'There isn't really anything to tell. It was scary and then Adam had me and I knew that it was going to be okay. Like, I didn't think I was going to die of the sting or anything.'

'They were so calm. Both of them, Adam and Ben. It was pretty hot.'

I laugh. 'So while I was almost dying, you were questioning your sexuality?'

'Absolutely not. I just have, like, a competence kink, you know? Adam saw you, he jumped in, he saved you. He got back to work. Totally chill.'

'I can't believe they carried me.'

'Adam looked terrified.'

'I'm not surprised,' I say. 'He's the reason I'm here. He'd have to explain to my mum that I'd been offed by a jellyfish.'

'The more you joke about it, the more I think you're hiding deep trauma.'

'You're so American. This is how Scousers deal with trauma.'

She looks at me. 'I've been meaning to ask why you're called "Scousers".'

'It's to do with sailors actually,' I tell her. 'Obviously Liverpool was an important port. And I think the sailors ate this, like, stew? Made with lamb, I think, cos it was a cheap meat back then.'

'When was this?'

'God, I don't know.' I wave my hand. 'You know . . . olden times.'

She snorts. 'I'm familiar.'

'The stew's called "scouse"; you can still get it now.'

'So they were Scousers because they ate a lot of scouse?'

'I love the way you say "scouse",' I tell her. 'There's no "zed" in it.'

'Scouse?' Berry tries again, dragging out the second 's'.

'That's it. And yes, I think so? I should probably google it.'

We sit in silence for a few minutes as the sky and the sea

shimmer golden in the morning sun.

'I'm very glad you're okay,' Berry says.

Me too.

She leans against me. And I lean back.

19

'This has been the absolute best holiday,' Marni says as we all line up on the dock to say goodbye. 'It's been a dream, truly.'

Marni and Paul's boys all look adorable in matching red T-shirts and navy-blue shorts, stood in a row behind their parents to shake all our hands.

'The food was incredible and you all went above and beyond,' Paul says.

'The film, the picnic, Sóller,' Marni adds. 'The cake! We really can't thank you enough.'

Paul tells us they'll be back and hope to see us all again and then he gives a fat envelope to Captain Liz and they leave, the children turning to wave until they're almost out of sight.

'They were adorable,' Captain Liz says. 'Now everyone get changed and meet me in the salon for the tip meeting.'

They've given us the best tip we've had so far – almost two thousand euros each – so everyone is in a buoyant mood as we pile into two cars and head into town for our night off.

I end up sitting next to Adam, unintentionally, but he did save my life so I can't be too annoyed about it.

'How are you feeling?' he asks me once we're on the road.

'I'm all good,' I tell him. I shift slightly so I can look at him. 'Thank you. For, you know, saving my life and everything.'

He smiles, almost shyly, and my heart thumps. No matter what, I think I'll always love him at least a little bit.

'It was nothing,' he says. 'All I ask is that you nominate me for a Pride of Britain Award.'

I laugh and despite everything it feels good to laugh with him.

'I'll get right on that,' I tell him.

The restaurant is in a town square that's buzzing with both tourists and locals. Children run around squealing and giggling, riding bikes or driving tiny electric cars. Elderly Mallorcans line a row of benches along the edge of the square. White-haired men in pastel shirts and Bermuda shorts, walking sticks propped against the bench between them, women wearing pinafore aprons over patterned cotton dresses, watching the children and smiling, sit either side of tourists in sunglasses, bumbags worn across their chests, holding their phones up to photograph the rows of frilly white bunting stretching across the square and dancing in the breeze.

Adam is sitting at the opposite end of the table, next to Liam, and Berry is next to me. She's wearing loose, black, wide-legged trousers and a hot pink vest.

Berry and I both turn our chairs a little so we can watch the happenings in the square without having our backs to anyone. We order wine and a selection of tapas, and the waiter brings us small glasses of a traditional Mallorcan aperitif called Palo. I wince as I sip it. It's thick and bitter and tastes like burnt caramel.

'Oh, yikes,' Berry says, her voice low. 'Liquid liquorice.'

I watch her tongue as she licks it off her lips. 'That is . . . something.'

'Tastes like the stuff my mum used to make me drink for constipation,' Nico says, leaning towards us. 'She had to hold my nose to get me to open my mouth and sometimes I'd still spit it out after.' He downs the rest of his drink. 'Important to keep regular!'

'Here.' Berry pours me a glass of Rioja. 'Take away the taste of Nico's poop meds.'

'I can already feel it working,' Nico says, rubbing his stomach. 'Gross.'

The food arrives and we all pounce on our preferred dishes, spooning some onto our plates before passing them along and waiting for the next one. Chunks of Mallorcan bread with wafer-thin slices of Iberico ham, Mahón cheese and pear; charred Padrón peppers, crunchy with shards of salt; meltingly soft calamari; burrata on a pile of basil leaves, glistening with honey oil; fat prawns, sizzling in garlic butter.

'This totally makes up for the . . . what's that drink in the UK that motorbike gangs like?' Berry asks me.

I shake my head. 'Motorbike gangs?'

'Yeah, I think so. Traditionally. It's like a black syrup thing. I think you can drink it with something else too . . .' She screws her face up in thought.

'Nico.' I bump his arm with my elbow. 'What do bikers drink back home?'

'Jäger?' he says immediately. 'Love a Jägerbomb.'

'Jägermeister,' I tell Berry. 'I don't know if bikers drink it, but my mum drank some by accident one Christmas and we didn't hear the end of it till New Year. She thought it was Kahlúa apparently. I didn't know what Kahlúa was either.'

'Coffee liqueur,' Nico tells us. 'Goes in a White Russian. The Dude drinks them in *The Big Lebowski*.'

'You are a font of information,' Berry tells him.

'I worked as a bartender for a few months,' Nico says.

Food is still being delivered to the table – anchovies and red pepper on olive oil toast; steamed mussels; and something I think the waiter says is called grandmother's croquetas – and no one's even passing it along now, it's a total free-for-all. More wine is ordered and the waiters bring jugs of water and top up our tumblers.

The entire outside seating area is full and everyone else seems to have ordered just as much food, and possibly also as much wine, as we have. Conversation in Spanish, English and German is interrupted by barks of laughter and shrieks of excitement from the children, who frequently run back from the square to their parents to report an incident or ask them to go and watch.

Adam leaves the table and goes inside with his phone in his hand. I don't know how many shots he's had, but when he comes back, I notice he's already swaying slightly on his feet. As he sits down, he bumps the table and Liam cheers as the water bottles rattle.

'It's like *The Fast and the Furious* out there,' Nico observes, gesturing at the square where tiny children are lined up in tiny cars, headlights flashing. Other kids run around throwing rubber balls that also flash with coloured lights as they bounce. A guy with a beard and a man bun is playing guitar and singing, despite being drowned out by all the other sounds coming from every other direction at once.

'This is perfect,' Berry says, shifting her chair closer to mine to make herself heard over all the noise.

'It really is.'

Ridiculously, my eyes fill with tears. 'Are you okay?'

I carefully wipe under my eyes so as not to mess up my make-up and tell her that yes, I'm fine; it's just a lot. 'I'm so tired and I miss home. And I'm worried about my mum. But this is just . . . It's exactly what I pictured when we planned this.'

'You didn't picture cleaning the loos?' Berry asks, smiling.

'Funnily enough, no. Or scraping gunk out of a washing machine filter.'

'Yeah, this makes it all worth it,' Berry says.

'Right,' Nico says, leaning back in his seat as if he's about to make an announcement. 'Never have I ever.'

Pretty much everyone groans.

'Seriously?' Louise says, leaning forward to look at the rest of us, as if she's looking for our support in voting the idea down.

'You just don't want to play because there's nothing you haven't done,' Nico says without looking at her.

She rolls her eyes.

'Fine,' Berry says. 'But we need more wine.'

'Easy one to start,' Nico says. 'Never have I ever fallen down the stairs.'

'Really?' I say. 'I thought everyone had done that.'

Nico shakes his head slowly. 'Nope. I'm very careful and responsible.'

The rest of us take a drink.

'When I was a kid,' Berry says, 'my dad came home from work and couldn't find me. I was lying at the bottom of the stairs with, like, my head on the ground and my body up the steps. I was going down there to paint – I was taking an art course at the time and thought I was the new Georgia O'Keeffe – and I had a tube of oil paint in my hand and when I fell I smashed it against the wall and it squirted everywhere. They couldn't get it off. They had to repaint.'

'Were you hurt?' I ask her.

She smiles. 'I was fine. I think I only stayed down for the drama of it all. I told myself I was being safe, you know, in case I'd broken my neck. But nah.'

'Adam broke his shoulder falling down the stairs,' I say without thinking.

When I look over at him he's looking back at me with this small smile, like he's happy I mentioned it, and it makes my heart twist – we've got so much shared history; I can't imagine not telling his stories and him not telling mine.

'I was wearing these Yoda slippers I got for Christmas as a joke.' His cheeks are flushed and he's already slurring slightly. We've all worked hard, we were all looking forward to coming out, relaxing, but I'm surprised he's got drunk so quickly.

'I skidded,' Adam continues, 'bounced down the whole lot and landed flat on my back in the hall. My mum came running so fast she almost tripped over me.'

More wine arrives as Berry says, 'Never have I ever stolen anything.'

'Me neither!' I say.

Adam clears his throat and when I look at him, he's got one eyebrow raised.

'What? I haven't!'

He holds up one finger. 'San Miguel glass from outside that pub.'

'That wasn't stealing!' I argue. 'That had been left outside like rubbish. I took it, but I didn't steal it.'

Everyone laughs.

'It would have gone in the bin!' I argue.

'You keep telling yourself that,' Liam says.

Adam holds up a second finger. 'A shot glass and a weird little glass that looked like a Petri dish from Prezzo.'

I laugh. To be fair, I had forgotten about them.

'Technically . . .' I start, and everyone hoots, 'I didn't steal them, you did.'

'Because you asked me to!' Adam says.

I shake my head. 'You put them in your pockets; you're the one who stole them.'

'Fine!' Adam drinks, draining the glass.

'I once stole a basket of underwear from M&S,' Louise says.

'Tell us more!' Nico says. 'About the underwear . . .'

She rolls her eyes again. I'm surprised she doesn't have permanent eye strain from being around him. 'I had the basket thing – one of those flimsy bag ones, you know? I had it over my arm and I was wandering around, picking things out, like you do. And then my dad phoned cos he'd gone for a walk and forgotten his keys and he was locked out. He only lives about ten minutes away from the shops, so I went to go and let him in. It was only when he said, "What've you got there?" that I realised I still had the basket over my arm.'

'Did you go back?' Berry asks.

Louise nods. 'Once I let him in, I went straight back. I thought they'd be pleased I was being honest, but they didn't seem bothered.'

'You didn't steal them then, did you?' Nico says. 'You just borrowed them briefly.'

Louise shakes her head. 'I stole them and then returned them.'

'You did not,' Nico says. 'You drank under false pretences. Your turn now.'

'Never have I ever shit my pants,' she says.

Everyone howls with laughter and she looks pleased.

'I was not expecting that,' Nico says, grinning. 'Fair play.'

And then he drinks. And so does Liam. And Adam. And then Adam stares at me until I drink too, which makes everyone cackle again.

'Okay,' I say. 'I was in London with my mum. I don't know if it was something I ate or a bug or what. We were by Trafalgar Square, I can't remember where we were going, but I suddenly . . .' I press one hand to my stomach, remembering. 'I just knew I was in trouble. And I told my mum, and she was all practical, like, "There must be a loo here somewhere!". But there wasn't. She almost went into the church – this big church at the side with all these steps and columns.'

'St Martin-in-the-Fields?' Nico suggests.

'I think so, yeah. I talked her out of that, because, come on. But then we saw this little cafe, like a greasy spoon? Just across the road.'

'I know the one,' Nico interjects. 'Great hangover breakfasts.'

'And Mum grabbed my arm and almost frog-marched me over and, just as we crossed the road . . .' I shake my head. 'It was too late.'

'That's happened to me,' Liam says. 'Held it until I got home and as soon as I put the key in the door . . . I think your body relaxes just that bit too quick.'

We are spared Nico and Adam's shit stories by the waiter asking if we want dessert. Despite having already eaten a ridiculous amount of food, it turns out we do. We order crema Catalana, panna cotta, almond cake, ice cream with hot raspberries, and a fruit salad. There is some debate about a cheese board, but we come down on the side of absolutely not.

'Your turn,' Nico says, shifting in his seat to look at me.

I groan. 'Okay.'

There are so many things I've never done, it's hard to choose one.

'Never have I ever jumped in the water,' I say and Nico boos. 'We already know about that. Give us a new one.'

'Fine. Never have I ever gone skinny dipping.'

'Never?' Berry says immediately, her glass already halfway to her mouth.

I shake my head. 'I've always kind of meant to, but never really had the opportunity.'

'You neither?' Nico asks Adam.

'Where would we?' Adam says, topping up his glass. 'The Mersey?'

Everyone laughs.

'Did you drink?' Nico asks Louise.

'Yep.' She drinks again, looking smug.

'Where?' Nico asks her.

'Iceland. In a glacier.'

'Damn, woman!'

She pouts at him.

Liam did it in Australia. Berry and Nico have done it all over the place, including California (both), Cornwall (Nico) and Thailand (Berry).

It's Adam's turn.

'Never have I ever got a tattoo.'

Everyone drinks apart from me and once again Nico is stunned to learn that Louise has a tattoo.

'Where?'

She shakes her head.

167

'What's it of?'

'If I'm not going to tell you where, I'm certainly not going to tell you what.'

'Does it say "Nico" in a heart?'

She rolls her eyes for a third time.

'"Nico was here"...' he says. 'On your inner thigh.'

Louise's eyes flash at him then and he mumbles, 'Sorry,' before pushing his chair back and heading into the restaurant to the bathroom.

We all stare pointedly at Louise.

'God, yes,' she says. 'Nico and I had a bit of a thing on a previous programme, but it wasn't anything serious. Obviously. No need to make a meal of it.'

Right on cue, the waiter arrives with our desserts.

'I can't believe it,' I tell Berry, once we're back on the boat, in our cabin. 'Louise and Nico.'

'There's always something going on with someone. I think the sea air makes everyone horny.'

She pulls her top off and drops it in the laundry bag. I'm used to seeing Berry in her underwear now. She's completely unselfconscious and there's no point in being shy when we're living in such close quarters. And yet, when she turns around to get her sleep T-shirt out of a drawer, I stare at the lavender tattoo on her shoulder and find I can't quite catch my breath.

She straightens up. Turns, pulling her top on. Hooks her hair out of the collar and smooths it down and I'm still staring.

'What?' She smiles at me, dimple popping. 'Have I got something on my face?'

I shake my head. I want to say something, but I have no idea what to say.

I've been thinking about when you kissed me. I want to kiss you. I lied to you. Can I kiss you?

'I lied,' I say and it's almost a whisper.

Her eyebrows pull together but she doesn't move.

'At the club that night. When you kissed me.'

Her lips part a little. Her eyebrows flick up.

'When I said I'm not into girls.'

My breath is coming too fast. And she's not saying anything, just studying me. She puts her head on one side. 'Hope . . . I don't know . . .'

'I want to kiss you,' I make myself say. 'Please can I kiss you?'

She laughs then and it makes me laugh too. But, god, what if she says no?

'Are you sure?' she says instead.

And then I can't speak. I nod. And I close the small space between us and press my mouth to hers. I feel her gasp, but then one hand comes to the small of my back and pulls me closer. I turn my head, my lips moving over hers for a better fit. And we do fit; it feels soft and easy.

I haven't kissed anyone but Adam for so long and I was scared it would feel wrong, weird, but it doesn't at all. It feels entirely right. I drift my lips over her jaw, down the side of her neck. I can taste the salt on her skin and I want more; I want to kiss her until our lips are sore.

The fingers of her other hand touch my jaw gently as I run my tongue over her lower lip, sighing into her mouth. And then she's pulling away.

'Hey,' she says, her eyes flashing in the semi-dark. 'So let me just . . . You lied? That night?'

'Yeah. I was . . .' I can't tell her about Adam, even now. It's all so complicated now. And I promised. 'I didn't think it was a good idea and I just . . . I have been. In the past. Into girls, I mean. Or one girl. And it didn't go well. So I wasn't even sure, because I'd never . . .'

'You don't have to,' she says. 'You don't have to prove anything. If you want to, that's enough.'

I nod. 'The girl at uni. I told you. But I really blew it with her.'

'Charlie was a girl?'

I nod again. 'And I don't want to do the same with you. But I just . . .'

My thoughts are so jumbled – things I want to say and things I know I shouldn't, can't, say – all crashing and piling on top of each other. And I'm so, so tired.

'I just wanted to kiss you,' I finish, not looking at her.

'To see if you liked it?' she asks.

I shake my head. 'No. Well, maybe. But really just because I like you and I wanted to. I've thought a lot about when you kissed me.'

'I've thought a lot about that too.'

My stomach lurches to think Berry might have been thinking about me too, the way I've been thinking about her.

'I felt guilty,' she says. 'I thought I'd misread. And I don't usually.'

I nod. 'That was my fault. I'm sorry. You didn't misread. I am very into you.'

She barks out a laugh and then covers her mouth with her hand, eyes going wide.

'I didn't mean to say that,' I tell her.

She steps up to me again. 'I'm glad you did.'

She's so close. I can smell her cherry perfume, the toothpaste on her breath. If I reach out I can slide my hands over her skin, her bare arms, down to her waist. I could lift her top, push it up over her bra, dip my head down to her breasts.

I shudder, scrunching my eyes closed, and she laughs.

'I think you really need to sleep.'

I slump, even though I'm still standing. 'I really do.'

She curls her hand around the side of my neck, fingers pressing into the hinge of my jaw and I shudder again as she brushes her thumb over my lips. I want to suck it into my mouth.

'Sleep now,' she says. 'We can talk tomorrow.'

20

There's a new charter arriving tomorrow, so Louise has given Berry and me the day off. Berry said she wants to show me the market, so we get a cab to the same town square where we had dinner a couple of nights ago.

The square and surrounding streets are filled with market stalls, with locals and tourists jostling to buy fruit and vegetables, leather bags and beaded jewellery. Berry and I walk up one side, pointing out towers of oranges with the leaves still attached, violet-and-white-striped aubergines, bunches of herbs, loops of chorizo hanging from the stalls' canopies, an enormous wheel of Parmesan, the guy selling it holding out a sliver to tempt us over.

We haven't talked about last night yet, or touched or kissed, but I want to. I want to hold her hand, to tell her I can't stop thinking about her, to run my tongue over her tattoos.

Streams of bunting stretched over the top of the square cast lines of frilly shade on the ground and across Berry's face as she smiles at me, pointing to a selection of huge pastries in the window of a bakery in the corner of the square.

'Have you tried these?' She points out a giant pastry that's round and swirled like a shell, golden and dusted with icing sugar. 'Ensaïmadas. They're unbelievable.'

I shake my head. 'Are they kind of like croissants?'

'I guess . . .' Berry says. 'Wait, no, I think they're softer. And sweeter. More like brioche?'

I follow her into the small bakery through a curtain of rainbow strips of plastic to keep out flies. There's a tiny woman behind the counter with dark bobbed hair and a welcoming smile. Most of the space is taken up by two tall men who seem to be asking questions about every item on the tilted wooden shelves.

The woman answers their questions in rapid Spanish, gesturing to us that she'll be with us when she can.

One of the men steps backwards, bumping into me, and then they turn and leave, without acknowledging us or thanking the woman.

'Men!' she says in Spanish-accented English and we both laugh.

'Which do you want?' Berry asks me, pointing at an array of pastries in a glass case. 'I think we should get a plain one. And I'm thinking chocolate?'

I choose an ensaïmada studded with halved apricots and the woman says, 'My favourite' as she passes it over the counter to me in a white paper bag.

Berry is already biting into her plain pastry as we step out of the cool shop and back into the hot sun.

'Oh my god,' she says, almost doubling over with happiness. 'I'd almost forgotten how good these are!'

She straightens up and I smile because her face is dusted with icing sugar.

'You've got a bit of . . .' I gesture towards her mouth. And chin. And cheeks.

'Oh yeah?' She grins at me and takes another huge bite. 'Want to make something of it?'

I really do. Her eyes widen as I take a step closer and look down at her mouth.

'Oh shit.' She laughs.

'Don't say that!'

'I meant . . . good shit.' She's still grinning.

I press up closer and she swallows, looking down at my lips.

'Wait,' she says, reaching for my wrist. 'Not here.'

She's probably right. There are a lot of people around. She tugs me down the side of the bakery and into a narrow and deserted lane; the buildings painted pink and terracotta and tan. We can still hear the bustle of the market – and somewhere a band is playing a song about how Sunday morning is easy – but for now we're alone.

Berry steps back into a wide doorway and smiles at me, waiting.

I study her for a second – her black sundress, yellow sandals, sunglasses pushed up on top of her head, as she stares back at me in anticipation – and I can't believe I'm about to do what I am absolutely about to do.

Her breath hitches as I take a step closer so I'm almost right up against her. And then I lean in and slowly run my tongue over her lips, tasting icing sugar and butter.

'Hey,' she says, smiling against my mouth. 'You've got your own.'

'I'm trying to be sexy,' I tell her, pulling back a little. 'And you're ruining it.'

'You're doing a great job.' She hooks a finger into the waistband of my shorts to tug me closer.

I brace one hand against the wooden door behind her to steady myself as I lick her mouth again and she sighs. I turn my head to deepen the kiss, slipping my tongue between her lips. She curls her tongue around mine, still pulling on my shorts and I relax against her and into the kiss.

I curl my hand around the back of her neck, my thumb brushing her jaw, the corner of her mouth, as she runs her tongue along my bottom lip, her hands on my hips now, holding me against her.

I pull away as the church bells at the end of the square start to ring.

Berry's breathing heavily, her pupils wide. She's still got some icing sugar on her face and I brush it off.

'You've got some now too,' she says. She runs her thumb over my lips then sucks it into her mouth and my knees actually go weak.

'That was extremely hot,' I tell her.

She smiles. 'I hoped it might be.'

It's only when we both straighten up that we notice Berry had been holding the bag of ensaïmadas between us and they're crushed. Apricot has oozed through the paper and all over the front of my T-shirt.

'Oops,' Berry says.

We spend the rest of the day wandering around the town. We have lunch at the bottom of a steep flight of steps that leads up to a small chapel and afterwards we walk up the steps and get an ice cream next to the chapel, while wild cats brush up against our legs and gaze up at us hopefully and the man who runs the cafe stands in an open doorway smoking and yelling at the cats to go away.

Berry brushes her thumb over the red lines the jellyfish sting left on my leg and it sends shivers through me.

'Does it still hurt?'

I shake my head. 'I can feel it; I know it's there. But it doesn't hurt.'

I don't, can't, tell Berry, but that's also how I feel about everything that has happened with Adam. Something doesn't feel quite right – if I stop and think about it, there's a sort of hollow in my stomach – but it doesn't hurt. Not like it did when he first told me about the kiss. Not like I thought it would.

'What are you thinking about?' Berry asks me.

I smile. 'How lucky I am to be here. With you.'

'Funny,' she says. 'That's what I was thinking too.'

'Can we . . . ? I know we haven't really had a chance to talk.'

'No.' She rests her warm hand on my thigh.

'I don't want to tell anyone.' I look down at one of the cats curled up under the table. 'If that's okay. I just . . . it's new. And I want to keep it just for us.'

'Yeah, I was thinking the same thing.'

I look at her and she's smiling at me, her sunglasses pushed up into her hair.

'Everyone's always in your business on board. And Nico with the jokes.'

I roll my eyes. 'Right.'

'Anyway,' she says, leaning towards me, her hand drifting further up my thigh, 'it'll be our own sexy little secret.'

When we get back to the *Serendipity* – soft and relaxed from the sun and the sugar and the kissing – before we're even back on board I can hear Adam shouting as we walk up the passerelle.

'Oh shit,' Berry says. 'What now?'

'It's not even about that,' Ben is saying, as we cross the aft deck. 'Yes, of course everyone makes mistakes, but you have to own up to them.'

'I said I'll go and talk to the captain!' Adam says, exasperated.

'But you should have come to me first,' Ben says.

'Better steer clear of that,' Berry says, heading for the doors to the salon.

Part of me wants to stay, to see if I can learn anything about what's been going on, but another part of me – the part that kissed icing sugar off Berry's mouth and shivered in the sun as she stroked my leg – doesn't want to break the sunny spell of the day, so I follow Berry down to the crew mess.

Louise is sitting at the table, her hair pulled back off her face with a wide stretchy band, her skin is shiny with moisturiser. In front of her on the table are two trays of nail products, including an LED lamp.

'I didn't know you did this!' Berry says, sitting on the end of the bench and reaching for one of the bottles of varnish before pulling her hand back.

'Can I?'

'Go for it,' Louise says. 'I got sick of having to fit appointments in around charters so I decided to just do it myself. I can do yours if you like? You too, Hope.'

I make coffees for Berry and me and a green tea for Louise then sit opposite Berry, on the other side of Louise.

Louise finishes her own nails and then starts on Berry's, removing the Barbie pink varnish and applying the peachy-orange shade Berry chooses.

'Do you know what's happened with Adam?' I can't resist asking Louise, as she paints Berry's nails.

177

'He broke the davit,' Louise says, without looking up. 'Wasn't concentrating, pulled it at an angle. Expensive repair. Captain's going to be furious.'

'Ben sounded furious,' Berry says.

'Yeah.' Louise caps the varnish and slides Berry's hand into the LED lamp. 'The thing is, everyone makes mistakes but Adam gets an attitude when anyone talks to him about it.'

'He's always been like that,' I tell them. 'He's angry with himself but he turns it on everyone else.'

'I get it,' Louise says. 'But it doesn't work in a job like this. You have to be part of a team. And I don't know if he's a team player.' She drinks some of her tea before swapping Berry's hands. 'Anyway. What did you two get up to?'

I look over at Berry. The corners of her mouth are twitching. I think about her fingers on my thigh under the table earlier. About leaning up against her outside the bakery, the sound she made when she knew I was about to kiss her.

'Not much,' Berry says, still looking at me. 'Walked around. Had lunch.'

My breath catches as, under the table, her bare foot slides up my calf.

'It's so nice there,' Louise says. 'There's this gorgeous deli at the bottom of the Calvari Steps. The apricot balsamic is incredible.'

I think about the apricot ensaïmada Berry and I crushed between us outside the bakery.

'I don't think I'm going to get my nails done,' I tell Louise and watch Berry's eyes widen. 'I think I'm good for now. Thanks though.'

Louise smiles at me. 'Actually that works out pretty well. I need to start getting ready.'

'Going somewhere nice?' Berry asks her.

'Wine and cheese-tasting evening in Alcúdia.'

Louise finishes packing her manicure stuff away.

'Alone?' Berry asks.

Louise smiles at us both. 'No. With Nico. He's trying to butter me up.'

'Wine and cheese should do it,' Berry says.

Louise slides to the end of the seat and stands. 'Can't hurt! Have a good night, ladies.'

Berry laughs. 'You too.'

21

'Been dying to do that for hours,' Berry says, the following day, crowding me up against the sink in the main guest suite, where I've been furiously cleaning the bathroom. She slides her hands into my hair and kisses me, sighing into my mouth.

Back in our cabin last night, we kissed all the way through an episode of *Woodwork Bake Off*, stopping only to see the final reveals, but then we slept in our own beds, agreeing that we should take it at least a little bit slow.

'This is extremely unprofessional.' I smile now.

'Oh, you think *this* is unprofessional?' She catches the hem of my shorts between her fingers and pulls it up. 'I'll show you unprofessional.'

I kiss her back, not touching her because I've still got a spray bottle of vinegar in one hand and a microfibre cloth in the other.

'Do you have a cleaning kink I don't know about?' I ask her.

'I've got so many kinks you don't know about,' she says, running her lips along my jaw. 'I'm going to lick all your freckles.'

She flicks her tongue just under my ear and I make a sound that's almost a growl.

'This is really unfair getting me all riled up when I'm trying to work.'

'I've been ironing,' she says, pushing one thigh between mine. 'I was all hot and bothered anyway.'

'God, Berry.' I tilt my pelvis and the friction is agony. 'We can't . . .'

'We could . . .' she says, kissing me again.

'We'll get fired.'

'Eh. It's just a job. We can run away and become beach bums.'

I yelp as she runs her hand down my ribs.

'Are you ticklish?' She looks delighted.

'No,' I lie. 'You just startled me.'

'I'm not ticklish,' she says, her lips up against my ear. 'You can touch me anywhere.'

I'm about to drop the cleaning stuff and risk my job when the captain radios.

'Berry, Hope, can you come to the bridge please?'

My stomach lurches.

'She doesn't know anything,' Berry says, stepping away from me and straightening her uniform. 'She can't do.'

I look up as if there's going to be a camera in a guest bathroom, but of course there isn't.

I put the cleaning stuff away in the cupboard under the sink and when I stand, Berry quickly presses her mouth to mine.

'You worry too much.'

I smile. 'So I've been told.'

When we get to the bridge, Captain Liz looks tense. She's leaning back against the command deck, her phone in her hand.

'I'm afraid Louise has just had some bad news. Her father passed suddenly last night. She's flying home immediately.'

'Oh no,' Berry says. 'Poor Louise.'

'It's terrible for her,' the captain says, 'but also it obviously means we're going to be short-handed. I'm of course going to try to find someone, but in the meantime, I'll need the two of you to step up. So Berry, I'm making you interim chief stew since you have the experience. Any problems, come and see me. I'm relying on you both.'

The two of us nod.

'Oh, and I might need to do some shuffling of the sleeping arrangements, depending on who's available,' she says. 'Are you two happy to keep sharing a cabin?'

'Yes, absolutely,' I tell her.

Berry nods. 'Yep. We get along great.'

'Excellent,' the captain says. 'Thank you.'

'God, poor Louise,' I whisper as we head back to the salon.

'I know,' Berry says. 'It's so sad.'

But then she snorts.

'What?'

'"Are you two happy to keep sharing?"' she mimics Captain Liz.

'Oh god, don't,' I say. 'I tried so hard to keep my face neutral.'

'More than happy, captain,' Berry says, deadpan. 'You wouldn't believe how happy.'

'Some might say too happy,' I joke.

'No such thing.'

We're having lunch together in the mess when Louise comes through with her bags. She looks pale, her eyes rimmed red.

We all tell her how sorry we are and she shakes her head.

'I'm sorry to have to leave you all in the lurch.'

'Don't be silly,' Ben tells her. 'Of course you have to go.'

'What happened?' Liam asks. 'Was he ill?'

Louise shakes her head. 'He was cycling. He rides every day. He's always been really fit; he still goes to the gym.' Her big eyes well with tears. 'Mum said he came home, said he didn't feel well and he was going for a lie-down. When she went in later to check on him . . .' Her face crumples and she brushes the tears away with her thumbs.

'I'm so sorry,' I tell her.

She nods. 'It doesn't feel real. It will when I get home, I suppose.'

Nico appears behind Louise with his backpack hanging off one shoulder. 'Sorry, lads, but I'm going too. I've spoken to the captain. Sorry for leaving you in the shit, but I can't . . .'

He reaches out and rests a hand on the back of Louise's neck and she makes a tiny move to lean into it. It makes my heart clench. I didn't know they were serious. I didn't know Nico was capable of being serious. But I'm glad Louise isn't going to have to go through this alone.

'Look after each other,' Ben tells them.

'We will.' Nico shakes Ben's hand, and claps Adam and Liam on their shoulders. Berry and I shuffle along the seats and stand up to hug Louise. Carlo pulls both Louise and Nico into a hug, his face wet with tears.

'I know I don't know you long, but I'm so sorry,' he says. 'I'm so sorry for your loss.'

Once Carlo lets them go, I hug Nico too and then they leave.

'Bloody hell,' Adam says, breaking the unhappy silence. 'That's rough. I need to go and ring my dad now.' But he doesn't move; he just drops his head.

I'd just been thinking the same thing. I want to talk to Mum. To Mick. To the kids.

Out of the corner of my eye I see Carlo rest his head on Ben's shoulder, Ben's hand comes up and squeezes the back of his neck.

I guess 'Don't screw the crew' really is more of a guideline. Adam was the only one who took it seriously.

Once we've changed into our whites, we line up on the dock to welcome the new charter guests. We'd been briefed on them earlier by Liz – it's a couple, Bec Bailey, founder of a skincare company, and her girlfriend Morgan, who owns a chain of gyms. They're not celebrating anything; they're just burned out and need a break.

Bec is short with long dark hair and a heart-shaped face. Morgan Carter has cropped blonde hair and a wide smile. They're both wearing shorts and vests and look relaxed and happy. They greet us all with enthusiastic hugs and tell us how thrilled they are to join us.

Berry takes them to their cabin, while I reread the preference sheet. Bespoke cocktails, karaoke and a trip to the local casino, but other than that they just want to relax. I'm hoping it's going to be an easy charter, since we're so short-handed.

Once they come up from their room, I serve them lunch and drinks on the daybed at the bow.

'We're relying on you for all the gossip,' Bec tells me, popping a gherkin-stuffed olive into her mouth. 'Who hates who. Who's sleeping with who.' She waves her hand. 'You know, the good stuff.'

'I apologise,' Morgan says, smiling at her girlfriend. 'She watches too much TV.'

'It's definitely not like it is on TV,' I tell them, smiling, as I pour them glasses of cucumber water. 'Not so much drama.'

'But a little bit of drama, right?' Bec says.

I smile. 'Maybe a little.'

'I can't believe we're actually here,' Morgan says, relaxing back against the seat, her arms spread, her face tipped up towards the sun.

'We're really here, babe.' Bec shuffles over to lean against her and Morgan wraps an arm around her.

They look so comfortable and relaxed that it's a while before I realise I'm staring.

'I'm just going to pop downstairs for some more food,' I tell them.

Morgan sighs. 'The food. I'm so excited about the food.'

'You're excited about everything,' Bec says. 'It's one of the many things I love about you.'

They've finished lunch and they're lying on the bunny pad – Bec on her back with a T-shirt over her face and Morgan on her front, reading something on her phone – when the captain announces over the radio that there are dolphins on the starboard side of the boat.

'Did she say "dolphins"?' Morgan's already swinging her legs off the pad to stand up.

As we cross to the other side of the boat, I'm low-key worried that the dolphins will have gone, but as soon as we reach the railing we spot them gliding smoothly just under the water. And then, as if they'd been waiting for us to arrive before putting on a show, they rise up, arching above the surface, before splashing back down again, the water shimmering in their wake.

Bec and Morgan both yell with excitement. Bec runs back to grab her phone, but Morgan just holds on to the rail, staring down into the water.

'Did you see the rainbow?' Bec says, excitedly, when she gets back.

Morgan looks up at the sky, understandably, but Bec says, 'No! In the water! When they jump!'

The next time they jump, I see them too: tiny rainbows where the sun shines through the spray.

'Oh my god,' Morgan says. 'Gay dolphins. This is already the best trip ever.'

22

I'm setting the table for dinner when the captain calls me up to the bridge. She's leaning against the command deck, her phone and a notebook next to her.

'So –' she gives me a tight smile – 'I haven't been able to find a deckhand who can come in on such short notice. Nico really screwed us over. I understand why . . .' She shakes her head. 'But it's not ideal. I've just spoken to Kelsey. She can come back as second stew.'

I try to keep my face blank but apparently I don't manage it.

'I know,' she says. 'But beggars can't be choosers. So I was wondering how you would feel about trying out the deck? I've spoken to Berry and she doesn't want to lose you, but she says you'll do a good job. Ben says the same.'

'Of course,' I tell her. 'Thank you for the opportunity.'

It means working alongside Adam, and I'm not sure how I feel about that, but I don't want to let the captain down either.

She grimaces. 'Born of desperation, but I appreciate your enthusiasm. Have you got five minutes to have a chat with Ben?'

'It's going to be challenging physically,' Ben tells me when I get up on deck. 'But I think you're up to it.' He smiles.

'I hope so,' I tell him. 'I'm excited to learn.'

'If I'm not around, you answer to Liam,' he tells me. 'Because obviously Adam's still learning too.'

I nod. That shouldn't be a problem. And I guess if I'm around Adam a bit more, I can see if I can find out what's going on with him. Because something definitely is.

I can't start on deck until Kelsey arrives – hopefully tomorrow morning – so I get back to setting the dinner table with candles and flowers, pink and orange to match the branding of Bec's skincare range.

The women exclaim when they see the table, laughing when they realise Bec is wearing a pink halter dress and Morgan is in a white T-shirt and orange shorts. Captain Liz is joining them for dinner tonight and the three of them talk as if they've known each other for years.

Morgan is equally as obsessed with Nordic crime, but Bec can't stand it.

'I don't understand people who like being scared,' Bec says. 'Like, being scared is my worst thing. I hate it. I hate thinking of people I love being scared. I just do not understand why anyone would do that to themselves deliberately.'

'For me it's because it's in a safe setting,' Morgan tells the captain, and it's clear that she and Bec have had this conversation many times before. 'Obviously, I don't like being scared in real life. But on TV? Or a horror film? It's not real. It's safe.'

'And I kid myself I'm learning from them,' the captain says. 'Like I know the signs and it makes me safer.'

'That's like me thinking I could perform a tracheotomy because I've watched so much *Grey's Anatomy*,' Bec says. 'And let me tell you, that is not true.'

As the sun starts to set, I head inside, turn the lights on low and do the turn-down service in Bec and Morgan's room, closing the blinds, preparing the bed, checking the fridge and bathroom are fully stocked. Berry radios for me to collect dessert from Carlo, so I come back via the galley and take up a tray of lemon and rosemary sorbet, served in half a scooped out lemon.

Once they've eaten dessert, Captain Liz leaves and Bec and Morgan move out to the bunny pad. I bring them Martinis and bowls of olives and they praise everything: the yacht, the captain, the food, the drinks, Berry and me.

Bec asks us how we got our jobs, where we're from, what we did before. They both suggest we get drinks and join them, which obviously we can't, but we can talk and we can listen.

Berry asks them how they got together and Bec says she was married to a man for almost twenty years.

'He cheated on me, repeatedly,' she says. 'But I kept thinking that if I could just be better, nicer, smaller, quieter then he would stop, you know?'

I nod. Even though I don't know. Not that.

'And then we moved to a new area for his job. I was terrified because I didn't know anyone and just imagined that I'd be stuck at home with the kids and he'd have this amazing new life. Anyway, I was walking our dog one morning and there was this cute little terrier outside a plant shop. Just sitting there, beaming away. My dog went straight over, of course, and I was checking the terrier's collar – I didn't know if it was lost, abandoned or what. And then the door of the shop opened and out walks Morgan.'

'It was my dog,' Morgan says, glancing up at me. 'Rufus.'

'And I'm there, like, on the ground,' Bec says, 'and I look up at this woman and . . . boom. I just knew. Like my life changed instantly.'

'You knew . . .' I start before I can think of how to end the question.

'I knew she was my person. I know how that sounds. It's ridiculous. Totally. But I knew. And I thought, "There she is!" As if I'd been expecting her. And I cannot tell you how much I had not been expecting her.'

Morgan snorts.

'I thought I was straight,' Bec says. 'Like, I'd never questioned it. I mean, looking back now I should have done. There were signs, you know?' She laughs. 'But at that point, no. It was literally – boom, there she is.'

'So what did you do?' Berry asks.

'Well, it took me a while to tell my husband,' Bec says, popping a prosciutto-wrapped olive in her mouth. 'I didn't know how any of it was going to work. Our kids were teenagers and I thought they'd lose their shit.'

'They were great,' Morgan interjects.

'They were. Husband, not so much, but once he got over himself, it was fine. He's remarried now. She's half his age. Why am I telling you this? I can't remember.'

'No one knows, baby,' Morgan says, and Bec laughs, nudging her with her shoulder.

'I think I just wanted to say you never know who you will fall for.'

I can't resist looking over at Berry.

She's looking back at me and the expression on her gorgeous face makes my stomach flip.

23

Kelsey arrives in the morning, looking the same as she did when she left, but with her hair unbraided and piled in a loose bun on top of her head.

'Welcome back!' I say, as she hefts her suitcase onto one of the daybeds.

Kelsey pulls a face, laughing. 'Thanks. Can't quite believe it. I feel bad for the captain because she was totally right to sack me.'

I laugh then too.

She shakes her head. 'I kind of have a problem with not being able to do what I want to do when I want to do it.'

'That does tend to be a problem in a job,' I tell her.

'I know, right?' She grins. 'This keeps happening. But at least I got to come back.'

'What have you been doing? Did you go to the Caribbean?'

She shakes her head. 'God, no, that guy was an absolute dick. He didn't even have a boat! I went to Paris for a bit, got food poisoning there, so came back. And I've been working at the club. We went there, right?'

'With the barman who looks like Jason Momoa?'

She cackles. 'Alvaro? Yeah. He's great. Not for, like, long-term, but very fun. So what about you?' she asks me. 'Any gossip? Any romance?'

I don't even know where to begin.

Kelsey goes inside to unpack, change and start work with Berry. Ben tells me my first job every morning will be washdown, which Adam will also be doing but starting at the other end of the boat. So eventually we'll meet in the middle.

'First we rinse, to get rid of any loose dust or dirt,' he tells me. 'Then we wash thoroughly. Rinse again, get rid of all the soap. And then we dry.'

I nod. Sounds doable.

He tells me to start with the port-side main deck. It all needs to be done quickly so it doesn't dry in the sun and create water marks.

I rinse everything with the hose, then fill a bucket with soapy water and use an extendable mop to wash everything, including the deckhead, which is above me. My arms ache as I swipe the mop from side to side, soapy water dripping down on me.

I squeegee the windows, rinse everything again and then dry with a chamois. By the time it's done, I'm soaked with soapy water and sweat and my arms feel like wet noodles.

'How you doing?' Ben asks, before laughing at the state of me. 'First time is the worst.'

'Not sure my arms will work next time.'

He grins. 'You'll get used to it. Top tip here . . .'

He takes out his phone and shines the torch on the windows and I cringe as it highlights all the spots I missed.

'Sorry. I thought I'd got everything.'

'Don't worry. Happens to everyone. You just need to go over the windows again. The rest looks great.'

I go over the windows again, stopping after every pane to shake out my arms and stretch my shoulders and back. I thought scrubbing the stairs was hard work but it's nothing compared to this.

And then it gets even worse – I have to do the same on the outside of the boat. Because we're in port, there's another yacht next to us, so I can only do it from the deck with the hose and a long-handled mop, leaning over the railing. It seems to take forever, but Ben's happy with it once it's done and sends me off for a break.

I'm walking round the stern when I hear Adam's voice. He's on his phone on the sun deck.

'I told you,' he says, his voice low. 'As soon as I'll have it, I'll send it you.'

I can't imagine who he's talking to, and I can't make myself walk away.

'I know. But what else do you want me to do?'

I should leave. If he comes down, he'll find me here.

'Yeah. Stop hassling me. I'll send it as soon as I've got it.'

A short silence is followed by a loud, emphatic 'Fuck!', which I assume means he's ended the call and will be coming back down.

I don't want him to catch me eavesdropping, so I run downstairs to the mess. What the fuck was that about?

'Hey!'

Berry's sitting at the table, a plate of sliced fruit in front of her.

'How's it going?' she asks me, popping a slice of kiwi into her mouth.

I wish I could tell her about Adam, instead I say, 'I need a coffee but I've ruined my useless arms.'

I lift them a little and flop them down to my sides.

She laughs. 'Washdown is brutal.'

'I can't believe we have to dry the outside of the boat! That's where the water is!'

'Salt water though. Very bad for boats.'

'Feels like quite a serious design fault.'

'Here.' She slides out from behind the table and steps closer. 'You sit down. I'll make the coffee and then I need to get back. Being this short-handed is no joke.'

'Is there anything I can do? I do need this coffee, but then I can come and –'

She shakes her head, smiling. 'No, babe. You're a deckhand now. You're out of my jurisdiction.'

A butterfly in my chest flutters at the 'babe', and then Berry is guiding me over to the table, her hands on my upper arms, and she gently pushes me to sit down.

'When they tell you to take a break, you take a break.'

I reach out and tangle my fingers with hers. There's no one around and I can't resist.

She squeezes my fingers and then brushes her thumb over my palm, which, somehow, makes a pulse beat between my legs. We stare at each other for a second and I want nothing more than to forget work and pull her into our cabin.

When I get back up on deck, we're about to set sail. Ben shows me how to release the lines and check the fenders. He talks with Captain Liz via radio the whole time and I'm not sure I even understand half of it.

'You'll pick it up,' Ben tells me, even though I didn't say anything. 'There's a lot to learn, but if there's anything you don't understand, just ask. No winging it.'

We anchor in the most beautiful bay and Berry radios to say the guests have had breakfast, they're getting changed and then heading to the swim platform.

Ben shows me how to prepare the water toys – Morgan wants to go on a jet ski and Bec would like to try the Seabob.

I stay on the swim deck to watch them and make sure they don't get into any trouble and it's nice to have a short break. My arm muscles thank me.

'Have you had a go on one of these?' Bec asks when she gets back, and I haul the Seabob out of the water. 'It is wild!'

I don't tell her that they terrify me – I hate the idea of being pulled down under the water – instead I say I haven't had a chance.

'Oh you must,' she says. 'I can't believe it's a real thing! I felt like I was dreaming. I'm going to be singing *The Little Mermaid* all day now.'

Morgan comes back and convinces Bec to go out on the jet ski with her, so I get to hang out a bit longer and then, once they're done, I have to rinse and dry everything.

Adam comes down to help put the jet ski away – it's too heavy for me to manage on my own. He looks tired and tense. In the past I would have teased him, made him laugh, given him a shoulder massage and pretended I was going to dig my fingers into his armpits, which he really hates. Now, though, I just give him a weak smile and thank him for coming down.

'You okay?' he asks me. 'How are you finding it so far?'

'You were right. It's really hard.'

He nods. 'You'll be fine.'

Adam attaches the winch to the jet ski and, once it's out of the water, the two of us guide it into place. We don't talk, concentrating on manoeuvring a 500-pound piece of equipment but once it's done, I tell him that I overheard him on the phone.

'Adam, what's going on?'

He shakes his head and runs one hand back through his hair. 'You're spying on me now?'

'Adam, come on. Something's obviously going on. Why won't you tell me? Maybe I can help?'

'You always want to fix everything.'

'I don't,' I say. 'But maybe –'

He shakes his head. 'You can't fix this, Hope. I'm sorting it. Just leave it. Okay?'

'Okay.'

I don't want to leave it. But if he won't let me help, won't let me in, there's nothing I can do.

When I get back to our cabin, Berry's in my bunk. I climb in next to her and rest my head on her shoulder.

Even if I can't fix whatever's going on with Adam, I hate not knowing. And even though we're broken up, I hate to think of him going through something alone.

'What was the other *Bake Off* you told me about?' Berry asks, pointing the remote at the TV.

'Make-up.'

Berry finds the first episode of *Glow Up* and then takes my hand in hers. I sigh as she starts to massage my fingers, squeezing and tugging. She presses her thumb in the palm of my hand and I stop thinking about Adam.

'Slide down,' she says, her voice low.

I roll onto my stomach and lie flat, moving my pillows to the side, gasping as Berry straddles me and runs her hands over my shoulders. She presses the muscles at the base of my neck, digs her thumbs into my shoulder blades.

I want to turn over, pull her down on top of me, run my fingers up her inner thighs, but I feel like I'm melting into the bed.

I moan as she presses her hands flat against my lower back and she shushes me.

'No sex noises.' She says, her mouth by my ear, her breasts brushing my back. Did she take off her shirt? 'Don't want to start any rumours.'

I try to reach back to touch her, but after my first day of deck work, my arms are basically useless.

She kisses the back of my neck, drifting her tongue along my tight muscles. Her hands are kneading my hips now and I tilt my pelvis, trying to get some friction against the mattress.

'Can you turn over?'

'No.'

She laughs. And then I do. I shift onto my back, feeling boneless, heavy, exhausted and incredibly turned on.

'Can I touch you?' she asks, her hand on my side, fingers pressed into the spaces between my ribs.

I tell her yes, please, and she glides her hand down over my stomach. I turn my head, press my face into the curve of her neck as her hand slips into my underwear and she curls her fingers between my legs.

'Oh my god,' I whisper against her skin. 'Oh my god.'

Her other hand comes up to cradle the back of my head, her fingers tangling in my hair, while she circles her fingers. I tilt my pelvis to rub against the heel of her hand, my breath speeding up, tears burning the backs of my eyes.

It's too much. I can't take it, but I don't want her to stop. I roll half onto my side so that I can kiss her as she circles her thumb where I am hot and wet and throbbing. She gasps into my mouth as I arch my back, put my hand on top of hers to keep it in place.

She whispers my name against my lips as she curls her fingers inside me and I can't stop myself from crying out as everything goes black.

24

I wake up curled around Berry, one arm numb from being trapped under her body, the other floppy and aching from deckhand work. Her phone is blurting the old-style ringtone she says is the most likely to wake her up and the mattress shifts as she stretches her legs down the bed and rolls over to face me.

'Morning. How are you feeling?'

'Weak as a kitten,' I tell her.

She kisses me quickly before rolling off the bed and stepping straight into the bathroom. I stretch and turn my own alarm off before checking my messages.

Riley has sent me a series of Reels from a woman who found eight baby skunks abandoned under her house. Maddie's sent me a message asking if she can run away and join me. 'If I see one more in-growing toenail . . .'

Mum's sent me a photo of Riley, Alfie and Mick on a ride at the fairground, all three of them crammed into one car. Mick is looking startled, his body turned towards the little ones, his hand braced on the safety rail; Riley's head is thrown back, her eyes squeezed shut, her mouth open with laughter; Alfie is looking straight ahead, his face serious but arms thrown up in the air.

I message her back, telling her about my first day as a deckhand – rinsing, washing, rinsing, drying – obviously I don't mention the mind-and-body-shattering orgasm it ended with.

Berry comes out of the shower, wrapped in a towel, skin still gleaming with water droplets and I stretch out one almost useless arm.

'Come here.'

She laughs. 'We definitely don't have time.'

Groaning, I clamber out of bed. A hot shower. Coffee.

Berry is bending over, taking her crew uniform out of a drawer. I run my finger over her lavender tattoo and she rolls her shoulders back, straightening up and turning round. I'm already leaning in. I kiss her quickly and she tastes like toothpaste.

'This is called a Sunset Serenade,' Liam tells Bec and Morgan as the sun is setting that evening. We're on the main deck, which is decorated with a gold fringe curtain and glitter balls, and Adam has set up the karaoke machine. 'It's bourbon, peach liqueur and lavender bitters, garnished with lavender.'

They each take a glass and rave about how delicious it is.

'And you gave it the perfect name!' Bec gestures at the orange, peach and lavender sky.

'Not my first rodeo!' Liam says, throwing a quick glance my way. While I was washing and drying the sun deck earlier, Liam was watching YouTube videos on how to create a cocktail.

'This is bliss,' Bec says, holding her drink out and taking a photo. 'We're so lucky, babe.'

'We are,' Morgan says. 'I am.'

She puts her drink down on the table. Stands. And drops down to one knee on the deck.

'Oh my god,' Bec says, staring down at her.

My breath catches and I grin at Liam who beams back at me.

'You are the love of my life,' Morgan says, looking up at Bec. 'I can't believe I get to do life with you. I know we said we didn't need to get married – and we don't – but I just want to marry you. I want to be your wife and call you my wife and also have a huge, fuck-off party for all our friends. What do you say?'

Bec laughs through her tears and touches Morgan's face. 'Yes. Of course. Of course!'

Morgan stands up and Bec jumps into her arms and I turn and run down the stairs, hoping to find Berry, who I know will be gutted to have missed it. At least if I get her now we can run back up together and join the celebration.

But instead I run smack into Adam.

'Oh, hey.' I take a step back. 'I'm sorry. Are you okay?'

He doesn't look okay. He looks terrible.

'Yeah, I'm . . . Hope, I need to talk to you.'

'I know,' I tell him. 'I want to talk to you too. Tomorrow? Or, I don't know, later tonight maybe? I don't know how late this is going to go.'

'I've fucked everything up,' he says, his voice low.

I shake my head. 'You haven't. It'll be okay. We can talk later. I'll find you after service.'

Adam nods. 'Okay. Thanks.'

I feel awful leaving him like this, but I remember why I ran downstairs in the first place. 'Morgan just proposed. I need to get champagne.'

He nods. 'That's cool. I can go if you want?'

'That would be great, thanks.'

He heads off to the galley and I find Berry doing the turn-down in Bec and Morgan's room.

'We should do something for them in here,' Berry says, once I've told her. 'How are you at towel animals?'

I snort. 'I don't think I'm up to a "congratulations on your engagement" swan.'

'Rose petals?' Berry says. 'Too obvious?'

'Maybe more champagne? More chocolates?'

We always leave a chocolate on the bedside along with a bottle of water.

'Ice bucket and champagne,' Berry says. 'To begin with. And then I'll see if we have petals?'

While Berry investigates, I go back up to the deck and find Morgan and Bec giddily FaceTiming friends from the daybed.

I put some music on quietly and switch on all the fairy lights, now that the sun's even lower.

'This is all perfect,' Bec tells us, once they're off the phone. 'You'll have some champagne with us, right?'

They get me to invite everyone else and Berry, Ben and the captain all come up. Carlo is cooking and I don't know where Adam is. We toast them with the champagne we can't actually drink, posing for photos that they post online. They insist we stay for the karaoke, and Captain Liz says just for one song and then she has to go. She sings 'Ironic' by Alanis Morissette and even though she speak-sings most of it, she belts out the chorus and it's amazing.

'Wow,' Morgan says. 'Who's gonna follow that?'

'You are, baby,' Bec tells her.

Morgan rolls her eyes and puts on 'Jolene'. She mostly can't sing it for laughing, but she gets through it and hands the mic directly to Bec. Bec sings 'Single Ladies' with attempts at the dance moves while Morgan films her and cries with laughter. Bec says she's going to give the mic to Liam, but sings 'My Life Would Suck Without You' to Morgan instead.

Liam is uncharacteristically reticent about singing anything, but since Bec won't let it drop, he eventually sing-shouts 'Smells Like Teen Spirit' badly, before scurrying back behind the bar to mix up some more cocktails.

Bec and Morgan sing 'Islands in the Stream' and then Carlo comes running up to sing Dua Lipa's 'New Rules', which is one of the funniest things I've ever seen in my life. He can really sing, but also totally commits, performing the whole thing with a straight face and dance moves.

Ben does an appalling version of 'I'm Gonna Be (500 Miles)' by the Proclaimers and then Berry sings 'No Scrubs'. She's got a good voice, but acts like she doesn't, covering her face all the way through. The version that plays is the one with the rap and Berry shakes her head, claiming she doesn't know it, and Morgan grabs the mic from her and does the whole thing so brilliantly she gets a spontaneous round of applause.

'Oh!' Berry shouts, holding up a cocktail. 'We need to find some yacht rock for Hope to sing.'

I shake my head. 'I don't want to sing.'

'Oh my god,' Bec says. 'You have to! Everyone else has, right?'

'Some of us more than once,' Morgan adds.

'What can you do?' Berry asks me.

'Nothing!' I tell her. 'I just like listening to all of you, I don't need to sing.'

'Sorry,' Bec says. 'This is our engagement party and I must insist.'

'I don't know any yacht rock,' I tell Berry. 'You wouldn't let me listen to the playlist!'

'You made her a playlist?' Bec says. 'That's adorable!'

'Doesn't have to be yacht rock then,' Berry tells me. 'I'll do that. You do whatever you want. Pick something!'

I scroll through the screens, trying to find something I know and think I have a chance of being able to sing. My mum always does Neneh Cherry's 'Buffalo Stance'. There doesn't even have to be karaoke. Sometimes she just puts it on and stands in the middle of the pub to do the whole thing.

I scroll through a bunch of Taylor Swift songs and Morgan yells that we have to do 'Love Story'.

I shake my head. 'I can't sing that.'

'We'll help you,' she tells me, and I don't even get a chance to agree before it's playing and Berry's given me the microphone.

I've lost my place by the end of the first verse and cringe at how terrible I am and it doesn't matter because first Morgan joins in, almost yelling the chorus, and then Bec takes the mic from her for the bridge. By the time we get to the key change and the line about the proposal and Morgan sings 'Marry me' directly to Bec, we're all laughing through tears.

As soon as everyone's in bed, as soon as we've tidied everything away, as soon as the boat is locked up and the lights are out and the door of our cabin closes behind us, Berry kisses me like she's been thinking about it all day. Like it's all she's been wanting to do.

She kisses me slowly, softly, and I can hear myself making little sounds, which she seems to like because she turns her head to deepen the kiss, her fingers on my neck. I part my lips, run my tongue along her bottom lip until she's sighing into my mouth.

She grabs the hem of my T-shirt and lifts it up, pulling back from the kiss to yank it over my head. I lean forward, chasing her lips, as she drops my T-shirt to the floor.

'Come here.'

She crawls into my bunk, pulling me after her and I lie on my back, Berry on her side next to me. She traces circles on my stomach with her fingers as she kisses my neck, my shoulder, down my arm, leaning up over me to lick along my collarbone and the dip at the base of my throat.

I roll onto my side to face her and hook my leg over hers, pulling her closer. We both moan as our bodies press together and then Berry whispers, 'We have to be quiet,' directly into my ear. 'These walls are so thin.'

I roll her onto her back and straddle her, leaning down to kiss her throat, her chest, tasting salt on her skin.

'Let me . . .' she says, wriggling under me to pull her vest top up and over her head. I hook one finger into her bra strap and slowly slide it down her arm and she shivers.

'Yeah?'

I look down at her. Her pupils are wide, cheeks flushed, as she nods.

I move down until my feet are pressed against the wall at the foot of the bed and kiss her chest, between her breasts, the skin soft under my lips. I lick over her bra and she pulls her legs up, wrapping them around my waist. It's too much and I have to take a second to just breathe, resting my forehead against her ribs.

'Want me to take it off?' she whispers.

I shake my head, lick along her ribs, run my tongue under the edge of her bra. I feel like I'm going to explode into tiny pieces, bits of me embedded in the glossy wood of the cabin.

I push myself up on one elbow, running my other hand up Berry's side until I'm cupping her breast, my thumb brushing her nipple.

Her eyes are squeezed shut and she's breathing fast, her chest fluttering under my hand. I lean down and run my tongue across her other breast, over the lace of her bra, and she whimpers.

I smile as I shush her and lick along the upper edge, the lace scratchy under my tongue. She arches her back, pushing her chest up towards me and I gently push her back down. She squeaks as I pinch her left nipple and lick the right one through the bra.

'Come on!' she mumbles.

I laugh. 'Impatient.'

She squeezes me with her thighs and I run my hand down her side, her leg, feeling the muscles flexing.

She tangles a hand in the back of my hair, not pushing my head down, but holding it still. I take a second and then suck her nipple through the bra and she moans, arching up towards me again.

'Thin walls!' I whisper. 'Everyone's in bed.'

'I don't give a shit.'

Giggling, I slide the other bra strap down her arm.

She goes still as I push the bra down to her waist, shifting over her so our hips are lined up.

'You're so beautiful,' I say, looking down at her.

She opens her eyes, still breathing fast. 'How are you so good at this?'

I laugh. 'I've thought about it a lot.'

'Yeah? Me too.'

The thought that Berry's been thinking about me too, the way I've been thinking about her, makes me shiver.

I kiss down her ribs, bite her hip bones, slide her underwear off. She pushes herself up on her elbows to watch me lick along her inner thighs and then she drops back down against the pillows, her arm over her face, as I dip my head between her legs.

25

Berry groans as my alarm goes off.

'Ignore it,' she says, her mouth against my neck. 'Let's stay here. They'll never find us.'

I laugh, leaning over the edge of the bed to turn off the alarm. 'I'm not sure that's a *great* plan . . .'

'Pack your bags. Let's steal a jet ski. Adam and Liam can manage.'

Adam. Shit. I was supposed to find Adam last night.

'Although I doubt Liam's made a bed in his life.' She stretches and then rolls on top of me. 'Tell me you set the alarm early enough that we can . . .' She ducks her head to kiss my neck.

'I didn't. Sorry.'

She pouts. 'I guess I'll get in the shower then.' She rolls off me. 'Want to join me?'

God, the thought of joining Berry in the shower is wildly hot. But I can't right now. I need to go and find Adam.

'He's gone to collect the tuxes,' Ben tells me when I find him on deck.

Tonight we're taking Bec and Morgan to a casino and the dress code is 'Black & Red Bond'. The men have hired tuxedos from a shop in the port.

'Anything I can help with?' Ben asks.

I shake my head. 'No. But thanks.'

I text Adam, apologising, telling him I was so tired after service I was dead on my feet, that we can talk when he gets back to the boat. He reads it but doesn't reply and I feel like shit.

'You look great,' Berry says.

She's still doing her make-up, a smoky eye, and she's not dressed yet, she's just in her underwear. I'm dressed already in a black dress with lace sleeves. I'm wearing it with red heels, but I haven't put them on yet, because they hurt like hell. My hair is piled up on top of my head and I've gone with minimal eye make-up and red lipstick.

'What do you think?' Berry says, turning back from the mirror and pouting at me.

'I think we should skip it and stay here.'

I step towards her, reaching out, and she grins, holding her hands up to fend me off.

'Do not ruin your lipstick!'

'Again,' I say.

She'd done it for me and then spent about thirty minutes kissing it off.

She reaches behind herself and undoes her bra, letting the straps fall down her arms.

'Oh, come on!' I say, taking a step back. 'This is cruel and unusual!'

She laughs, dropping her red dress over her head. My stomach swoops as I watch it shimmy over her curves. It has one thin strap and the other side is a bustier, so she's going braless. She turns around and wiggles at me. 'Can you see my underwear?'

'Do not even think about going commando!'

She laughs and I reach out and smooth my hands down her sides, pressing up against her.

'You look beautiful.' I kiss the back of her neck, next to her lavender tattoo, and then have to wipe the lipstick mark off with my thumb.

Turning round to face me, she tips her head to press her lips against the side of my neck, just under my ear. I shiver.

'Seriously, let's not go,' I say. 'The boys can take them.'

'We'll get fired.'

She drifts her nose along my jawline and I imagine gathering her dress in my hands and lifting it higher and higher.

'We can get new jobs! Where's the jet ski hijacker from this morning?'

She laughs, stepping back. 'Come on. We'd better go.'

I groan. 'Great. What's the female equivalent of blue balls.'

'There isn't one because blue balls is a made-up thing.'

'You are giving me nothing!' I tell her, smiling.

I bend to pick up my shoes and when I stand, she's moved closer.

'So we have to go out now.' She presses a finger to my collarbone. 'But later we'll be back.' She drags her finger across my chest to touch my collarbone on the other side. 'And first you can take off those shoes. And then you can take off this dress.' She hooks her finger into the neckline off my dress. 'And then you can take off *my* dress.'

* * *

'This is wild,' Morgan says, gesturing at everything.

The casino is in an art deco former palace – we enter through a square covered courtyard stretching up three floors. It's all gold leaf and marble columns with arched stained-glass windows and a stained-glass ceiling. The effect is pretty much ruined by the rows of slot machines lined up against the walls.

I haven't had a chance to talk to Adam – I'm pretty sure he's been avoiding me – and he stays away from me now; he won't even meet my eyes. I feel horrible that I forgot to find him last night, but I apologised. I don't know what else I can do.

From the courtyard, we're shown into the Royal Ballroom, which looks like something from a Disney film. The walls are flocked pink between arched windows. Gold and crystal chandeliers hang from the cloud-painted ceiling. The carpet is patterned with multicoloured butterflies.

There's a row of rectangular roulette tables under black-fringed pendant lights, and a second row of small round tables surrounded by red chairs – some empty, some with people sitting and drinking – and lit with lamps. At some of the tables croupiers are waiting, wearing white shirts with black trousers and waistcoats.

I feel completely out of my depth. I've never even considered going to a casino before and can't believe I'm in one now, but it's also sort of fascinating – who even knew about any of this?

The main room is surprisingly quiet, given how many people are playing. I guess they're concentrating on the gambling. Roulette and blackjack tables are separated by a long bar and we get drinks for Bec and Morgan while they buy their chips.

'I thought it was going to be louder,' Bec tells me, looking around. 'And, I don't know, sexier? This is like something from *The Crown*. But tackier?'

I laugh. 'I know what you mean.'

'Not exactly James Bond, is it?' she says. 'Fun though!'

I get the impression that Bec is the kind of person who can find fun anywhere.

Adam, Ben and Liam are the only men in tuxedos. Almost everyone else is in ordinary suits.

'Ben is really wearing that tux, though,' Bec says, gesturing at him across the room. 'All three of them look great, but Ben . . . ahooga.'

She says 'ahooga' with a completely straight face.

'Worst. Lesbian. Ever,' Morgan says, drily.

Bec is right, though – Ben manages to look like a film star in his normal clothes, so in a tuxedo he's absolutely dazzling. But it's Adam I keep looking at. I've never seen him in a tux before. I saw him in a suit at graduation and a couple of weddings, but a tux is a whole different thing. It's almost unbelievable to me how different he looks. I keep thinking how grown-up he is, even though he's been like this for a few years now, but there's something about it that doesn't feel like Adam to me.

It makes me think of when Mum went to hospital to have Mae and afterwards I took the other two in to see her and she was freaked out at how much bigger they suddenly looked, like the toddlers they'd been just the day before had gone and been replaced by these huge kids, all long limbs, that she worried about around the tiny new baby.

Somewhere along the way, Adam grew and changed into someone I don't quite recognise and I can't even work out how or where it happened because I've been here the whole time.

Bec plays roulette, fully throwing herself into it, cheering when the wheels spins and groaning when she doesn't win. I make sure she has drinks and casino chips.

'Your turn,' she tells me. 'Pick a number.'

My mind goes blank.

'Any number!' She laughs.

'Four.'

'Red or black?'

'Red.'

She pushes a pile of chips to the square and the dealer spins the wheel. I watch the ball as it clatters around the top of the wheel, before bouncing into the centre and stopping in twenty-five black.

'Bad luck,' Morgan says. 'Want another go?'

I shake my head. 'No, thanks. It's stressful!'

She laughs. 'I love it.'

Berry is across the room with Morgan, who I think is playing poker or maybe blackjack. There's a tiny line between Morgan's eyebrows, as she stares intently down at her cards. Berry looks up, catches me staring at her, and smiles.

'She's bad at it,' Bec says, gesturing towards Morgan. 'She always loses a ton of money. But she loves it. She's convinced if she just keeps playing she'll suddenly get good.'

'How long's she been playing?' I ask.

Bec laughs. 'About fifteen years.' She crosses her fingers on both hands. 'But any day now!'

Waiters walk around with trays of finger food, sliders and prawn tempura and tiny roast potatoes with crème fraiche and caviar. I don't take anything, I'm not sure if I should, but Bec tells me to help myself and so I do.

'What's his deal?' she asks me, gesturing at Adam, who is standing at one of the tables where players are seated all around. 'You're friends, right?'

My mouth is full of potato – the crème fraîche coating my tongue, caviar bursting saltily – so I gesture as I nod and chew fast.

'Yes,' I tell her. 'Since school.'

'That's great,' she says. 'You came here together?'

I tell her how Adam found out about it on TikTok.

'Oh god.' She grimaces. 'I had to ban myself from TikTok. Fourth of July weekend, I sat out on our porch and thought I'd have a quick look with my coffee. Morgan went out for the day. When she got back, I was still there. I'd been sitting there all day! Just on TikTok! And I'd had, like, four coffees. She said my eyes were like . . .' She makes spirals with her fingers as I laugh. 'I deleted it from my phone. Sometimes friends will send me a link and from that one link I can lose hours. So addictive. But then it's designed to be. It's like this place. Some people can just come for a night out and have a good time. And other people come once and then can't stop.'

'Hey, babe.' Morgan comes over, takes a potato from the plate, and slings her arm around Bec's shoulders. 'Win big yet?'

'Nope,' Bec says. 'How are you going?'

Morgan shrugs. 'Not great. Fun though. Jeez, these are delicious.' She reaches for another potato.

'Are we staying in here or are there other rooms?' Bec asks.

'I think the other rooms are, like, slot machines and I think they have electronic poker?'

'You wanna stay analogue?'

Morgan nods, her mouth full of potato. Bec wipes a bit of cream from the corner of her fiancée's mouth and Morgan dips her head to kiss her quickly.

'Pick a number,' Bec says, gesturing at the table.

'Twenty-two,' Morgan says immediately.

'Our anniversary,' Bec tells me. 'But does that make it less likely to come up? Like a random number is more probable than a number that's meaningful to us?'

'All the same probability, babe,' Morgan says, which I know is true but feels like it can't be.

Morgan's number doesn't come up either and, after taking another potato, she heads back to the poker tables.

We've been there a couple of hours and I'm starting to wonder how much longer we're going to be staying, when I become aware of someone shouting at the other end of the room.

'What the fuck, man?'

I stand on tiptoes to see and, when I do, it's Adam.

He shoves the table where he's been playing alongside Morgan and it tips over with a clatter of plastic chips and a muted smash as a bottle falls over and rolls onto the carpeted floor.

'He stacked the deck!' Adam is yelling, gesturing at the dealer.

Ben is gripping Adam's arm, trying to steer him away from the table. Adam's face is red and he looks like he's about to cry.

'Oh dear,' Bec says, kindly. 'Too much to drink?'

I can't even believe what I'm seeing. Adam's always been so even-tempered; it's one of the things I love about him. I know girls who enjoy volatile relationships, enjoy fighting and making up, but I've never been into that. I hate conflict. I can't stand raised voices.

'You're in on it with him,' Adam shouts, his Liverpool accent coming out with his anger, as he gestures at one of the other players, pulling himself away from Ben.

The other player stands quickly, his chair crashing to the floor and approaches Adam, his hands held up in front of him. It looks like he's trying to reason with him, but then Adam pulls his arm back and I let out a shout as Adam punches him in the face. The man staggers, crashing into the table and Adam grabs his shirt, as if he's planning to hit him again. I feel like I'm going to be sick.

'Oh shit,' Bec says. 'What do we do?'

I don't know. I can't even think. I can't believe what I'm seeing.

Ben steps back as two security guards approach, but before they reach the table, the other player punches Adam back. Adam hits the floor and then security is there. One of them pulls Adam up off the ground. He slumps between them, all his anger apparently spent.

'Sorry,' I hear him say. 'Sorry, sorry. You don't need to . . .'

'What the hell?' Berry says. She's next to me but I don't know how long she's been there. 'What happened?'

I shake my head as I watch Ben follow security leading Adam out of the room.

'Are you okay?' Berry asks me. 'Do you want to go after him?'

My throat is so tight and I feel like I can't quite catch my breath. What *happened*?

'I think we're happy to go too,' Bec says.

Morgan pushes her chair back. 'Yeah, I'm done here.'

'Hope?' Bec says. 'Are you okay, honey?'

I swallow hard. 'I'm so sorry about this. I have no idea what just happened, but it's so wildly unprofessional and –'

Bec squeezes my arm. 'Honestly, don't worry about it. Gambling brings out the worst in some people. It's not your fault. Let's go and make sure those goons aren't kicking the shit out of him in the car park.'

I hadn't even thought of that and I feel terrified as we leave the room and cross the courtyard to the main doors. The slot machines are loud, bells ringing, music playing, lights flashing. It makes it all feel even more surreal, more like a nightmare.

Outside, Ben and Adam are sitting on a stone bench at the side of the path. Adam with his elbows on his knees, his head in his hands. There's a pool of vomit on the floor between his feet. Ben is texting but glances up when we approach.

He stands, apologising to Bec and Morgan, who once again assure him that it's all part of the authentic casino experience. I walk around to Adam, put my hand on his back, but he shrugs me off. My hands are shaking and I just want this night to be over, to be back on board. To wake up tomorrow and find none of it really happened.

'Are you okay?' Berry asks me, once we're back in the cabin.

I shake my head, the threat of tears closing my throat again and she wraps her arms around me. I relax for a second and then say, 'I think I need a shower.'

She squeezes me. 'Okay. You can do that.'

I strip off in the bathroom, letting my dress drop to the floor. I don't bother to take off my make-up; I just let the hot water run over my face, my mascara stinging my eyes.

I've never seen Adam like that before. I didn't even know he knew how to play blackjack, never mind well enough to be able to accuse someone of cheating. It makes no sense to me. It doesn't feel like Adam. I never would have expected him to gamble, to start a fight, to punch someone.

A sob bubbles up and I try to swallow it down, hoping that the sound of the running water muffles it. I can't believe he punched someone. And he got punched. A stranger punched Adam in the face and knocked him to the ground and I just stood there and watched. I didn't even do anything to help. I didn't even say anything. And then when I tried to comfort him, he shook me off.

Despite the hot water running over my skin, I shiver.

When I wake up in the morning, Berry's not in bed, but then the door opens and she brings me a coffee, climbing back into bed next to me.

'How are you doing? Did you sleep?'

'A bit,' I tell her.

I dreamt about the casino. The metallic jangle of the slot machines. The rattle of the ball on the roulette wheel. When I woke up I had a second of relief, thinking the fight had been a dream, but then I remembered. No, it really happened. It was real.

I blow the top of the coffee.

'Ben's up,' Berry tells me. 'Seems a bit freaked out by what happened.'

'Is Adam getting fired?'

She grimaces. 'He's in with the captain now.'

I sip the coffee and it burns as it goes down. 'I can't believe he did that,' I tell her.

'You've never known him to –'

I shake my head. 'I don't think I've ever heard him shout. Not in anger. Since we came here though . . . There was that day he lost his temper with Ben. He was throwing the lines and kept missing and he stormed off. I know he gets frustrated when he can't do something. But nothing like that. He punched someone!'

'I know,' Berry says. 'Obviously I don't know him as well as you do, but it seemed out of character. Some guys you expect. Like Liam. If Liam got punched at a club, I'd just be like, well, someone's jealous boyfriend found him. But I never got that impression with Adam.'

'I think something's really wrong,' I tell her. 'He doesn't seem like himself.'

She shifts on the bed, turning more towards me. 'Was everything okay at home, do you think? Like, you told me he suggested you both do this and then it all happened fast. Do you think he was running away from something?'

I take another sip of coffee before I answer.

'I didn't think that before. I thought he just wanted us to do something cool together, you know? Because neither of us had found anything we wanted to do back home. But now I think maybe you're right.' Tears burn the back of my eyes. 'I overheard him on the phone. It sounded like someone was threatening him? I don't know.'

Tears are spilling down my cheeks now. Adam. My Adam. Who's always been so gentle.

Berry squeezes my hand.

'He wanted to talk to me,' I tell her through my tears. 'I promised I'd find him the other night after service. But then there was the karaoke and we came back here and I completely forgot.' I shake my head. 'I let him down. And I tried to talk to him yesterday, but he was avoiding me.'

'It sounds like it's something he wants to deal with on his own.'

I nod. Maybe. I just wish I knew what it was.

26

I'm meant to be working, obviously, but instead I wait for Adam outside the bridge. I can't bear the idea that he's going to get fired and I can't just get on with work while I wait to hear.

I scroll through the selfie folder of my phone. So many of them are of the two of us. Me beaming so widely that my eyes have all but disappeared, Adam's mouth pressed against my temple so fiercely that it looks like he's trying to suck out my brain. His chin on my shoulder on the big wheel at the Liverpool Christmas market, against a background of fake-snow-covered log cabins. Lying on the grass, squinting against the sun, just before we noticed we were surrounded by enormous slugs.

He's in so much of my history. It's hard to imagine he might not be part of my future.

The door opens and he smiles weakly when he sees me waiting. He doesn't seem at all surprised.

'How did it go?'

'I'm not fired,' he tells me, and I sag against the wall with relief.

'I should be,' he says. 'I would be. But we're too short-staffed.' He blows out a breath.

'Adam. What's going on?'

He shakes his head. 'Not here.'

I nod and follow him down to his cabin.

It's a mess, clothes piled on what was Nico's bed and all over the floor.

'Sorry,' Adam says, picking up a couple of coffee mugs and taking them into the bathroom where he flushes the loo and then closes the door.

'It's me,' I tell him. 'I know how disgusting you are.'

He smiles a smile I feel like I haven't seen for a while before his face creases again and he sits on the floor.

I kick a space through the clothes and sit opposite him. 'Tell me,' I say. 'And I promise I'll just listen. I won't try to fix anything.'

'I was a dick about that. Sorry.'

I shake my head. 'I'm sorry I didn't come and find you that night.'

'It wouldn't have made any difference.' He rubs both hands over his face. He keeps breathing short sharp breaths through his nose and I wait, forcing myself not to speak, to let him tell me in his own time.

'I have –' he sucks in a breath – 'a gambling problem.'

I have no idea what I thought he was going to say, but it wasn't that. Maybe that there was something wrong at home. That his mum was ill or struggling with money, but gambling?

'Wha . . . ?' I start. 'How? Or . . . I don't know. Since when?' I shake my head. 'Just . . . tell me whatever you want to tell me.'

He glances over at me then and he looks stricken. It makes my heart hurt.

'It started at uni.'

'Adam. Oh my god.'

He winces. 'I know. Can you not . . . ?' He shakes his head. 'I feel bad enough. Could you just listen and not –'

'Yes,' I tell him. 'I'm sorry. I'm just surprised.'

He nods. 'I know. I'm sorry. It started with . . . Have you heard of matched betting?'

'A bit.'

Some of the boys in our year talked about it. Once a guy called Jude who I didn't know but had heard a bunch of rumours about, turned up at a party with a literal wedge of cash, fanning it out in his hand, flicking people with it, generally acting like a massive wanker. Someone said he'd made it doing matched betting. I'd googled it and read it's basically placing opposing bets, so, say, on both teams in a football match, using the free bets offered by bookie sites. I didn't really understand how it worked and I certainly wasn't going to be signing up to any bookie sites and I forgot all about it.

'There was a club,' Adam tells me now, 'at uni. Started with matched betting, branched out into other types of betting. I won a bunch of money to begin with. Remember when we went to Panoramic 34?'

He'd taken me for my twenty-first birthday. It's one of the highest restaurants in the UK and much posher than either of us were used to. The bill came to more than two hundred pounds and the thought of it made me feel panicky, but Adam had assured me it was fine and that he'd saved up to treat me.

'I'd had a win,' he tells me now. 'I thought about telling you that night – I was kind of proud of myself, you know? I thought I was doing something clever. Once I got into it, it was so easy and it just felt like free money. I mean, it *was* free money at the start.'

'What happened?'

'The sites I'd registered for to get the free bets had online games and sometimes they'd offer free goes on them too. Like bingo and poker. So I started playing a few of them. And, again, I won a bit. And then I started losing. So I played more to try and make back the money I'd lost.'

'Shit.'

'Yeah. It's embarrassing. Like, if someone else was telling me this, this is the point where I'd be saying stop now. Get out. Forget the money you lost; it wasn't even that much. But I was sure I could win it back. And then Jake suggested going to a casino and I won there too. And then the same thing happened. It's why I wanted to do this.'

Everything he's said has shocked me, but I think maybe this shocks me the most.

'This job?'

He nods, blowing out another slow breath. 'I needed to get away from temptation. And also to make some money to pay people back.'

'Adam. Oh my god.'

'I know. I'm so sorry. I've been a fucking idiot.'

'No,' I say. But then I change my mind. 'I mean, yes, you have. But also, I can't believe you didn't tell me any of this before now. I could've helped.'

'How? Like, I thought about it. I thought about telling you and I know you would've asked Mick for money or done something to bail me out. I know that. But then what if I'd just run it all up again? I bailed myself out more than once and promised I'd stop, but then I'd wake up in the early hours, pick up my phone and play poker again. It was bad enough losing my own money, I couldn't risk losing yours or Mick's.'

'But you could've told me that's why you wanted to do this job.'

He shakes his head. 'I couldn't. I just needed to get away.'

'I can't believe I didn't know.'

'I worked really hard to hide it from you. I feel like shit about that too.'

'God.' I can't even think about any of that. About how much he's lied to me. About how this whole thing – this big adventure, the two of us together, our future – the whole thing was a front to cover up his gambling. That he felt like it was easier – or, I don't know, better – to lie to me. To get me here under false pretences.

I thought he was planning this amazing future for the two of us together when he was actually running away and taking me along for, what? Cover? Company? Because he was afraid to do it alone?

First, I lost the future I thought we'd have together, and now he's rewritten some of our past.

27

We have another charter in a couple of days, so the captain gives us the day off and I'm so relieved. I can't deal with Adam right now. I just want to stop thinking about all of it. Pretend, at least for a little while, that none of it ever happened.

'What do you want to do?' Berry asks me, curled up against my side, her fingers drifting slowly back and forth over my ribs.

'This.'

'We can't spend the whole day in bed.'

'We totally can.'

'Everyone will wonder where we are. What we're doing.'

I hook my leg over hers. 'They won't. They're all too busy with their own shit.'

Berry walks her fingers up my inner thigh. 'So you don't want to get off?'

'Yes.'

'The boat?'

'No.'

She dips her head and kisses the tip of my shoulder. 'I want to go to the beach.'

'Which beach?'

'A tiny one. Where no one knows us. Where we can lie in the sun and then swim in the sea and drink cocktails and not think about work at all.'

'That sounds like a plan. But not yet.'

She squeaks as I roll on top of her and I kiss her to keep her quiet.

The beach is not far from the marina, but it's small and there's hardly anyone around. We buy drinks, sandwiches, watermelon and crisps from a snack bar at the top of the steps and find a space between some rocks to throw our towels down.

'This is good, right?' Berry says, stretching her arms wide and staring out at the glittering blue-green ocean.

'It's perfect.'

I slide my hands around her waist and I'm leaning in to kiss the back of her neck when she tips forward, her arms still wide, and shouts, 'I'm the queen of the world.'

I lie on my stomach on my towel and Berry straddles me. I hear the snick of a cap and then she's smoothing suncream over my shoulders and back.

'What is it you call this?' she asks.

'Hmm?' I try to turn to look at her but it's too bright and also she's sitting on me.

'Sunscreen. You call it something weird, right?'

'Suncream.'

She snorts. 'That's it. "Would you like some suncream on your strawberries?"'

'Wow, that is one of the worst English accents I've ever heard.'

'You'll have to teach me.'

Her hands move down my sides and I gasp as her fingertips graze the sides of my breasts.

'I dreamt about this,' I tell her.

'About what?'

'You, sitting on me. Putting suncream on my back.'

'Oh yeah? Was it hot?'

I curl up a little so my forehead's resting on the towel.

'Extremely.'

'I can't believe you had a dirty dream about me! And we were being sun safe.'

'I'm very responsible.'

'Oh, I know. Did I do this?'

She smooths the suncream up my thighs and I gasp into the towel.

'Actually I think you did.'

'Wow. Dream me was very thorough. Turn over.'

She lifts up onto her knees and I roll over underneath her.

'Want me to do your front?'

'I don't think that's a good idea,' I tell her. 'Not in public.'

She grins down at me, her hair falling down around her face, blue sky bright behind her. I reach a hand around the back of her neck and pull her down on top of me.

We talk and read and turn over and over in the sun like rotisserie chickens and then, when the heat becomes unbearable, we tuck our stuff behind a rock and walk out into the water.

We swim out towards a buoy and I remember that day in Formentor. It seems like so long ago now. I barely knew her at all.

We tread water, beaming at each other from behind our sunglasses.

'You know what you could do,' Berry says, turning in a circle.

'What?' I turn too.

Blue water as far as I can see. And then the beach, the rocks, the buildings behind.

'The thing you haven't done.' She grins.

'There are so many things I haven't done.'

'We could tick one off the list right now.'

She waggles her eyebrows and I realise what she's thinking of.

'Skinny dipping? No!'

'No one's looking,' Berry says. 'And even if they did, they wouldn't be able to see anything under the water.'

There's a man swimming front crawl across the bay further out towards the buoy. There's a group of people who look to be in their sixties, treading water and talking and laughing, but they're not close by and, Berry's right, they're not paying any attention to us.

'We could just take our bikinis off,' Berry says.

I stare at her. 'And if we drop them?'

'We won't drop them.'

She stares at me as if in challenge, mouth quirking at the corners.

I look back at the beach. Tourists lying on sunloungers. Children digging with bright plastic spades. A toddler sitting at the edge of the water, filling a yellow bucket and dumping it out again while an adult squats next to them, filming them on their phone.

I kick my feet to stay afloat as I reach around and undo the clasp at the back of my top, letting the straps drop down my arms. The water rushing over my bare breasts immediately feels amazing, better than I expected.

'Feels good, right?' Berry says.

Without me noticing, she's taken off her top too and pulled the strap over her head so it's dangling down her back.

She swims a few strokes further out and I follow her. The water feels different on my bare skin and it doesn't make sense because I've had water on my skin before, but this feels sort of silky, as if it's fabric running over me, not liquid.

'Ready for the bottoms?' Berry asks, treading water again.

I pull mine down carefully, making sure to keep tight hold the whole time. The last thing I want is to have to walk back to the beach naked from the waist down. Once I've hooked them off my feet, I slip my hand through and hold on tight.

Berry ducks down under the water and then pops up closer to me.

'So what do you think?'

Obviously, I've seen Berry topless before. But much like the water feels different like this, seeing her topless here feels different. Wildly hot. Have I been staring at her tits this whole time?

When I look at her, she's grinning at me, biting the corner of her mouth, which means, yes, I have been staring at her tits this whole time.

'Shut up,' I say, even though she hasn't spoken.

'Yours look great too,' she says.

I laugh. 'I get why people like this. It feels really free.'

'Right? You get used to it fast too. I went to this nudist beach once and at first most people are a little shy.' She curls over herself, hiding her chest with her forearms. 'But then you realise no one cares and it's just bodies. People were running, playing frisbee. There's like a concession stand there and I put a cover up on but when I got there, other people were standing around naked, drinking beer, eating pizza, just having regular conversations with boobs and dicks dangling.' She grins. 'It was so cool.'

'When Alfie was little he hated wearing clothes,' I tell her, smiling as I remember. 'He used to take them off as soon as he got a chance. Like, in shops. I'd be trying to choose cereal or something and I'd hear a gasp or a laugh and I'd look and he'd stripped off. He'd be standing there in his nappy and shoes and socks.'

'He sounds awesome.'

'He is. We finally convinced him that he had to wear clothes in public, which just meant he never did in private. We'd get home and before the door was even shut he'd be naked.'

'I could go for that. Especially in this heat.'

I picture myself in an apartment. White. Big windows. Filmy curtains billowing in the breeze. And Berry. Naked. All the time.

I lean back and relax. And let myself float.

28

I can't believe this charter is our last. It's gone so quickly. I'm dying to get home – to see Mum and everyone – but I'm not ready for this to be over. Adam and I have stopped avoiding each other – it's almost impossible when we're both working deck anyway, particularly when he's working even harder, trying to make up for his fuck-ups – but I'm still pissed off at him.

But first: our last guests.

'Kent Hogan and his wife, Babs, are celebrating selling their jewellery business,' Captain Liz tells us at the preference meeting. 'They're also bringing Babs's brother Marc and his wife Jenny. Marc is a gynaecologist and Jenny has a boutique in Los Angeles. She's also an influencer with over four million followers on TikTok.'

She pushes the bio pages across the table and I scan the photos. The primary, Kent, is good-looking with a swoop of greying hair and a salt-and-pepper beard. His brother-in-law, the gynaecologist, looks similar but less handsome, like if you ordered the primary from Wish. His hair isn't as full, his beard a little stragglier, eyes a bit too close together. Babs is blonde and glossy with a wide smile. Jenny, the gynae's wife, has a brown bob with caramel streaks and a lot of filler in her face.

'They want to go to Deià,' the captain tells us. 'And they're looking forward to trying out the water toys. The men both want to try waterskiing. They like all kinds of food,' she tells Carlo. 'Love steak. Hate sushi. Would like to be low-key drunk the whole time.' She rolls her eyes. 'Not while waterskiing they won't be.'

The guests arrive looking rich and being loud.

'Everyone's so gorgeous!' Jenny exclaims, stepping back and gesturing at us all lined up in our whites. 'This is going to be fun!'

Berry gives the guests the tour while the rest of us bring their luggage on board. We're sailing as soon as possible, so I go back to the deck to release the lines and then we're on our way.

I'm washing the stern when Marc comes out and leans against the railing.

'Is everything okay?' I ask him. 'Do you need anything?'

He smiles. He's got a drink in his hand – short, brown, looks like whisky.

'Just admiring the view.'

I look out over the ocean. 'I know,' I say. 'It's beautiful.'

But he's not looking at the ocean; he's staring at me.

'Don't let me disturb you.' He gestures at the squeegee in my hand.

I don't know what else I can do but carry on working while he watches.

'Did you get changed?' he asks after a few minutes. 'You weren't wearing that when we arrived.'

I look down at myself, even though I know what I'm wearing – my uniform polo shirt and a skort. 'We greet the guests in our dress uniforms,' I tell him. 'But then change into this for work.'

'It's nice,' he says. 'But aren't you too hot?'

'It's not too bad,' I tell him, even though sweat is pooling in the small of my back.

'You don't need to dress up on my account.' He drains his drink. 'Feel free to work in a bikini.'

I laugh. Even though it's not funny.

'I'll suggest that to the captain,' I tell him. The creep.

On my break, I'm hiding out in our cabin when I get a text from Mick asking me to call when I can. I call immediately, my stomach twisting with anxiety.

'Mick? Is Mum okay?'

'I wouldn't go that far.' He turns the phone and I can see my mum in a hospital bed.

'Oh my god! Mum! Have you had the baby?'

She shakes her head and it's only then that I can see how red her face and sweaty her hair is.

'I'm only six bastarding centimetres,' she says. 'They've given me two paracetamol. And someone forgot the bloody Bluetooth speaker, so I can't even listen to my playlist.'

'I offered to go and get it!' Mick says.

'And miss the birth of your child?' Mum says, appalled.

'Can you talk to her?' Mick asks me. 'While I go and try to find original Lucozade in the shop downstairs.'

'He bought me an orange sport one,' Mum tells me, as if he'd presented her with a bag of dog pee.

'Wow, what an idiot,' I say, smiling.

'Thanks for that,' Mick says, before passing the phone to Mum.

'And get me a Snickers as well,' she tells him.

'You're not meant to have peanuts,' Mick says.

'Bloody hell, it's nearly out! I'm not going to give it an allergy now, am I?'

Laughing, Mick kisses her on the forehead and says 'good luck' to me.

'I'm so sorry I'm not there,' I tell my mum.

She shakes her head. 'Don't be daft. How's it going? What are you up to today? Distract me from the literal human trying to crawl out of me.'

I tell her we have new charter guests, but they've only just arrived and we don't know yet what they're going to be like, but first impressions weren't great.

'How's Adam?' she asks me.

'He's okay,' I lie. 'Busy. It's really hard work.'

'Yeah, his mum said that when she popped round with . . .'

She makes a sort of keening sound and for a second the phone swings and I'm looking at the ceiling – tiles, an extractor fan, strip lighting.

'I'm okay!' she says, before reappearing.

'How bad is it?' I ask her.

She shakes her head. 'The anticipation is almost the worst part. Like I can feel it building like a wave and each time I think I'm going to breathe through it, but then the wave hits and I forget to breathe and then it goes and I have, like, a minute to relax before I start worrying about the next one. Well, as relaxed as you can be when strangers keep coming in to look up my chuff and there's a cardboard hat full of pee on the floor next to me. How much do you bet Mick steps in it before someone remembers to take it away?'

Between pauses for pain and breathing, she brings me up to date on everything the kids have been doing – Riley won Star of the Week at school and it gave her airs; Alfie fell out with one of his friends because he called him a 'shitcake'; Mae is insisting the new baby is going to be a penguin and they need to build him an igloo.

Mick comes back – he couldn't find an original Lucozade, so he's got her a Cherry Coke and two Snickers to be safe – she gives him the phone while she swings her legs out of bed and leans forward with her elbows on her knees.

'She's tried to book me in for a vasectomy,' Mick tells me. 'Literally asked at the desk when we came in.'

'Yeah, well, I'm not doing this again,' Mum says without turning round. 'And if they can't fit you in, I'll give you the snip myself.'

I have to get off the phone when a doctor arrives to examine Mum, but I ask Mick to keep me updated. It's hard to be so far away, but it's not for much longer. Soon I get to go home.

And I don't know how I feel about that.

Over dinner, the expensive wine flows and the guests get louder and rowdier. There's no way to avoid Marc on a boat this size and with a relatively small crew, but he seems to be on his best behaviour in front of other people. It's a warm night and the darkness is velvet soft, the sky a deep cornflower blue. Carlo has made a seafood banquet with oysters and shrimp and a centrepiece of lobster, deep red and glistening with melted butter.

I'm topping up Marc's wine when I feel a sharp pinch on my hip. I flinch, stepping away, unsure at first what it even was; it felt a little like a bug bite.

Marc is looking up at me, laughing, his face flushed from the alcohol, from showing off in front of the others. He holds up a lobster claw and clicks the pincers together. 'Snap, snap!'

I blow a breath out through my nose, not sure of how I'm meant to respond. Do I have to laugh? Can I tell him not to do it again?

Berry appears and briskly snatches the claws from Marc's hand, dropping them on the pile of plates she's already cleared to take back to the kitchen. 'Didn't anyone teach you not to play with your food?' she asks him, lightly.

Marc stretches back in his chair, looking between me and Berry. 'You two a couple?'

I scoff again. 'What? No!'

I sense rather than see Berry turn to look at me. There's no way I'm planning on telling this particular guest anything personal.

'Shame,' he says.

Oh my god. Gross.

29

Mum had the baby while I was asleep. He was born around 4 a.m. They'd thought she was going to have to have a C-section, but Mick said Mum was so determined not to that she forced the baby out by sheer will.

Mum was sleeping when Mick texted, but by the time I'm up and out on deck with my coffee, she's awake and FaceTiming me.

'I don't know how they expect you to sleep in hospitals,' is the first thing she says. 'It's boiling hot, the lights stay on, people are in and out all night long. Some fool woke me up to feed the baby and then realised she'd got the wrong bed.'

I smile at her through my tears. 'How are you, though? How's the baby?'

Her face softens. 'Oh, he's delicious. He fell asleep with me when I fed him and I woke up with him stuck to my boob. Had to peel him off like a plaster.'

'What are you calling him?'

'Haven't thought of anything yet. We said we'd wait to see what he looks like, but he just looks like a baby. Mick said I can't call him "Baby" cos everyone'll think it's after *Dirty Dancing*.'

'Also,' I say, 'it's not a name.'

'Mae wants to call him "Cocomelon".'

'Also not a name.'

'Hang on,' she says, shifting on the bed. 'I'll show you.'

'God, don't get out of bed!'

'I've already been out of bed. Breakfast's on a trolley in the corridor. I asked if they could bring it to me, given that I just shat out a human, but they said no. Good to get moving early doors. Someone did bring me a brew though, thank god. I was gasping.'

She turns her phone to show me my littlest brother. He's asleep, his face red and scrunched under his little white cap. One tiny shrivelled red hand poking out from his swaddle, fingertips resting on his chin.

'He's perfect,' I tell her.

'What time do you get off?' Marc murmurs to me from over the top of his glass of whisky at dinner that night.

Berry and Liam took them to Deià today, so after I did the washdown, I helped Kelsey with the cabins.

I force myself to smile. 'Not until the last guest's gone to bed.'

'That's not what I asked,' he says, smirking up at me, clearly pleased with himself. 'I asked what time do you get off. Or, more importantly, what gets you off. I'm a gynaecologist. I know the anatomy. It's what I do.'

I can't believe anyone talks like this. I can't believe he could possibly think I – anyone – would go for it. I can only assume he thinks because I'm staff I have to listen to his gross bullshit. I catch Adam's eye across the deck and he raises one eyebrow. I shake my head at him; I can handle this myself.

My fingertips tingle with adrenaline and I briefly fantasise about punching Marc in the face, but instead I say, 'I'm just trying to get to the end of my shift.'

He raises his hands as if in surrender, but he's still grinning at me, like the creep he is.

'Want me to go and fart on his pillow?' Berry asks when both of us are in the galley collecting yet more nibbles.

'Thanks. I might go and do it myself.'

'I can hot sauce in his undies,' Carlo says.

Berry and I burst out laughing.

'Do you even know who we're talking about?' I ask him.

Carlo looks sheepish. 'No. But I always want to hot-sauce someone's undies.'

'Stay away from my undies,' Berry says, grinning at him.

He holds his hands up, smiling, and on him it's endearing whereas on Marc . . .

'I don't know about your undies,' he says. 'Do we have the . . . ?' He screws up his face in thought. 'The glue that is forever?'

'Superglue?' I guess.

'You can put in his shampoo.'

'You're too good at this!' I tell him. 'And you look so sweet!'

'I am not sweet,' he says, sweetly. 'I am Italian.'

I was hoping that by the time we got back up on deck, Marc would have gone to bed or fallen asleep where he was sitting, but no. He has the whisky bottle now and I'm pretty sure he's undone another button on his shirt, his chest, pale and hairless, peeps out.

'Gonna be a late one,' Berry mutters to me.

Looks that way, yeah.

Marc's wife, Jenny, and Babs are dancing. Arms in the air, eyes half closed, staggering a little either due to the rocking of the boat or the amount of cocktails they've put away.

'Can we swim?' Babs asks me, gesturing out at the black water.

'No, sorry. It's not safe at night,' I tell her. I don't add *or when you're shit-faced*.

'Fancy going skinny dipping?' Marc asks them.

They both giggle.

'How about you?' he asks me. 'And Cherry. Ever go skinny dipping?'

I top up his glass, not bothering to correct him on Berry's name. Better for him not to know it.

'No,' I lie.

'Shame.' He curls one hand around my ankle and slowly slides it up my calf to the back of my knee.

'Have you tried the crab toasties?' I ask him, stepping away again.

His hand drops back to his lap.

Kent gives me an apologetic look and I feel another stab of fury. He clearly knows what Marc is like. He knows it's shit and rather than tell Marc to stop, that his behaviour is unacceptable, he's wordlessly apologising to me.

'I don't eat that shit,' Marc grumbles and takes another swig of his drink.

He ate the lobster, though, didn't he? Or did he just use it to bother me?

'Come and dance!' Jenny calls.

At first I think she's talking to me. Or to her husband. But, no, it's Adam and Liam. Jenny grabs Adam and Babs hooks her arms around Liam's neck, shimmying against him.

'The party's still going, eh?' Liam says, smiling down at her.

'Just started now you're here.' She takes one of his hands and twirls herself under his arm. 'I heard you like older women.'

'For fuck's sake,' Marc mutters, shifting to the edge of his seat.

I think he's had enough, that he's going to get up and go to bed and hopefully the women will follow and we can all finish up, clean up and finally get to bed ourselves.

I'm wrong. He grabs me again, his big hand around my thigh this time, and yanks me. It's so sudden that I don't have time to brace myself against it. I'm pulled off balance and he uses that to drag me down and onto his lap, wrapping his arms around my waist.

I wriggle, trying to pull away, and he says, 'Yeah, that's it. Give me a lap dance.'

Kent is laughing. The wives aren't paying any attention; they're dangling off Adam and Liam, twirling themselves out to arm's length and then pulling themselves back in.

I'm trying to work out the best way to deal with this. I can't hit him. I don't even know what I can say. And he's holding me so tightly it's almost painful so there's no way I can get myself free. I see Berry crossing the deck towards us. She looks furious.

And then Adam is in front of me, blocking her from my view. He grabs my hands, pulls and says, 'I'd appreciate it if you'd let go of my girlfriend.'

Marc doesn't let go completely but he loosens his hold enough that Adam can pull me free and to my feet. The momentum makes me stagger and I fall into him, against him. He wraps his arms around me, holding me, my face against his chest. I have a moment of relief that I'm okay, Adam's got me like he has so many times before,

241

before I realise what he said, what he did, in front of everyone. In front of Berry.

I push him away and twist myself to look for Berry.

She's staring straight at me, her eyes wide and stunned.

I think I say her name, but I'm not sure I actually make a sound. She turns and heads inside, into the salon.

'This is all very exciting,' Marc says. 'But who do I have to fuck to get a drink around here?'

Adam jerks as if he's going to push past me to get to Marc.

'Don't,' I tell him. 'You can't.'

And then Ben's there, steering Adam away.

'I can get that for you,' I tell Marc.

I take his glass, and by the time I get to the bottom of the stairs to the galley, tears are streaming down my face and I'm struggling to catch my breath.

'What's wrong?' Carlo asks, coming towards me, concern all over his face, his hands reaching out for mine.

'Everything,' I tell him. 'Everything's falling apart.'

He pulls me into a hug. 'I think it's maybe not so bad. You're tired, yes?'

'Always.'

'My mama says that it always looks better in the morning. Anything. At night things . . .' He mimes an explosion with his hands and blows out a breath.

'I need whisky,' I tell him.

He frowns. 'I think you should not drink.'

I smile, shaking my head. 'Not for me. For a horrible guest.'

'The man with the pepper underwear?'

'That's the one.'

Carlo passes me the bottle of whisky and I blow out a breath.

'Do I look like I've been crying?'

'No. But maybe . . . fix the lip.' He points to his mouth.

I quickly reapply my lipstick and when I get back up on deck, the guests have gone. Kelsey's clearing the table and Liam is brushing the deck.

'We've got this,' Kelsey tells me.

'Are you sure? I can –'

She waves me off. 'It's fine, really.'

I'm glad, because I need to talk to Berry. I can't believe Adam called me his girlfriend. She must know it's not true. But her face. She looked so shocked, so hurt. I hate that I made her feel like that.

As I walk around the stern towards the stairs, I see Adam leaning back against the flagpole, staring out over the water. I almost ignore him and sneak past to get to Berry. But he sees me and gives me a weary smile.

'You okay?'

I nod. Even though I'm not.

'I'm sorry about that guy,' he says. Piece of shit.'

'It's okay. I'm glad you didn't punch him.'

He huffs. 'I wanted to throw him overboard.'

He rubs his face and when he takes his hands away his eyes are wet.

'I don't think this job is for me.'

My stomach lurches like the boat's hit a swell and I walk over. Sit down next to him. I so want to see Berry, but I know Adam needs to talk to me right now.

'I think it's just such a big learning curve. You'll get it. You just need more time.'

He shakes his head. 'You always do that.'

'I always do what?'

'Encourage me. Tell me I can do anything.'

'You *can* do anything.'

He smiles. 'I can't. But also I don't want to. And I don't need you to fix this.'

'I wasn't trying to fix it. I just think –'

'Hope –' he turns towards me – 'I have hated pretty much every minute on board this yacht.'

I shake my head.

'It's true. It wasn't just for the money. I thought I'd love it. I thought I'd love being here with you. Sailing. Meeting people. Even the work. I knew it would be hard, physical. But I thought it would be fun. I'm not having fun. I know you are. I know you love it. But I don't. I hate it.'

'Do you have enough money? For . . . whoever you needed it for?'

He blows out a breath. 'Not enough, no. But I've told my mum. She's going to pay it. I'm going to pay her back. And I will.'

'I know you will,' I tell him. 'Do you know what you're going to do? When you get back?'

He shakes his head. 'I don't think I can stay home, not for a while. I don't trust myself not to go back to gambling if I'm with the same lads, you know?'

I nod. I'm glad of that, at least.

'Liam was telling me about the football coaching he did in America, so maybe that? Or maybe something completely different. I don't know. My head's wrecked. I need to think. I don't get time to think here.'

'You know where I am if you need to talk about any of it,' I tell him. Even though none of it has worked out like I thought, I can't imagine doing this without him.

'You love it, yeah?' he says. 'The job?'

I nod. 'I really do. Not tonight. Not these guests. But the rest of it, yeah. It feels right.'

'I fucked everything up,' he says, his voice cracking. 'I'm so sorry, Hope.'

He reaches for my hand, sliding his fingers between mine. I know him so well. I know his face. I know his scent. I know the sounds he makes in his sleep. I know his family and friends. I thought I knew his dreams, his thoughts. I thought I knew everything. I didn't. But I still know him. Better than almost anyone.

His eyes flick down to my lips and my breath catches. He's been mine and I've been his for so long, before we ever even thought about anyone else. He was always it for me and I know I was it for him.

I don't see him move and I don't think I move, but then his mouth is on mine and it's so warm, so familiar, so easy. I feel everything in me relax, all the tension from the evening, from the guests, from the work, just drifting away. I feel like I'm melting as his hand curls around my neck, smooths down over my shoulder. I press closer to him, feeling the muscles in his chest, sliding my fingers into the back of his hair. He moans into my mouth as I tug at his curls. He needs a haircut, but I like it. I like him.

I love him. I've loved him for so long. I can hardly remember a time when I didn't love him. But that's not a good enough reason.

'Wait,' I tell Adam. 'Stop. Sorry, I . . . I can't do this.'

'Ah, go on,' he says, grinning, and despite everything, I laugh.

'I'm going to bed,' I tell him. 'And you should too.'

I stand, turn around, and that's when I see Berry standing at the back of the deck. Even from here I can see the tears on her face. She turns and disappears through the doors to the salon and I leave Adam on the bow and follow her.

I have to talk to her. I have to explain.

But when I get to our cabin, the door is locked.

30

I sleep in Adam's room. But not in Adam's bed. Nico's bunk is empty and so I sleep there. Or at least that's where I spend the night. I don't sleep much.

My eyes are hot and gritty and I can barely keep them open, but whenever I close them I see the hurt and shock on Berry's face.

Does she think I've been with Adam this whole time? Does she think I cheated on her tonight? I can't bear it. My chest aches and tears run from the corners of my eyes to soak the pillow behind my head.

I sleep eventually, my alarm waking me for work. I get dressed in my clothes from last night and step out of the cabin when Adam's in the shower.

I knock on our door. Say Berry's name. But she doesn't reply.

The guests don't come out of their rooms all morning. I do my deck duties as usual – wash down and dry everything, polish all the chrome, scrub the deck, but it takes me so much longer, my physical and mental exhaustion making me slow and clumsy.

There's no sun today: the sky is grey, the humidity is heavy and oppressive. Ben radios to tell us a storm is predicted. He thinks it will miss us, but we should make sure to keep everything locked up either way.

I'm on my break, making a coffee and mentally rehearsing what I'm even going to say to Berry, when Captain Liz comes in.

'Tell me what happened with Marc last night.'

I drink my coffee as I tell her everything he said to me. How he grabbed my leg. And eventually pulled me into his lap. How Adam told him to take his hands off me.

'Did Adam touch him at any point?' she asks.

I shake my head. 'No. He grabbed me, my hands, and pulled me up off Marc's lap.'

'Did he swear at him? Call him names?'

'I don't think so. I can't say a hundred per cent because it happened so fast and I was . . .'

She nods. 'You were shocked.'

'I was. I mean, I knew he was a creep, but I didn't expect him to grab me like that. His wife was right there.'

'And what was she doing?'

'She was dancing with Liam.' I remember. 'Or maybe with Adam? I'm not sure. But just before Marc grabbed me, Adam and Liam came out on deck and Jenny and Babs were dancing with them. I'm pretty sure it pissed Marc off.'

'I'm not surprised.' She scrapes her hand back through her hair. 'I know men like Marc Summers. He's going to try to put all this on us. He won't take responsibility for his behaviour, that's for sure. He probably won't for his wife's either. He'll blame you and Adam and Liam.' She shakes her head. 'You're confident neither you nor Adam did anything wrong?'

'I'm pretty sure we didn't.'

She nods. 'Thank you. I appreciate that. Unfortunately we get some guests who think the staff are included in the price. It doesn't happen often, but it happens. I'm sorry he treated you that way – it's totally unacceptable.'

I nod, tears pricking my eyes. 'Thank you.'

'I'll be telling them they won't be welcome on one of my charters ever again.' She covers her hand with mine and squeezes. 'It hasn't put you off?'

I shake my head. 'No. I love this job.'

She smiles. 'Good. Because you're very good at it.'

'Thanks,' I say again, grateful for her kindness.

I'm leaning off the side of the boat, scrubbing at the black marks on the white finish with a long brush, when Adam comes up behind me and grabs me around the waist.

'Hey,' I tell him, straightening up. 'Don't do that.'

He removes his hands instantly. 'Sorry. Just don't want you falling off the boat.'

'I won't,' I tell him. 'Sorry to snap. There's just a lot going on and my head's all over the place.'

I put the brush back in the bucket and pick up the hose to rinse off the soap.

'I don't like the look of that sky.' Adam gestures behind me and I turn to see heavy dark clouds on the horizon.

'God,' I say. 'That's all we need.'

'Still predicted to miss us, apparently,' Adam says. 'I don't know though . . .'

'Ben's the expert,' I say. 'I guess we're sailing away from it. And the sea's calm, at least.'

It turns out that the expression 'the calm before the storm' is literal, because when the rain starts a little while later, it's an instant deluge, as if we've been hit by a wave.

'Shit,' Adam says. 'What do we do?'

I don't even know. Our radios are crackling, so we both move to get undercover. I skid slightly on the teak, clutching the edge of the table as I go. Adam grabs the salon door but now the wind has hit too and he can't open it.

Ben tells us over the radio that the guests have been advised to stay in their cabins. I hope they do.

I don't know where Berry is and I need to find her. She's scared of storms. I can't bear the thought of her alone and afraid.

I press my radio mic and say, 'Berry, Berry, Hope. Where are you?'

Someone's keyed their mic. I can't get through.

The boat is pitching and rolling and, along with the water hammering down, waves have started crashing up over the deck. There's a sheet of water pouring down from the awning too, sloshing over the deck, picking up cushions and a jacket someone left on the back of a chair. A glass slides off the bar and smashes.

I move around the table, holding on, until I get close to the bar and launch myself across. I'm expecting Adam to come too, but instead he lurches across the deck to throw up over the side.

The wind is making an eerie whistling sound now and with the creaking of the boat and the flapping of the awning the *Serendipity* almost sounds alive, like it's roaring back against the storm. A crash of thunder makes me jump and then I see a fork of lightning over the sea.

'Adam!' I shout. 'We need to get inside!'

I pile the glasses into the cupboard and lock it. I've got most of the bottles into the fridge when the wind catches the door and knocks a bottle out of my hand, it hits the deck and rolls, rattling across the deck before falling off the edge. I lock the fridge too and then make my way, holding on to anything I can find, to Adam who has done the same in the opposite direction.

Between us, we manage to open the salon door and throw ourselves inside. Adam pulls the door closed behind us and for a second the silence is almost a sound in itself. But then I can hear shouting downstairs, something banging, something creaking.

'Have you keyed your mic?' I ask him.

He shakes his head, pointing to the radio on his belt. 'You okay?'

'I need to find Berry,' I tell him. 'I'm going downstairs.'

I try the radio again, but there's nothing and then Carlo shouts from the galley and I go in there instead, to help him secure everything that wasn't already locked down. Waves crash against the galley window, the boat lurches and I stagger sideways, my stomach tilting along with it as I smash my hip into the counter.

I need to get to Berry, but I can't leave Carlo until everything is secure.

Kelsey appears in the doorway, holding out her left hand, her right hand wrapped around her wrist. Blood is dripping from her fingers.

'I'm okay,' she says immediately, although all the colour has drained out of her face. 'I just need a plaster.'

Carlo takes her arm and guides her to sit on the floor, opening the cupboard for the first-aid box. The cupboard door swings wide and bangs back against the counter, making us all jump.

'Have you seen Berry?' I ask Kelsey.

She's propped her hand on her knees now, still holding her wrist. She shakes her head.

'Are you okay here?' I ask Carlo.

He nods. 'Andare. Go. Go.'

In the crew mess, boxes have fallen off the shelves and there's cereal all over the floor. The cupboard and fridge doors are open and banging and there's broken glass from somewhere, along with coffee spilled across the table, but I ignore it and go straight to my cabin. Mine and Berry's cabin.

The door is unlocked and Berry is sitting on the floor, her back pressed against the wall. She's pulled the duvet off my bed and wrapped it around herself. Her bare toes are peeking out from under the hem. Her eyes are wide and her face is streaked with tears. I drop down to my knees and crawl over next to her.

'I'm being pathetic,' she says immediately.

I slide one arm around behind her – she moves forward to let me – and pull her towards me with the other. She goes easily, almost falling into me.

'You're not.' I curl my hand around the back of her neck and hold her still. 'Don't say that.'

'Is everyone okay?' Her voice is so small. She doesn't sound like herself.

'Everyone's fine. You're fine.'

The boat rolls and Berry sobs.

I hold her tighter. I can't bear to think that she was here alone and afraid.

'I can't stay,' she says. 'I can't do this.'

My eyes are hot and my breath catches in my throat. 'That's okay. You don't have to stay if you don't want to.'

'I shouldn't have come back,' she says. 'I should've known.'

'It's okay,' I tell her. 'You're safe. Everyone's safe.'

The boat rolls again and I want to distract her. I want to make her feel safe, not just tell her.

I say, 'Tell me about the superbloom.'

'What?'

'Tell me about the flowers. What flowers did you see?'

She's quiet for a second and then she says, 'Poppies.'

'Oh yeah? I love poppies. What else? Which flowers are you going to have tattooed?'

'Marigolds.'

Her breathing seems to be slowing.

'You mentioned purple,' I prompt. 'What are the purple flowers?'

She sucks in a breath. 'Bluebells.'

'Your tattoo is going to be so beautiful.'

I picture it: the rainbow of flowers curling around her arm.

'There's some called popcorn flowers,' she says. 'I always remembered cos I thought it was funny.'

'Yeah? I've never heard of them.'

'I don't know the real name,' she says. 'They're white with yellow at the centre. And they're kind of fluffy. They look like when popcorn pops, you know?'

My radio buzzes into life, the captain giving more instructions for securing the boat.

'Go,' Berry says, turning her face up to look at me. 'I'll be okay.'

'I can't leave you like this.' I want to kiss her, but I know I can't, not yet, not until I've explained what Adam said, what she saw.

She gently pushes me away. 'You can. You helped. It's okay. I'll be fine.'

'I'll come back and check on you,' I tell her. 'Stay here.'

She nods. 'I'm not going anywhere.'

31

The storm blows itself out almost as quickly as it started, but there's a ton of clean-up to do.

Adam, Liam and I sweep up the broken glass and take inventory of everything that got broken or lost – some of the cushions blew overboard, a lot of the food and alcohol is ruined and will need to be replaced.

There isn't time to talk to Berry, because we're heading straight back to port to drop off the guests who are shaken by the bad weather and desperate to get back to dry land. I'm pretty sure they're also pissed off following a conversation with the captain, but it's not my problem. I'm just glad I'll never have to deal with Marc ever again.

When I eventually make it back to our room, Berry's packing.

'What are you doing?'

She doesn't look at me. 'We're in port. The guests are gone. I'm leaving.'

'Wait, what? Now? Why?'

She shakes her head. 'Don't even pretend to care about this, Hope.'

She crouches down to pull a drawer out from under the bed, grabbing handfuls of clothes and shoving them into her backpack.

'About what? About you? You know that's not true.'

She edges past me into the bathroom and comes back with her *Pickle Slut* bag.

'I don't know that.' She won't meet my eyes. 'Were you two together this whole time?'

'God, what? No. Of course not.'

'But you were together when you got here?'

'Yes. But we broke up. And because no one knew we were together, I couldn't tell anyone when we split up.'

She shakes her head, her face twisted with hurt. 'He called you his girlfriend. I saw you kissing him.'

'He called me his girlfriend because he was pissed off at Marc. And he kissed me. You saw him kiss me. But I stopped it. I stopped it.'

I reach out for her then, but she holds her hands up to prevent me from touching her.

'You knew I was upset. But you didn't come after me. You went after him.'

'We were together for a long time,' I tell her. 'I'm sorry I didn't tell you. I promised him I wouldn't tell anyone. But it's over, I promise. Properly over. I want you.'

'I don't think you know what you want.'

She bends to pull the last of her clothes out of the drawer and then zips up her backpack.

I shake my head. My heart's racing. I can't let her leave without explaining. But I can't think of what to say to make her understand.

'How long were you together?' she asks me.

I tell her six years and her breath catches, tears springing to her eyes, as she grabs her bag and reaches past me for the door.

'Six years and you didn't tell me. You promised him, but what about me? You didn't think I deserved to know? That you were with him. That you came here together as a couple? Who broke up with who?'

I shake my head. 'It doesn't –'

Tears are running down her cheeks now. 'Who, Hope?'

'He broke up with me.'

She laughs, humourlessly. 'Great. Get out of the way of the door.'

I shake my head. 'Don't leave,' I tell her. 'Don't leave like this.'

'You owed me!' she almost shouts. 'You owed me this information. You owed me an explanation.'

'I'm trying to give you an explanation!' I tell her, my voice thick with tears.

'No,' she says. 'You're trying to give me an excuse. You wanted to know what it would be like with a girl and weren't you lucky there was a girl right here in your bunk while your long-term relationship was falling apart?'

'That's not fair.'

I don't know how to make her understand that it wasn't like that. That what happened with me and Adam has nothing to do with what happened with me and her.

'Isn't it?' She yanks open the cabin door so hard that it rebounds against the wall. 'It's not even the first time you've done this, Hope. What was her name? Charlie?'

I'm so shocked, so stunned, that I don't even react when she walks out, pulling the door closed behind her.

'How are you doing?' Kelsey asks me the following morning. She's standing in my half-open doorway as I pack, her head tilted to one side, her eyes wide in sympathy.

'Not great,' I tell her, my own eyes immediately welling with tears. My face feels tight after crying myself to sleep.

She pulls me into a floral-scented hug. 'She'll come round,' she tells me. 'Anyone can see she's really into you.'

The thought of it makes my heart hurt. She was. I think she really was. I don't know if she is any more.

'Are you going out there?' Kelsey asks, releasing me.

'Where?' I open another cupboard and lift out a pile of T-shirts, dropping them straight into my case.

'Barcelona.'

I straighten up and look at her. 'She's in Barcelona? I thought she'd gone home to LA.'

Kelsey shakes her head. 'Nope. She sublet her rental place while she was here, so she's gone back to sort it out. Going to be there a couple of weeks, I think.'

'I don't have the address,' I say, my heart a rock in my chest.

'I do,' Kelsey says. 'I probably shouldn't give it to you. But she didn't tell me not to so . . .' She shrugs.

She scrolls through her phone and texts me Berry's contact. 'The flight's, like, less than an hour. From Palma.'

'I have to go home first,' I tell her. 'My mum had a baby.'

'Oh, cute! Congratulations.'

'Thanks.' I can't quite believe I'm going home.

'What are you going to do?' I ask Kelsey.

'Ah, remember Alvaro? Works at the club? Looks like Jason Momoa?'

I nod. Once seen, never forgotten.

'I think I might have underestimated him. I'm going to stay at his place for a while. See if it could be a thing.'

I hug her. 'Good luck. Hope it works out.'

'Thanks,' she says. 'And if it doesn't, something else will.'

Once I've finished packing, I zip up my case and stand at the door of the cabin. It doesn't feel like long ago that I got here. That Berry came in, pulled off her shirt, that I stared at her tattoos and felt something that changed everything.

I think about Harry's tarot reading. About rose-tinted glasses. About not resisting reality. Finding out what's actually true. He was right about all of it. But he didn't tell me how much it would hurt.

Even though I had to sit on my case to close it, I open it again and find the tarot pack Harry gave me when he left. I shuffle the cards, close my eyes and pull one out.

It's the Eight of Cups.

'*Time to move on*,' I read in the accompanying booklet. '*If there's something missing in your life, you're not going to find it by keeping everything the same. To seek means picking a direction and moving on with no guarantees you'll get a better deal. Hard, but the alternative is to stay stuck in an old life and an old self forever.*'

Fucking tarot.

I knock on Adam's door and push it open when he calls out. The floor and beds are clear of clothes and his backpack is leaning against the closet door.

'Hey.' He smiles. 'You packed?'

I nod. 'What are you going to do, Ad?'

'I'm going to go and stay with my dad for a bit. Probably not a good idea to go back to Liverpool just yet.'

I nod. I hate that. Adam loves his family, his friends. But he's right – it's probably for the best.

'Be nice to spend some time with him,' I say.

He pulls a face. 'See how long till we're at each other's throats, but I'll give it a go.'

We stare at each other and I can see him at sixteen on the back seat of the bus with his mates, all of them jeering as he got up to come and sit with me. Lying in his room, doing my uni reading while he played *FIFA* and put his hands up my shirt between matches. Pushing him up against a palm tree on the way here and thinking this job, this new experience, would change everything.

He holds his arms out and I only hesitate for a second before I step into them, relaxing against him.

He squeezes me. Kisses the top of my head.

'Keep in touch,' he says into my hair.

And I nod against his neck.

The only thing I have left to do is see Captain Liz.

She asks how my first season went and I find myself telling her everything – how Adam told me we had to pretend not to be together, how I had no idea about his gambling addiction, how he dumped me because he couldn't deal with any of it, and how I found myself falling for Berry. And now she's gone and I don't know what I'm going to do.

Tears drip off my chin as she passes me tissue after tissue.

'I can't believe he told you to pretend not to be together.' She shakes her head, a combination of incredulous and amused.

'On the course we did, the guy kept saying –'

'"Don't screw the crew",' she interrupts.

'Exactly. And so Adam said we shouldn't tell anyone we were a couple and that made sense to me.'

She nods. 'Often programmes actually prefer couples, you know. Established couples.'

'I didn't know that,' I tell her.

She smiles. 'No reason you would. He's right that there's a better chance of getting individual jobs when you're pretending to be single because couple jobs are in demand. But it's certainly not unheard of. And it wouldn't have been a problem for me.'

I shake my head. 'He was so insistent. I didn't even question it.'

'Maybe if you'd done your own research . . .' she suggests, gently.

I wince. 'I know. I should've done. But Adam was so excited . . . I thought he was keen on the job, you know? I didn't know it was because he was kind of desperate.'

'I feel for him. It's easily done. As for you, I'd be more than happy to have you back next season and I know Louise would too.'

'Oh, wow. That's . . .' My stomach flutters at the thought of it. 'I think I'd really love that. As a stew or deckhand?'

'Which would you prefer?'

My first instinct is deckhand. I like how strong it made me feel. But I don't want to make any sudden decisions.

'Can I think about it?'

'Of course. Take some time and let me know. You're going home?'

I nod. 'To see my new baby brother.'

She beams at me. 'How wonderful! Congratulations. So, yes, do that. Take some time. Have a think. Go and sort things out with Berry. And then give me a call. Like I said, Louise will be back and so will Nico. Having those two as a couple on crew is going to be interesting.'

I laugh. 'I can't even imagine it.'

She pulls me into a hug. 'Look after yourself.'

I hug her back. 'Thank you. I will. Are you going home?'

She nods. 'But first I'm having a holiday with some friends. I go away with the same group of friends for a week every year. This year we're going to the Bahamas.'

'Oh, amazing.'

'It will be, thanks. Enjoy Liverpool.'

32

It's so strange to be home. I feel like I've done so much and changed so much and everything here is just the way I left it, but of course that's not true, because there's a baby.

But before I can hold him, I have to sit on the sofa so Riley can show me Reel after Reel of Uncle Bao, a cat she's obsessed with, while Alfie squeezes up against my other side, asking me if I know the Spanish word for poo (he does) and if I saw any sharks. Mae is shy at first, standing next to the baby's Moses basket with her thumb in her mouth and a blanket wrapped around her hand, occasionally going up on tiptoes to peek inside, before looking back at me as if she's not sure I know what's in there.

'Everyone out,' Mick says, once he's extricated me from the sibling sandwich and hugged me hello. 'Let Hope have a bit of peace.'

The kids all complain until he tells them he'll take them to the LEGO Store at Liverpool ONE, and then they can't get ready quick enough.

'Here,' Mum says, once they've finally left. 'Have a hold while I make you a brew.'

I slide my hands under his tiny, soft body and lift him out of the Moses basket, holding him against me, his little face resting against my neck.

'Oh, he's so tiny,' I sigh.

'Didn't feel so tiny when he was getting dragged out of my arse,' Mum calls from the kitchen.

'I'm pretty sure that's not where babies come from,' I tell the baby in a sing-song voice.

'That's what it feels like,' Mum says. 'Tea or coffee?'

'Oh my god,' I tell her, bringing the baby with me into the kitchen. 'Tea. Obviously.'

I drink coffee from a machine on a boat when I haven't had enough sleep. At home I drink tea, like I always have.

'I'm thinking "Bob",' Mum says, filling the kettle.

'Do not call this baby "Bob",' I say, stroking his soft hair with my finger.

'I don't know,' Mum says. 'He looks like a little old fella, I thought I'd give him an old fella's name. Amos. Cecil. Archibald. Basil.'

'Basil.' I roll my eyes. 'I'm so sorry, baby.'

'Wilf,' Mum says.

'I quite like "Wilf".' I sniff the top of his head. 'Hello, baby Wilf.'

'I don't think Mick'll go for it, but I'll stick it on the list.'

I put my baby brother back in his basket and Mum and I sit at the dining table with our teas.

'So,' she says, 'tell me everything.'

I tell her everything.

About Adam and Berry and how it all ended.

Mum squeezes my hand, gets up to bring me a box of tissues, then gets up again for biscuits.

'I used to worry about the two of you,' she says eventually. 'That you'd got too serious too soon. Adam's great, he's always been great, and he was good to you, which was a relief. So I used to feel guilty sometimes for worrying. But . . . you were so young when you got together. I worried you'd get married and pregnant and that would be it – you'd be stuck.'

I don't tell her I had the same worries myself, despite everything.

She takes a sip of her tea. 'You've always been so responsible, so conscientious. A lot of it was my fault. I put a lot of pressure on you. At first out of necessity and then I told myself it was fine, you didn't mind, you were coping with everything. But you shouldn't have had to look after the little ones while you were at uni. That wasn't fair. It was only when you left and I didn't know how to do half the shit that needs doing I realised how much I relied on you. And I'm so grateful. But I'm so sorry you had to.'

I shake my head, my eyes brimming with tears again. 'I didn't mind. I like helping.'

'You did more than help.' Mum brushes her thumb over the back of my hand. 'I honestly couldn't have done any of it without you. But that makes me feel like shit. Because you shouldn't have had to do any of it. You had to grow up too soon. I used to say you were born grown-up and it took me a long time to realise it wasn't that; it was because you had to be.'

'Mum,' I say, shaking my head, 'I don't –'

'No,' she says. 'Listen to me. And then you're texting me from a bloody yacht, beating yourself up cos you couldn't be with me when I had little Cyril here.'

'No. Not Cyril.'

She smiles. 'I didn't need you here. I love you and if you'd been home it would've be nice to have you there, but I've got Mick. I don't want you worrying about me. I want you to be free. I want you to make mistakes and fuck up. To get drunk and dance and laugh and kiss the wrong people at the wrong time and then find the right people to kiss and kiss them as much as you want.'

I smile through my tears. 'I've done some of that. And I got stung by a jellyfish.'

Mum laughs. She's tearful now too. 'Well, that's something, I guess. You've always taken care of everyone else. Including me. Including Adam. I want you to forget about everyone else and think about what you want.'

When I wake up the following morning, I remember there is one thing I want. And when I call, there's been a cancellation so I'm able to get it today.

I'm home just before dinner time. It's pouring down outside and Mick is singing a song about the rain to the baby, holding him up against his shoulder and bouncing on his feet while rubbing Wilf's back.

'That's the stuff,' he says when Wilf burps. 'You like a bit of Supertramp, don't you?'

'That's Supertramp?' I say. 'That song?'

Mick nods. 'Good band. Look them up. They look like a bunch of supply teachers, but they had some great songs. "Breakfast in America", that's another one.'

'My friend told me about them.' My chest clenches when I call Berry my friend, but I don't think I can call her anything else now. I probably shouldn't even call her that. 'She made me a yacht rock playlist.'

'Are they yacht rock?' Mick says, squinting one eye closed as he thinks. 'I've never thought of them as yacht rock. That's more . . . the Doobie Brothers, no?'

'God,' I say. 'What is it with middle-aged men and yacht rock?'

He laughs. 'It's good stuff. What else is on this playlist?'

I connect my phone to the kitchen speaker and put Berry's playlist on shuffle while Mick dances around the kitchen, smoothing his hand down Wilf's back.

I want there to be a message in the songs. I want Berry to have chosen them to tell me how she felt about me. But they're almost all love songs and none of them are specific to our situation. Or all of them are. And I know how she felt about me. I just hope she still feels the same way.

The next song that plays is the one Berry said her parents still dance in the kitchen and my eyes prick with hot tears. Much as I love Mick and Wilf, I don't want to dance in the kitchen with them.

I want to dance in the kitchen with Berry.

And if she doesn't want me, then that's fine. But I have to tell her how I feel. I'll regret it forever if I don't.

33

It's hot in Barcelona. Hotter even than it was on the yacht. There, at least, there was almost always a breeze. Here it's humid and there's sweat trickling down my back within minutes of getting out of the cab.

The address Kelsey gave me is on a narrow street with a single palm tree at the end like an exclamation mark. Most of the buildings are tall, painted lemon and peach and baby blue, but Berry's is shorter, with only two floors and an iron balcony in the centre of the first floor, the windows either side hidden with wooden shutters.

I stand on the other side of the street and try to make myself cross. To knock on the door. To see Berry and explain everything. To tell her I'm sorry I didn't tell her about me and Adam. I'm sorry about the storm. I'm sorry she left. I'm sorry I let her down.

The balcony is lined with plants in brightly painted pots. Mostly green, but one in the corner trails a veil of pink flowers over the railing and down the front of the building.

I take a deep breath, count to five, and make myself cross the street, stand in front of her door and press the buzzer, my hand shaking. I can feel my heartbeat in my face, in my teeth. If she's not here, I don't have much of a plan. I'll wait. I'll come back. I'll go home. I don't know what I'll do.

And then the door opens and Berry is standing in front of me in pink shorts and the 'Let's Summon Demons!' T-shirt she was wearing the first time I saw her. Her red-wine hair is piled on her head and she's perfect. Beautiful and perfect and looking at me like she's been expecting me. And, like Bec said about the first time she saw Morgan, I think, *There she is*.

'Come up,' she says.

I follow her up a short flight of dark, narrow stairs and into her apartment. Berry's apartment. It's so bright, so suddenly, that tears prick the corners of my eyes.

It's only when I've blinked them away that I see the dozens of flowers I sent from Liverpool. Pink, red, orange and peach dahlias that look like a sunset. Clouds of white hydrangeas, because I couldn't get popcorn flowers in the UK. Tall stems of purple veronica because lavender's out of season. Pink and white snowberries that look like balls of meringue.

'I wanted to make you a superbloom,' I say, my throat tight.

Berry nods. 'I got that, yeah.'

'I was thinking about your mum's metaphor about the bad thing bringing out the good.'

She smiles. 'I got that too.'

'I miss you,' I say, before I can stop myself.

She shakes her head. 'Hope, you can't just turn up and –'

'No. I know. I'm sorry. I didn't mean to do that. I just . . . I did, I missed you. But forget I said that. I want to explain everything.'

'Do you want a drink?' she says. 'I need a drink.'

She brings us both cold beers, condensation on the glass. We take them outside to her terrace and sit on an uncomfortable wooden bench shaded by a yellow-and-white-striped awning.

'Okay,' she says, turning towards me, leaning back against a cushion, her feet up on the bench between us, her knees pulled into her chest.

I tell her how it was when Adam and I were together and that we agreed to pretend not to be for the job. I tell her about his gambling addiction and debts and how that was partly why he wanted us to hide our relationship; he couldn't risk anything jeopardising the job because he needed to get away from Liverpool and he needed to make as much money as possible. I tell her that I was attracted to her from the first time I saw her, but I was still with Adam and it freaked me out. That it freaked me out even more when she kissed me because then I couldn't stop thinking about her and I dreamt about her and it was so hard to share a room with her, wanting her all the time. And how I told myself it was just a crush because Adam was being weird and I was totally out of my comfort zone, but then when I kissed her I knew I was kidding myself.

I tell her that it's over between me and Adam but that he was my first love and my best friend and he'll always be in my life and I'm not going to apologise for that, but I apologise for everything else. And that what she said about me using her, when she brought up what happened with Charlie, really hurt me.

By the time I've said everything, we've finished our beers.

Berry brushes tears from her cheeks with her fingers. 'So.' She smiles. 'That was a lot.'

I smile through my own tears too. 'I know. I'm sorry.'

Over another two beers, Berry tells me she thought about moving back to Barcelona, getting her tour guide job back, but since she's been here, she's realised she doesn't want to do that.

She's house-sitting for a friend from home for a couple of weeks, but then she needs to decide what's next.

'What are you going to do?' she asks me.

'I'm going back to the *Serendipity*. Captain Liz asked me and I told her yes.'

'Oh, wow, I didn't realise.' She takes a pull of her beer, her brow furrowed.

'What's wrong?'

She shakes her head. 'Nothing's wrong. I think part of me thought you wouldn't make plans until you knew where I would be.'

'I did think about that. Of course I did. But . . .' I sigh. 'All of this happened because I was following Adam. You know? It was his idea and I just went along with it. And, god, I'm so glad I did. I'm lucky that I love yachting and that I met you. But the next step needs to come from me.'

She nods. 'I respect that. So if I go back to California?'

My heart clenches like a fist. 'Are you going back to California?'

She smiles. 'I haven't decided yet.'

'Oh.' I twist the beer bottle in my fingers, trying to give her the space to tell me more.

'And we're not going to do long distance.'

It's not even a question.

'You really don't want to come back to the *Serendipity*? With me?' I can't help but add.

'It's not a no,' she says and my stomach flutters. 'But I need more time to think about it.'

We talk all afternoon. Berry orders in food from one of the places she used to take people on her tours. We eat sharp cheese and lavender honey, slivers of ham and bright, sweet, sundried tomatoes.

The air cools, the sky darkens, a crescent moon rises, surrounded by a scatter of stars.

'I downloaded an app,' Berry tells me, pointing. 'That one – see the sort of circle?'

I don't, but I tell her I do.

'That one's Neptune's Nutsack.'

I snort. 'Oh yeah? I think that's my rising sign.'

She laughs. 'That is not how rising signs work.'

'You're the one inventing fake constellations.'

'Listen, I googled and they pretty much all look like dicks.'

'Wow. The patriarchy is everywhere.'

I shield my eyes with my hand, squint, and try to tune out everything else and focus on the pinpricks of light that are actually long-dead planets. The past made visible, as Berry's mum said.

But I don't want to think about the past. I want to focus on the future.

I take a deep, slow, steadying breath. 'I think I'm probably in love with you,' I tell her.

I can't read her face, her perfect face, but she moves closer.

'You have to promise not to hide things from me,' she says. She's inches away now.

I nod. 'I promise. I never meant to –'

But I don't get to finish, because she kisses me. Slowly and softly and intentionally, like she's been thinking about it as much as I have. I make an embarrassing sound, my hands circling her wrists and she lets me hold on for a second before pulling away.

'I've missed you too,' she says.

We kiss until the moon is higher, the sky dark enough to reveal more constellations we know nothing about. The heat of the day has dissipated and the goosebumps on my arms aren't just from the kissing, from being here, with her.

'You know, there's a double bed in my room,' she says.

My stomach flutters. Nerves and excitement are the same emotion.

'Oh, I don't think I could sleep in one now,' I say. 'I've become institutionalised. Do you have anything in a cupboard? Maybe a steam trunk.'

'Hope,' she says, looking at me intently, her dark eyes twinkling, 'I'm asking you if you want to come and spend the night with me in an actual bed with room for both of us.'

'God,' I say. 'I really, really do.'

'I feel like I need to cover Dory's innocent eyes with a plaster,' I say later, stroking Berry's *Finding Nemo* tattoo with the tip of my index finger.

She laughs. 'It's okay. She has short-term memory loss.'

I giggle, dropping my head to rest against her hip bone. 'That just means we're traumatising her over and over and she'll never get used to it.'

'Maybe she's into it. You don't know her life.'

'I'm so sorry,' I tell the little blue fish tattoo.

Berry dips her head to kiss the new palm tree tattoo on my thigh next to the small scar left by the jellyfish sting.

'I was so scared when you got stung,' she says. 'And then you asked if the kids were okay. I couldn't believe it.'

'I was worried about them,' I tell her.

'I know. Because you're lovely. You know the scar kind of looks like a constellation.' She runs her finger over it gently.

'Please don't tell me there's a dick on my leg.'

She laughs and her warm breath on my skin makes me shiver. 'Never again,' she says, which makes me snort.

'I still can't believe you got a palm tree,' she says, smiling. 'So basic.'

'It's to remind me of the best summer of my life.'

She crawls up my body, caging me with her arms. She leans down and kisses me slowly and I kiss her back, brushing her jaw with my fingertips and curling my hand around the back of her neck.

'I don't know about that,' she tells me, smiling against my mouth. 'I've got high hopes for next summer.'

Acknowledgements

Thank you so much to Georgia Murray, Jennie Roman and Aimee White for the easiest and most fun edits.

To Jenny Richards and Beth Free at Nic+Lou design studio for the perfect cover.

And to everyone in sales, marketing, PR and production at Hot Key for championing my book.

Thanks as always to my agent Hannah Sheppard.

And thank you so much for reading. I really appreciate it.

HOT KEY BOOKS

Thank you for choosing a Hot Key book!

For all the latest bookish news, freebies and exclusive content, sign up to the Hot Key newsletter – scan the QR code or visit lnk.to/HotKeyBooks

Follow us on social media:

bonnierbooks.co.uk/HotKeyBooks